PRAISE FOR THIS BOOK

'All the charming and not-so-charming characters are back. Another great read by Nicola May – five stars'
Devilishly Delicious Book Reviews

'A story of emotion, drama, romance and life in general. Such a great read'
Me and My Books

'Nicola May expertly weaves together threads of drama, emotion, and romance in this delightful story'
Audio Killed the Bookmark

'A soap opera in story form – a whirlwind of a read'
Just 4 My Books

'Coming back to Cockleberry Bay was like coming back to a place I know and love. Great characters, perfectly descriptive location and a plot that has humour, romance, friendship and unexpected escapades. I predict that this too will become a bestseller'
Chocolate Pages

THE GIFT OF COCKLEBERRY BAY

NICOLA MAY

Lightning
Books

Published by
Lightning Books Ltd
Imprint of EyeStorm Media
312 Uxbridge Road
Rickmansworth
Hertfordshire
WD3 8YL

www.lightning-books.com

British Library Cataloguing in Publication Data
A catalogue record for this book is available from the British Library

Printed by CPI Group (UK) Ltd, Croydon CR0 4YY

ISBN 9781785632068

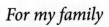

For my family

Is not the beautiful moon, which inspires poets,
the same moon which angers the silence
of the sea with a terrible roar?
Kahlil Gibran

PROLOGUE

'Rosa, Rosa, you have to come right now.' Jacob's voice was full of panic.

'What's wrong? Where are you?'

'Upstairs at the pub. The Duchess is about to give birth, and although I've watched *Call the Midwife* once or twice, my own midwifery skills are somewhat limited. Please, I need you!'

With a shake of her dark brown curls, the publican's younger friend answered with a smile-filled voice, 'Jacob, it's OK. The Duchess will know what to do.'

Then on hearing both him and the pregnant dachshund making irregular panting noises down the end of the phone, she said, 'I'm on my way.' Instructing her own dachshund, Hot Dog, to be good, she quickly headed for the door of the Corner Shop, slamming it shut behind her.

Rosa was walking so fast up the hill, she nearly missed her mother waving from the window of Seaspray Cottage. Mary Cobb dashed out, dressed in her supermarket uniform, ready to do a shift at the local Co-op.

'I'm just off to work but have you got a minute, duck?'

'I haven't actually. The Duchess is about to give birth and so too is Jacob by the sound of it.'

Mary tutted. 'Bloody drama queen, he is.'

Rosa laughed. 'Yes, and he'd be the first to admit it. I must go – but is everything OK?'

'Yes, apart from the weather forecast. Did you not hear? There's a massive storm on the way. The sea's likely to come right up and over the beach wall. You and Sara might need sandbags to protect the café.'

'A storm in July? And that bad – really?'

'Well, I personally can't wait. I'm sick of this bloody humidity. It plays havoc with my breathing.' Mary reached for the inhaler in her apron pocket and shook it. 'Merlin, that mad cat, has been tearing around the back yard in circles too, and he is all-knowing when the weather's about to change.'

'OK. I'll go down to the front and check with Sara about keeping the café protected, but I can't go until I've helped deliver these baby chipolatas.' Rosa turned to go.

'You'll be getting a reputation as a midwife in the village at this rate, what with bringing Titch's little Theo into the world too,' Mary called after her, a sudden gust of wind taking her words away over the rooftops of Cockleberry Bay.

As Rosa carried on up the hill, Ritchie Rogers was busy nailing single boards of wood across the big front window of the fish-and-chip shop.

'Morning, Rosa,' the young man hailed her from the top of his ladder. 'It's going to be a fiery one. The glass was blown clean out last time we had a storm of this predicted level. It was really dangerous – thank heavens no one got hurt.'

'Really? It doesn't seem possible with the sun still shining like it is now.'

'Yes. I guess you soft townies haven't encountered anything like a proper coastal storm.' He laughed. 'You wait and see.'

'Right now, I'm off to put a cold flannel on Jacob's forehead.

The puppies are on their way.'

'Aw, exciting. I'll let Titch know. She'll be beside herself.'

'Are you two still having one of the puppies, then?'

'That's the plan.'

As Rosa reached the Lobster Pot a huge gust of wind swept down the narrow street, causing her light summer dress to blow up and reveal her knickers.

Watching for her from the top window, Jacob had hurried downstairs and was at the door ready to greet her. He put his hand to his forehead in mock horror. 'If it's not enough dealing with a bitch in labour, I now get to see the next week's washing of another one.'

Rosa laughed. 'Come on, Grandad, let's do this.'

With an offended 'How very dare you!' from the handsome forty-something publican, they made their way inside.

CHAPTER ONE

Rosa could barely hear her friend Sara and co-owner of ROSA'S – the café formerly known as Coffee, Tea or Sea. The waves crashing to shore and the heavy rain that had just started lashing against the side of the glass-fronted café made it all but impossible to make out her words, even though they were standing facing each other. The force of the wind had already washed the apostrophe off the ROSA'S sign outside.

'I'm so glad you are here,' Sara said gratefully. 'I've never known a storm quite like this before.'

'I know,' Rosa nodded. 'It came in so quickly too. Madness! Trust the boys to be on the golf course when we need them. I can't get hold of Josh, his phone is off.'

'It's fine. I managed to reach Alec; they are seeing if they can get some sandbags on the way back. He said they literally ran like kids to the car when the first lightning bolt struck.'

Despite it being just four o'clock on a summer's afternoon, it was almost dark. Sara squealed as the whole café suddenly lit up with an impressive fork of lightning that appeared to dance right along the ominously black horizon. It was immediately followed by a resounding CRACK of thunder that made the whole timber building shake.

'I tried to sound calm when I suggested everyone made their way home from here as I needed to batten down the hatches, but I've always been terrified of storms.' Sara shuddered. 'Even the voice of the weather presenter on *South Cliffs Today* went a bit high-pitched at the first flash of lightning. I don't know why at the sight of bad weather they send all these poor reporters out into either pouring rain, a hurricane or the eye of the storm. They could quite easily present inside in front of a window. Anyway, I digress.'

'There's naught scarier nor more powerful than when Nature shows the dark side of her face.' Rosa quoted her mother in Devonian twang then began looking around the café for potential hazards in case the sea did come up.

She still had to pinch herself that her lovely husband, Josh, had invested in this partnership with Sara, so that as well as running her beloved Corner Shop – inherited just over eighteen months ago from a mystery benefactor, who had turned out to be her great-grandfather Ned – she could also work part-time here.

'Where's Hot?' Sara enquired.

'I phoned Titch to go and get him. Mind you, it's not Hot I should be worried about; his furry girlfriend was just about to give birth when you called me. I've left Jacob and Raff watching a YouTube tutorial on delivering dachshund puppies, while trying to keep the pugs Ugly and Pongo away from the delivery suite. Vicki the vet was busy with another emergency.'

'I can just imagine the panic,' Sara said.

'Thank goodness Raff is there; he's the calm one in that relationship. He'll sort it. I googled what should be happening and it looked like everything was going to puppy plan.'

Rosa checked that the café's red and white awning was safely stowed and that all the appliances were powered off and wires tucked away. She removed the tea-light holders from each table and packed the books from the *Read me, Replace me, Replenish me* shelf into a couple of boxes and put them on top of the ice-cream freezer.

'OK, what shall we do now?' Sara asked, starting to empty the dishwasher of china.

'Finish that, then let's stack chairs on the tables as a starter.' Rosa's common sense quite often belied her twenty-seven years. 'Can you call your Alec again and see if the pair of them can grab anything like bricks or blocks so we can lift the appliances off the floor when they get here.' Her phone rang and she added: 'Forget that, it's Josh calling now.'

Her husband's voice was full of concern. 'I can't believe this. Are you both OK, darling?'

'Yes, we're all right – how far away are you?'

'That's the thing: a tree has gone down at the top of the hill by the garage, so we are going to have to dump the car and walk. So, no sandbags, I'm afraid. Is the sea coming up?'

Sara screamed again as another massive clap of thunder boomed overhead. Then, 'Help! Water is coming in! Rosa, I'm scared.'

'I heard that.' Josh sounded urgent now: 'Get out, Rosa – get out, both of you and up the hill now. We can sort any damage, but you two are irreplaceable. Is Hot somewhere safe?'

'Yes, Josh, he's over with Titch. Don't worry, we're leaving now – see you at home. You be careful too.'

Dirty water was now swirling around their feet like a wildly angry serpent writhing around in search of its foe. Then, with another almighty flash of lightning, the lights in the café went off, and this time both women screamed.

'Rosa, come on.' With hands firmly clasped, they made their way to the door and wrenched it open. The roar of the sea was deafening, and the spray and driving rain felt as if pebbles were being flung in their faces. Even the seagulls had sensibly headed inland.

Thankful to have reached the solidity of the road, the pair were then faced with not only a torrent of water running down the hill at speed but also a woman doing the same, nearly mowing them down in the process.

'Stop!' Rosa shouted. 'What are you doing? It's too dangerous down there.'

'My four-year-old grandson!' the woman shouted back, out of breath and looking terrified. 'He's down there and I can't swim!'

'What? You mean he's on the beach?'

'The water took him off down the hill.'

Without any hesitation, Rosa threw her bag at Sara and ran back towards the sea, calling behind her: 'You two stay here.'

'Rosa, no!' Sara cried out. 'The sea is too angry. We should ring the coastguard.'

Rosa ran the fastest she had ever run in her life. Reaching the beach wall, she peered over it in the strange darkness of the storm, looking desperately up and down and in amongst the waves. Spotting a little head bobbing up and down, she snatched the lifebuoy off the side of the beach wall and, careful not to hit him, she threw it, hollering, 'Hold on, little man.' Then, without a thought for her own safety, she took a deep breath and clambered over the wall and jumped into the angry black waters that were already waist-deep. Fighting the current, she reached the half-drowned child, put the buoy over his head and clung on to him, only to have a huge wave surge forward and engulf the two of them. Using the might of both mind and body, Rosa maintained her grip on the child and the lifebuoy. Miraculously, and somehow managing to miss the edge of the wall, she then surfed them into the relative safety of the car park of the Ship Inn. Here, the water was coming up, but only ankle-deep, thus far.

Soaking wet and staggering, she managed to pull the life ring off the youngster and held him tight to her chest as he choked and screamed in fear, his teeth chattering from cold and shock. 'It's OK, little one,' she comforted him. 'Your granny's coming.'

At that moment, Josh and Alec came charging towards her. They had bumped into Sara on the hill and found out what was going on.

'Bloody hell, Rosa.' Josh was beside himself at his wife's state. Her tight brown curls hung like rats' tails, her summer dress clinging to her tiny frame tighter than the little boy was. She was shaking like a leaf.

As another gust of wind nearly blew them off their feet, he took the sobbing child from her and rugby-passed him to Alec. The big man deftly placed the little lad over his broad shoulder, then firmly grasped the hand of the now hysterical grandmother, who had finally made it down to the beach and was at the point of collapse. Their terrifying ordeal had ended safely, thanks to Rosa's quick thinking and courage.

Lifting his wife like a baby into the safety of his big, muscular rugby-player's arms, Josh squeezed her tightly to him for a second. Then with a loud, 'Let's get up this hill – and quickly,' he led the shocked and drenched quartet through the driving rain to the safety of higher ground.

CHAPTER TWO

Rosa awoke to the sound of cawing seagulls and her handsome six-foot-two husband leaning up on one shoulder staring down at her. A ray of light was sneaking its way through the chink in the bedroom curtains.

Since their wedding day, they had decided to carry on living in the modest two-bedroom flat above the Corner Shop. Rosa was quite happy with its quirky Victorian features, but Josh had insisted that the avocado bathroom suite should be replaced with modern white fittings, new tiles and flooring, and that the upstairs kitchen also be brought into the twenty-first century with modern grey units and a granite worktop and splashback replacing the old Formica. Rosa still loved the balcony that came off the lounge, and was adamant that the ornate railings around it should stay; a compromise that Josh was happy to accept.

As much as she did love living here, Rosa was getting quite excited about the prospect of moving to picturesque Polhampton, the local small town, where they'd have a house with more space, a garden and, hopefully, a direct sea view. She also wouldn't miss the staircase, which was the steepest she had ever encountered, and which went down directly into the shop.

She was surprised that her great-grandfather Ned had managed to stay there as long as he did – well into his nineties.

Sometimes, she still found it hard to believe that just two Christmases ago, she was renting a room in Josh's terraced house in Whitechapel, in the East End of London. At that time she had little money and few job prospects, and the future looked bleak – something she was used to after a difficult childhood. Now, not only did she have a comfy home and her own business, but she was married to Josh, a gem of a man, and there was a bright future ahead of them. Not a day passed when she didn't feel blessed with all the love and security that she now enjoyed.

'Here she is,' Josh said softly. 'Cockleberry Bay's little heroine.'

'Ow.' Rosa groaned, putting her hand to a bandage on her knee. 'I know I've just got cuts and bruises, but I'm bloody hurting. Anyway, I'm being a baby. Good morning, husband.'

Josh brushed her lips with his. 'Just because you don't drink like a fish any more doesn't mean you should think you can swim like one, especially in that sort of weather.'

'Oi.' Rosa stuck out her bottom lip. 'There wasn't exactly time to get the health and safety manual out now, was there, mister? And you like the fact I don't drink any more, don't you?'

He hugged her tight. 'My baby. Don't be sensitive. You know I do, but only because you are so much happier without the demon alcohol inside of you.' He kissed the top of her head. 'I bloody love you, Rosa Smith. Please don't be scaring me like that again.'

Rosa pulled away and yawned loudly. 'How is the little boy, anyway? And who were they, do you know?'

'I have no idea. Alec took the lead on getting them away from danger. Holidaymakers, I assume.'

Rosa sat up. 'Right. We had better go down and assess the damage at the café.'

'No rush. What's done is done. It's bright sunshine out there today so the drying out will already have started.'

'You know me, I have to get up and get things sorted. I can't believe I dropped off to sleep with the wind howling like it was. And that rain! I'm sure it's worse than any weather we ever had in London when we lived there.'

At that moment Hot came pattering into the bedroom from his basket in the sitting room. He'd heard the voices and knew it must be breakfast-time. Josh leaned down and whisked him on to the bed. 'Here's our little sausage.' He pushed his face into the mini-dachshund's velvety neck and breathed him in. 'Careful with Mummy,' he warned the little dog. 'She's hurt her leg.' Hot whiffled around them both and let out a bark.

'Come on then, my lad, let's get you some breakfast and then it's walk time, to view our estate.' At the mention of the W word, Hot started running around in circles on top of the covers.

'Oi!' Josh grabbed the excitable hound and held him tightly in his arms.

'Wait for me,' Rosa said. 'I've scratched myself on the sea wall, that's all, and I need to know what's happening.' She then crashed back down on her pillow. 'I do feel really tired though.'

Josh put Hot back on the floor and placed his hand gently on Rosa's arm. 'It's not surprising. I expect you are suffering from a bit of delayed shock.'

Ding! The shop doorbell signalled a visitor entering. Only two people had the front-door key apart from themselves.

'Rose? Josh? You awake? I'm coming up.' Titch Whittaker's Devonian twang filtered up the stairs. 'Put your tits and bits away, the pair of you.'

The nineteen-year-old paraded into the bedroom. Her cropped blonde locks and large breasts under her tight red T-shirt made her look like some kind of a computer game character. From the day they had met in the Ship Inn, when Rosa had only just arrived in the Bay, Titch had never called Rosa by her real name and 'Rose' had just stuck. As had their extremely strong friendship.

'I just saw your mum,' she told Rosa, as Josh went off to let Hot onto the balcony to do a wee. 'She's working in the Co-op till midday. She sends her love and said she'll pop by and see you when she's done. The damage is pretty bad down the front, evidently. The beach is a complete mess too. If you need any help with the café, I'll come down after my shift here.' When Hot scampered back into the room, she picked him up, cuddled him close and continued: 'The sun's out again, so I reckon the shop is going to be busy, especially now you've got those wildlife-shaped inflatables. The parrot one is my favourite, for sure.' She suddenly stopped and burst out, 'Oh shit, and more importantly, I forgot to say...' She ran out of breath.

'Take it easy, love, before you internally combust.' Rosa swung herself out of bed while a scrabbling Hot released himself from Titch's cuddles.

'Guess what?' Titch said importantly. 'You were mentioned on the radio this morning.' She assumed a newsreader-type tone. '"Local shop-owner, Rosa Smith, is the heroine of the moment after saving the young son of a London family who are down here on holiday." I cannot believe I missed all this. Mind you, Theo just wouldn't settle. The thunder scared him, and his crying drowned out most of the noise of the storm for much of the night, to be fair.' She gave a lengthy yawn. 'I'm bloody knackered. So, what happened?'

'You always said you'd be famous one day.' Josh poked his wife gently in the ribs as she walked past in her little nightie.

'I'd much prefer *in*famous. And, well – look, Titch, it's no big deal. A young kid ended up in the drink; luckily the surf was up so he had a soft landing. I just jumped in and managed to get hold of him before the tide swept him away.'

'You ARE mad – it's official. But, bless you, Rose, and thank goodness your arm is better now, or you'd have been swimming in circles like Nemo.'

Despite Rosa having a flashback to her drinking days, when she had fallen at West Cliffs and badly hurt her arm, she still managed to laugh.

'You wait, the *Gazette* will be wanting a piece of the action soon. In fact, a storm in the Bay *and* a dramatic rescue, that'll be at least six pages taken up and an award of some sort, I reckon.' Titch sniffed, then went on, 'Right, I'd better open up.' She headed for the stairs, singing a very out-of-tune version of the song 'Tell Me Why I Don't Like Mondays'.

Highly amused, Rosa got back into bed and cuddled into the lovely, warm body of her husband, who had snuggled back under the covers himself. Hot, scurrying around the side of the bed, broke up the cosy moment with a 'get up and take me out, you bastards'-type yelp.

Rosa put her hand outside the bed so that the impatient hound could lick it, made a little contented noise and shut her eyes momentarily before opening them with a start. 'Oh no! *Shit!*'

'What is it, angel?'

'I completely forgot about Jacob and the puppies.'

CHAPTER THREE

Before they went up to the Lobster Pot to see the new arrivals, Josh and Rosa's first duty was to check what had happened to the café. The beach, when they got there, mirrored a war zone. Rosa had never seen anything like it. So much debris had been washed up that the place was almost unrecognisable. What astounded Rosa the most was the number of plastic bottles and fishing line that were entwined with varying banks of seaweed. There were even dead fish and sea birds in the mix, and to her distress, some of the birds were still alive, flapping and cawing as they struggled to free themselves. Thankfully they were being attended to by people wearing branded green and white T-shirts with some kind of logo on them.

It seemed as if nearly half the inhabitants of Cockleberry Bay were also down there doing their bit. Some had begun placing the plethora of debris into different piles, while others were retrieving waste bins that had been blown around the Bay, and in the case of the Ship Inn, clearing up glass from windows smashed by the force of the storm.

Sara greeted Josh and Rosa at the café door and let them in.

'How are you feeling, chick?' she asked Rosa, hugging first her and then Josh. 'I can't believe you were so brave. I couldn't have done what you did.' Sara never failed to be astounded by Rosa's strength and determination. She put it down to her tough upbringing in children's homes and foster-care. A lesser person would be dining out for weeks on jumping into a turbulent sea and rescuing a child, but not Rosa.

'I'm fine – a scratch on the knee and feeling a bit tired, that's all.' She made a little groaning noise. 'I can't bear that so much wildlife has been affected. How on earth does all this plastic get into our waters, anyway?'

'That's a good question.' Sara put on her bright yellow apron. 'But if we as individuals can all try to do our bit, then that's a good start, at least. We need to stop using plastic for everything. I even saw an advert for bamboo toothbrushes the other day.'

Rosa nodded and looked gloomily outside. 'What are we doing to our planet?' she sighed.

Sara picked up some plastic-covered menus that were scattered on the floor. 'Maybe we should print fewer of these too?'

Josh was busy checking out the appliances in the kitchen area of the café.

'How's it looking?' Rosa noticed a broken window to the side of the seating area. The rain had come in and there were shards of glass lying around. 'Right, I'll get rid of those safely – and that floor is filthy.' She went to find the dustpan and brush as well as the broom, mop and bucket from the cupboard. After collecting up the shards of glass and tipping them into the recycling bin, she quickly swept around the floor, ready to wash it.

'We were lucky, you know,' Josh told them. 'I think the sea must have reached its peak when the little lad fell in, so the water didn't sit in here. The sea only came in a couple of inches, by the look of it, so all the appliances are in good working order, thank goodness. The floor in here is designed for wet feet anyway, so I reckon let's leave all windows and doors open for a few hours. With a day like today, once we've cleaned it, the place will dry out properly in no time.'

'That's a relief.' Sara started turning everything on. 'Let's fill all the urns up and get ready to give the volunteers hot drinks on us – and although I feel guilty saying this out loud, we've got plenty of plastic bottles of water too. Is that OK with you?'

'Of course it is,' Josh said immediately, Rosa nodding in agreement. 'We've got stacks of recyclable cups with lids out the back.' He looked around him. 'And only one window smashed – that's incredible. We can claim for that on our insurance if we need to, but it may not be worth losing the good premium we have. I'll check if one of the lads out there has got a spare board I can use for now.' Josh scratched his head. 'Where's the big lad this morning?'

'He's got a couple of clients first thing, said he'll be down later.'

Alec Burton was a counsellor, nicknamed 'big lad' because, at six-feet four, he was just that. With his thick mop of auburn hair and beard, he resembled some sort of Scottish gladiator.

Alec had helped Rosa through a very tough time earlier in the year, assisting her in facing her demons with alcohol, and also with confronting her self-esteem issues. Not only had she become stronger as a person but her relationship with Josh and her jealousy issues had also come on in leaps and bounds. Rosa had been delighted to pay this kindness forward in playing Cupid between him and Sara, who had also had her own struggles; namely coming to terms with the untimely death of her partner. Now, very much together, Alec and Sara appeared a perfect couple, and were direct proof that you could find love later in life.

Sara went on, 'Alec was just so good with that woman and her grandchild last night. He is an amazing human.'

'Aw, look at you, all in love and soppy.' Rosa grinned.

'And I have you to thank for that. It's not even three months yet and I do have to say I am rather smitten.'

'Life in the old dogs yet, eh?' Josh chipped in.

'Enough of your cheek, Mr Smith. Fifty is the new thirty, I'll have you know.' Sara in no way looked her age, with her natural beauty, trim figure and trendy dress sense.

'You'll be moving in together next,' Rosa teased.

'Er, this weekend actually.' Sara blushed.

'Really? You kept that quiet, lady.'

'If anyone ever said to me, "When you know, you know", I used to laugh and wonder what they meant. Yes, I was completely in love with my Steve, but it was a slow burner. This feeling has whipped *me* up like a storm, and I have not one single doubt about this man being The One.'

'I am so happy for you,' Rosa said, squirting floor cleaner into the bucket.

'Yeah, good on you. Alec didn't mention your co-habitation either.' With his last words, Josh sounded a little put out. His friendship had also grown with the big man in a very short time, but Alex hadn't shared that news with him. 'Do shout if you need a hand with the moving.' Josh started spooning instant coffee into the recyclable cups while Rosa mopped and pottered around, getting the café shipshape.

'So, tell me more about the lady and the little boy,' Rosa enquired.

'Well, her name is Tina Green and the little boy is her grandson, Alfie. They speak like you, Rosa – proper London people. They were holidaying down here, staying in the mobile park at the top. As the road was blocked, Alec put them up last night. Tina wanted to see you, to thank you, but they had a train booked back to London and couldn't afford to change the tickets. I just hope the road was clear enough to get to the station.'

'Oh yes, I forgot about the fallen tree. That's probably why so many people are down here helping with the clean-up: they couldn't get through to work.'

'Excuse me.' A deep voice caused Rosa to turn around from what she was doing. She was greeted by a guy in his early twenties, she reckoned. His face was tanned and friendly, and his long brown curls were being kept in order under a trendy striped bandana. He wore his long shorts well – like a European, not an Englishman. He wiped his hands down the side of them, then held one out to Rosa. 'Hi, I'm Nate.'

'Hi.' On shaking his hand, Rosa got a weird feeling run through her, as if she knew him already. 'Have we met before somewhere?'

'No, I doubt it. I work for these guys. Have done for a couple of years.' He pointed to his T-shirt, the Sea & Save logo crossing his chest. 'We're based on the north coast, but we saw the forecast for the eye of the storm, so we were all set to come down first thing this morning.'

'Aw, it's great, what you are doing.'

'Yes, they are a good bunch. My boss has asked if we can maybe have some drinks, but it would be easier if you could bring us a batch so that we don't have to stop what we are doing. We will pay, of course.'

'We are already on it, and no way are any of you paying; we're getting a table set up outside so please do tell everyone to help themselves. We are making some cheese rolls up too.'

'That's so kind.' Nate smiled at her for a long moment then hurried out of the café.

'Look at you being all bashful around the rescue team,' Josh noticed, kissing his wife on the cheek.

'Moi? Of course not. What's that saying: why would I eat a burger when I have steak at home?' she teased him then carried on with what she was doing.

Leaving the floor to dry, Rosa was just loading up the table outside with ready-made coffees, when the familiar white-haired figure of Sheila Hannafore, the landlady of the Ship Inn, walked past. There was no love lost between the two of them for many reasons – most recently due to Sheila's belief that Rosa had run her youngest son, Lucas, out of the Bay. Unbeknown to Rosa, that was in fact what had happened.

Rosa noticed how thin and stressed Sheila was looking as the woman greeted her curtly. Despite being in her late sixties, she had always looked well and sprightly, probably down to the new teeth and face-lift that she had paid for out of the money her husband had left her when he had died; today, however, that wasn't the case.

'Sheila,' Rosa acknowledged back. They hadn't spoken to each other for months and Rosa wondered what was coming now.

'In all my years down here, I've never known a storm like it. You didn't have too much damage, I hope?' Sheila asked.

'Er no, we were very lucky. You?'

'Some windows got broken, but it's not the end of the world. I'd prepared for far worse so I'm not complaining. Anyway, look, I'm not actually here for small talk.'

Phew. Situation normal, Rosa thought, feeling slightly unnerved by the previous pleasantries.

'Have you heard from my Lucas lately?' Sheila then demanded.

Rosa sighed. Even the mention of the woman's youngest son's name unsettled her. She hadn't heard from him since the awful incident last Christmas when Josh had been away and Rosa had got drunk, not knowing afterwards whether or not she had slept with Lucas. That incident had nearly broken up her marriage and was one of the key reasons why she had stopped drinking for good.

'I haven't, Sheila, no. Is he all right?' Rosa cringed at showing how much she cared.

'That's why I am asking *you*, Rosa. It pains me to have to do that, but I thought you might still be sniffing around him. He said he might be down in the summer, that's all.'

'He was never one for having his mobile on all the time.' Rosa cringed again at releasing yet another knowing comment about the woman's precious son.

She could hear Josh and Sara chatting and laughing inside.

'Well, you would know that, wouldn't you?' Sheila barked. 'I hope married life is treating you well,' was her final sarcastic comment before she turned and marched back across the littered beach to her pub.

Josh had caught the end of the conversation and appeared at the door, asking, 'What did *she* want?'

'Oh, er, nothing much. She was just being nosy, wanting to see what damage had been done. Probably hoping to nick some of our business – you know what she's like.' Rosa tried to shake the thought of Lucas out of her mind. She knew that whatever she and he had had was over, but it didn't stop her worrying about him.

Putting her face up to the sun and pushing thoughts of the handsome plumber to one side, she murmured, 'I cannot believe what a change there is in the weather. It's summer again. This breeze is so welcome too.'

'Yes, it's a perfect day. Might even get my Speedos on later.' Josh made a clicking noise with his tongue and winked.

'What a joy for us all.' Rosa laughed.

'Always treating the ladies, you know me... Anyway, now the

worst is cleaned up, Sara said she's fine to carry on with her shift today.'

On hearing her name, Sara herself came to the door and said, 'Yes, go on, the pair of you. You need to spend as much time with each other as possible, while you can.'

'What do you mean by that?' Rosa frowned, causing the tiny lightning scar on her left cheek to crease.

Sara grimaced. 'Sorry, eek – I didn't realise. I'm going back inside.'

'Josh?' Rosa cocked her head to the side.

'Come on, pretty lady, Jacob has just asked us to go and meet his new brood. Let's go.'

As they began to walk up the hill, Rosa linked one of Josh's big arms with both of hers and said, 'Husband? Please tell me what's going on.'

CHAPTER FOUR

'*Ciao-ciao!*' The chiselled Italian called Raffaele air-kissed both Josh and Rosa three times before telling them: 'I must get on, sorry.' He pointed to his chef's whites. 'We are very busy with lunchtime bookings today. His Lordship is upstairs with Her Ladyship, the Duchess.' He waved his arms around animatedly, his accent becoming more pronounced. 'I tell you – he is *obsessed* with those little cuties. *Per favore* – go on up.' And then Raff hurried back into the pub kitchen.

Josh and Rosa raced each other up the stairs to the swish private quarters above the pub where Jacob and Raff stayed when away from their beautiful home in Polhampton Sands. Tiptoeing now, Rosa opened the sitting-room door and peeped in.

'Oh, my goodness!' she cried quietly, without even greeting Jacob. She gave a little gasp. 'Just look at them!'

'Don't mind me, love. I've only been up all night playing nanny to this lot.' The smart publican camply flicked his hand at Rosa, then reached for Josh's hand and shook it firmly.

Rosa crouched down to take a better peek in the Duchess's comfy blanket-laden dog crate. 'Aw, they are miniature Hots,' she whispered. 'They are so cute! Just two?'

'Yes, two little boys, thank goodness. One bitch in this household is quite enough.' As Josh shook with laughter, Jacob continued, 'I'm surprised she could fit any in that tiny little belly of hers – thanks to your dirty dog taking advantage of her when she was so young.'

Josh then thought back to when Jacob and Raff had introduced the Duchess as Lady Dolce Vita Petunia Duchess Barkley. 'Have you thought of any names yet?' he enquired, bracing himself, wondering what the couple had come up with this time.

'Well, I dare say we should really let the future owners decide on their pups' names,' Jacob said reluctantly, adding, 'And with a pending last name of Rogers, I perish to think what Titty Titch will come out with for hers.'

'Has she met them yet?'

'No, I wanted you as the other grandparents to see them first. When are Titch and Ritchie getting married, anyway?'

'They haven't set a date yet, but she was hoping Christmas-time this year, I think.' Rosa gently stroked the exhausted Duchess.

'Exciting – I love a wedding. And where exactly is the absent father today?' Jacob asked, looking around for Hot. 'Trust that naughty dog not to be at the birth, or here now. A typical man.'

'What are you like?' Rosa smirked. 'He's with Mary, much to Merlin's disgust.' Merlin lived at Seaspray Cottage with Rosa's mother Mary; he was a huge, rather scary black cat with yellow fog-lamp eyes and too much attitude. 'Who's having the other puppy, anyway?' Rosa asked, and looked directly at Josh, who immediately put his palm up and out flat.

'No, no and *no*. Hot would hate not being the centre of attention and we've got enough to do with the shop and the café, without taking into consideration puppy training and raising a potential brood ourselves.'

'You're a miserable one today, aren't you?' Jacob tutted. 'I have to say that Raff and I are quite smitten with the smaller cherub, and with three already, what difference is a fourth really?'

At that moment, as if on cue, the couple's pugs Ugly and Pongo came running in and started play-fighting by the side of the crate. Whining softly, the Duchess watched them with interest and a degree of scorn.

'That's what I've been saying to Rosa. The bigger the family, the better.' Josh winked at his wife. 'And not through want of trying.'

'Ew.' Their host grimaced. 'It was bad enough being at the business end of a puppy birth, let alone hearing about you two at it like rabbits, or should I say dachshunds, in the circumstances.'

'But we won't be for a while, now Josh has announced he's decided to take some consulting work – without consulting me!' Rosa harrumphed.

Jacob frowned. 'That's OK, isn't it? He did it before, and London's not that far.'

'No, but New York is.'

Even easy-going Jacob looked taken aback at this. 'Oh. How long for, chap?'

'It's just for a couple of months. I'm helping out a former boss and the opportunity and money are just too good to turn down. I can fly home some weekends, and Rosa can come out to see me too, if she wants to.'

'Yes, I'll just drop everything and swan across the Pond, shall I?' Rosa sighed.

'Well, the Cockleberry gossip train tells me you are quite capable of swimming across after last night's heroics,' Jacob said fondly. 'You madwoman.'

Rosa shrugged. 'Oh, that. All in a day's work – you know me.'

Josh kissed his wife's forehead. 'She's not just a pretty face, this one. And to be fair, re New York, we did just discuss it and if you really don't want me to go, then I won't.'

'I was more bloody peeved that you mentioned it to Sara before me.'

Jacob mouthed 'oops' to Josh as Rosa continued, 'I get it. Financially, it should ultimately lead to you being home more, and if I am producing a football team, I will need all the help I can get.'

Josh lifted Rosa up and putting his big arms around her, he said, 'Let's chat this evening and make a final decision. I haven't signed anything yet and keeping my little princess sane and happy is the most important thing, you know that.'

At that moment there was a little yelp from the cage. The Duchess pulled one of her scamps back in line and the tiny puppy recommenced sucking furiously at the bitch's already sore little teats. Pongo and Ugly had settled down and were watching curiously and sniffing the new-borns through the crate.

'You tell them, Duchess.' Jacob looked at the feeding puppies proudly, then unfurling his legs he got up from the floor. 'Right, you lovely people, I'd better go and help my husband before *he* starts yelping at me. Are you staying for lunch?'

CHAPTER FIVE

Rosa was busily arranging stock outside the front of her shop, including doggie life-jackets and her bestselling animal-shaped Lilos. When she had first arrived in Cockleberry Bay, she hadn't realised quite how much scope there would be for selling pet products. Initially just sticking to food, accessories and designer dog-clothes, she had made a good living. However, now a whole new world had opened up, with products like pet nail varnish and hair slides, and she even had a full range of personalised pet birthday cards. Singing happily, she enjoyed the warm July sun on her back as she attached the sale items to a stand.

'Rosa Larkin?'

Startled, she turned around quickly.

'Sorry to make you jump. I thought you saw me there.'

Rosa checked out the young man in front of her. He looked around the same age as her, a surfer-dude type, of which there were many in south-west England, with shoulder-length bleach-blond locks and dark-blue twinkly eyes. He was a similar height to Lucas Hannafore and had a whisk of stubble on his firm jawline.

'It's fine. I was miles away and it's Rosa Smith – Larkin was my maiden name. Who wants her?'

'I'm Scott, Scott Wilde, reporter for the *South Cliffs Gazette*.'

'Just Wilde in name or in nature too?' Rosa said without thought, then, on recalling her own reckless and unhappy adolescence, filled with cider, soft drugs and hard knocks, she sighed unconsciously.

'I'm wild in the waves, baby.' Scott did a surfing action with his body. 'You said maiden name? You got hitched early, didn't you?'

Rosa found herself blushing slightly at his sexy accent. 'So you're a Scott from Scotland, and a cheeky one at that. Whereabouts are you from up there?'

'Glencoe. Not too far from Glasgow. You know it?'

'I do, actually. Many years ago, I went on a school trip to try and find the Loch Ness monster. We went up on a cable car when there was no snow and I was so frightened because it was so high that I had to be blindfolded to get me down again.'

'I know exactly where you were.' He grinned. 'That's funny.'

'To those watching, maybe. So, what brings you all the way down here?'

'I studied journalism in Exeter and just fell in love with this whole area, especially the surf.'

'It gets you here, doesn't it?' Rosa put her hand flat to her heart. Then she asked casually, 'Is Joe Fox still your Editor?'

'Ah, you know Joe, do you?'

Rosa winced at the thought of why and how she knew Joe, firstly their affair and then the awful business of him throwing a ball for his dog Suggs, causing both Hot and Rosa herself to take a tumble over West Cliffs.

'Yeah, I know him,' she said quietly.

'He interviewed me, but he's gone back to live in Manchester, I think. Family problems, I heard.'

Rosa felt a sense of relief. It was about time that karma had kissed the randy reporter. Becca, his wife, had said she was intending to move to Spain near her mother, taking the three younger kids with her but leaving their unpleasant teenage son behind. For Becca's sake, Rosa hoped she had followed through with her plan. She deserved some happiness.

'So, you have a new editor, then?' she asked politely.

'Yes, Kelly Daly. She's been around the block working for the national newspapers in a previous life, she told me. She's a right laugh.'

Scott realised maybe he'd given too much away about his new boss. He also noticed how beautiful Rosa was with her unruly dark brown curls and piercing green eyes. Adding pert breasts and brown toned legs to his list of pleasing observations made her easy to give away to. Even the bandage around her knee didn't deter his ardour.

'OK, I'm here to work.' Scott pulled himself together. 'Have you got a moment to chat? I hear you were quite the local heroine the other night and I would love to feature you in this week's edition.'

'Really?'

'It will make a lovely feel-good story and it was bloody brave what you did, girl. I spoke to Tina Green on the phone earlier. According to her, you saved her little grandson's life.'

'Anyone would have done it.'

'Nah, they wouldn't. I didn't even want to open my front door the other night, let alone jump in an angry ocean.'

Rosa shrugged. 'OK. I suppose I don't mind being interviewed. Josh, that's my husband, said he'd be back around midday to take over here, so could I meet you somewhere then?'

CHAPTER SIX

'Here comes the bride, all fat and wide,' Titch sang as she manoeuvred the baby buggy containing a sleeping Theo into the Corner Shop.

'Hardly,' Rosa replied. Patricia Whittaker was tiny in both height and stature, hence her nickname.

'I don't know any other words to that song.'

'You crack me up, mate. It's "all dressed in white", isn't it?'

'Shush, you'll wake the devil incarnate. I tell you, since he's started crawling, I need to be on full alert.' Titch walked into the back kitchen and filled the kettle. 'Nobody tells you that you also need eyes in the back of your backside to stop them getting into stuff.' She yawned hugely. 'In fact, Rose, nobody tells you how hard it is being a mother. I reckon it's a conspiracy: couples who reproduce don't put out a warning as they want everyone else to suffer as much as they do.'

'Don't be saying that to me,' Rosa objected. 'Not when I've just got my head around getting up the duff myself.'

'Ah, now *that* is an exciting revelation. And joking aside, Rose, just look at him.' They both stared down at the caramel-skinned, curly-haired sleeping little baby and said, 'Aw,' in unison. 'I wouldn't change him for the world. And now I've got

Ritchie, well, I can't complain. He does so much. I've lucked in with him, I tell you.'

'Remind me. How old is he now?'

'My fiancé? He's twenty, I think.' Titch grinned. 'Oh, my son, you mean. I can't believe you just asked me that, considering you helped deliver him on this very floor – and in a dog bed!'

'Ha! Oops, yes of course. That was a day neither of us will forget in a hurry. Wait a minute – he'll be walking before too long, won't he?'

'Thanks for that, Rose, I'm only just getting used to the crawling bit.' She looked around. 'Where's our Hottie today?'

'With Josh. They've gone into Polhampton to do some shopping.' Rosa's phone beeped. 'Talk of the devil.' When the conversation had ended, she said, 'That's a nuisance.'

'What's up?'

'I said I'd meet the *Gazette* reporter at twelve, and now my dear husband tells me he's going to be later than he said.'

'Theo shouldn't need his lunch until one, so I can cover until Josh gets back, if you like. Just let me make myself a cuppa before you go.'

'You're an angel. Make us both one, I've still got half an hour. I can't believe it's so quiet today. Everyone's down on the beach, no doubt. The calm after the storm and all that.' Rosa followed Titch into the back kitchen. 'How's it going, with all of you living at your mum's, anyway?'

'It's all right, but when we are married the plan is to get our own place. In fact, hurry up and move out of upstairs, mate – you know we want to rent it off you.'

'Patience, dear Titch, patience. That is the plan, especially once I start popping out babies too.'

'Babies plural? I'd like to see how you get on with just the one first, love.' Titch held up the biscuit tin and shook it. She frowned. 'Looks like we need to get Mary baking again with immediate effect.'

As Rosa headed home from her interview with Scott, she thought back to the day that had literally changed her life. It seemed unbelievable now, how so much could have happened in such a short time. This hot July day was a contrast to the cold and frosty December morning when she had stepped out of Evans, Donald & Simpson Solicitors in London, with the ancient leather briefcase she'd been given, along with the revelation that she was the brand-new owner of the Corner Shop in Cockleberry Bay.

Hurrying home to her rented room in the East End of London, she had confided in Josh, her landlord at the time, asking what on earth she would do with a rundown old shop located miles away in South Devon. And then she discovered the condition attached to the mystery inheritance. A note she had found among all the paperwork in the old briefcase had read: *One proviso of my gift to you is that you must NEVER sell the Corner Shop in Cockleberry Bay. When you feel the time is right, it can only be passed on to someone you feel really deserves it, and only then.*

Thinking this over, Rosa sighed then returned to the present moment. Scott had been a proficient interviewer – concise and straight to the point, which made it easy for her to answer. He took a few photos of her on the beach and outside ROSA'S, and had done his research about 'the proviso' since it had been mentioned previously on the *South Cliffs Today* radio show. He had said that if she wanted to tell him anything more about that, it would be completely off the record. In reply, Rosa had casually mentioned that it had been on her mind a bit recently but there was nothing more to be told.

However, it *had* been on her mind a lot lately. Yes, she was just part-time at the café now and yes, she did love sharing her shifts with Titch at the shop, although it didn't leave her much time for anything else. Having a family and moving to a bigger home were the obvious next steps for her and Josh. And as he had made a significant investment into the café, that was what she needed to concentrate on more now. Especially as part of their deal was that Sara, who had created such a good foundation for ROSA'S, wanted to start taking life a little bit easier.

There was no question now that she had to do right by her wonderful great-grandfather Ned and great-grandmother Queenie; the couple had not only loved her from afar and brought her back to her birth mother Mary, here in Cockleberry Bay, but they had also given her a chance of making something of herself in this beautiful part of the world.

And as much as her heart and soul were entwined with the shop, and despite having owned it for such a short time, realistically and practically, Rosa knew it was time. Time for it to be passed on to somebody who truly deserved it.

CHAPTER SEVEN

Titch appeared from the back kitchen with Theo in her arms. 'Shit! They don't tell you how much babies do that, either. I've put his stinky nappy in the bin, Rose, so the flies don't get at it.'

Relieved that there were no customers within earshot, Rosa took Theo's little hand in hers. He gripped it tightly, then smiled gummily at her.

'He's a bloody flirt already, too,' his mother said proudly. 'Right, I'm off. Did the interview go OK?'

'Yes, fine, thanks.'

'Good, good. I sold two flamingo inflatables so you'll need to put some more out. And it looks like you are getting low on the big bags of the posh dried dog-food.' Titch started loading stuff into the bottom of the pushchair. 'Now, what did I want to ask you? There was a reason for me popping in earlier. Oh yeah. Can we have the wedding reception in the café, do you think?' Before Rosa could answer, Titch added hurriedly, 'We will pay you and everything, as we realise we will need it exclusively. We were thinking the day after Boxing Day if that's OK?'

'What a fantastic idea. We can decorate it beautifully and make it look all lovely and wedding-y, as well as Christmassy. I'll have to run it by Sara, but I'm sure she'll be fine about it.'

Rosa picked up Theo's bottle, which he had just thrown to the floor. 'And if it suits, well then – that can be my and Josh's wedding present to you.'

'That would be amazing. Thanks, Rose. We were just going to do a fish-and-chip supper for everyone. That's Ritchie's mum and dad's present to us, seeing as they own the fish-and-chip shop and all that.'

Rosa bent down to Hot's basket to gently play with the snoozing hound's floppy ears. 'So, my wanderer husband did return?'

'Yes, he's just gone upstairs to put some shorts on.'

'Have you thought about your dress yet?'

'Yeah. It'll just be simple, like me.' Titch grinned. 'I actually saw one on eBay that I loved, so I bought it. It's designer and I could no way afford it normally, so it's a win-win really. I'm not bothered it's second-hand – it just needs a clean. I was thinking of powder blue for you, if that's OK? I obviously want Theo to be a page boy, so he can wear a blue bow-tie then. Choose whatever you want online, up to one hundred pounds, and we will give you the money.'

'How exciting! Show me a pic of your dress. And don't be silly, I can buy my own outfit.'

At that moment, Theo launched his bottle again and started to wail, causing Hot to wake up and dart from his bed in the corner and start barking.

'Here we go again,' Titch grumbled. 'I'd better take him home and feed him properly. Hot – shut it! I'll send you the link to the dress, Rose. Oh, and I've put your post on the stairs.'

'Don't forget, you'll soon be having one of these too,' Rosa reminded her friend, picking her noisy dachshund up from the floor to quieten him. He immediately began licking her face.

'Hmm. "Too" and "soon" being the operative words.' Titch bit her lip. 'I need to speak to Jacob, as I think I may have been a bit rash in my decision. A ten-month-old, a tiny new puppy and a wedding to plan might be just a wee bit too much all at once. OK, must go. See you, Rose.' And Titch made her way out onto the street, now bright with sunshine and teeming with tourists.

As soon as Rosa put Hot back down, he started to jump up at her legs, whining for more cuddles. 'Hush now,' she told him. 'If it's like father, like son, I don't think I could cope with two of you either.'

Josh was now calling down the stairs to her. She stroked Hot's snout and put a *Back in 20 minutes* sign on the shop door. 'Come on, let's go upstairs and see what your daddy wants.'

As Hot tore up the steep staircase ahead of her, Rosa glanced down at the post in her hands. A bright pink Jiffy bag stood out, with Rosa's name and address written on it in an untidy scrawl. She hadn't remembered ordering anything online. Intrigued, she ripped it open right away. Inside she found a one-page letter written on lined paper torn out of a notepad, and attached to a brown, hard-backed envelope. The note read:

Dear Rosa

We wanted to see you before we left for London – me and Alfie, that is. But our train tickets were for a set time and I couldn't afford to change them. We ended up climbing over the fallen tree and walking all the way to the station. Look at me talking about money, when what you did for me was priceless. I'm the sole carer of Alfie, see. His dad, my son, is away at the moment and his mum – well, she ain't around any more neither. I love both my boys to the moon and back. I didn't know what to get you. I mean, what is the price of a life? Alec gave me your details and I was just going to call you, but I felt words weren't enough for what you did, so I saw this and had to get it for you. I'm hoping to work some extra shifts so that we can come back down as we'd love to meet you properly.

May the brightest star always shine down on you and bring you happiness.

Yours gratefully,

Tina and Alfie Green

As Rosa stood, taking this in, Josh shouted downstairs: 'You coming up to see me, wifey, or not? I've got something to show you.'

'Ooh, promises! One sec.' Rosa opened the brown envelope and felt emotional as she looked down at the celestial certificate in her hand. Tina Green had named a star after her and called it ROSA'S STAR. An inscription underneath simply said:

You didn't just save Alfie's life, you saved mine too x

CHAPTER EIGHT

'Here, let me read it.' An agitated Rosa grabbed for the newspaper which Josh was now teasingly holding high above her pretty head. Hot was running around them excitedly on the landing, barking so incessantly that they didn't hear Titch coming back in downstairs to retrieve the bag of shopping she had forgotten to get out of the fridge.

The couple went into the lounge and sat on the sofa. Josh was busy quickly reading the article before handing it over. 'Wait a minute!' he exclaimed, a frown appearing on his face.

'What's up?'

Josh handed the local newspaper to Rosa. 'What would you want to say that for? We're not even sure what we are doing yet.'

Rosa read the headline aloud: *Brave Cockleberry Bay Resident Plans to Give Her Corner Shop Away for Free!* What the hell? I didn't say that, I swear. And that photo – my dress looks so short!' One of the two shots was of her reaching up to tie an inflatable to the pole outside; a little bit of her knickers was on show. The other was taken outside the café, near the beach wall, showing where she had jumped in to save Alfie. 'Little shit!' she said angrily.

'Who?'

'Oh, Scott Wilde, the reporter. He's not only mangled my

words, he's taken that photo without me even knowing. I look a right slut.' The more she read down the article, the more incensed she became. 'Stupidly, I trusted him, thought he was OK, not like the others. I should have known better.'

'Don't let it get to you.' Josh sat next to Rosa on the sofa, pushed her short dress up and rested his hand on the soft skin of her thigh. 'You do look hot though.'

Far more interested in the column inches that confronted her, Rosa brushed her husband's hand off and started reading intently. 'Blah blah about the rescue, but, oh no, he's obviously pulled this from the podcast of the radio interview I did all that time ago.' She read aloud:

'Not only is Rosa Smith a complete heroine of the moment, saving the life of holidaymaker four-year-old Alfie Green, she is giving away a little goldmine of hers, the Corner Shop in Cockleberry Bay – for free. Yes, readers, FOR FREE! Her great-grandfather Ned, who many inhabitants of the Bay will remember with fondness, left her the shop in his will, under the proviso that it must never be sold but given to somebody who truly deserves it. Here's a thought: maybe there are golden tickets in the dog food, Willy Wonka-style? I suggest you all go along, form an orderly queue and see what you need to do to get hold of it.'

'Maybe that isn't such a bad idea,' Josh interjected. 'Trial random people.'

'Josh, I'm surprised at you. You just don't get it, do you?' Rosa was close to tears. 'This is so important to me and my family.' The word 'family' didn't flow off Rosa's tongue easily. She had spent too many years growing up alone with just herself and her demons – not even realising she had any family of her own until she inherited the Corner Shop.

'I mean, how are we going to do this?' Josh continued. 'Titch would be your obvious choice, I guess.' Titch was just about to call out goodbye from halfway up the stairs, but on the mention of her name stood silently and listened as Josh went on, 'But although she's great with the customers, she's not the brightest spark in the box when it comes to management and figures. And you want the legacy of your great-grandparents to be a success, don't you, not a half-baked attempt at keeping the shop running.'

Titch's mouth fell open. Not wanting to hear any more, she quietly went back down the stairs and made a quick exit.

'Titch wants the flat, not the shop.'

'Have you asked her?'

'Not directly. In fact, I don't think we've ever discussed it. Josh, this is a huge decision for me to make, so I'd appreciate you being less flippant about it and not so rude about Titch. I'd trust that girl with my life, and remember, I had help with the figures side of the business when I first arrived. There is always a solution. She's a shrewd cookie, that one.'

'OK, calm down. Sorry, I love her too. That was just me with my business head on talking.'

Still annoyed at her husband's instant dismissal of her friend, Rosa told him, 'Anyway, Ritchie's parents have set their son's sights on running the chip shop when they retire soon, and Titch has already said to me that she's happy to help part-time here while Theo is not of school age, but with a view to eventually working with Ritchie.'

'That makes sense, so whatever happens, she will be fine.'

'Yes, of course she will. Titch is always all right. She's a survivor, like me.'

'There's a flat above the chip shop, isn't there?'

'Yes, but Ritchie's parents love it in the Bay so they are going to stay living there, I think.'

Hot, who had gone off to sun himself and watch next door's cat on the wall from the balcony off the lounge, came running in and pushed his wet nose against Rosa's bare legs. She began playing with his silky brown ears. 'What do you say, boy? Or shall we just stay here and be done with it?'

But the dachshund had spotted a favourite toy peeking out from under the sofa – a smelly piece of rag that used to be a squeaking squirrel – and he now began to systematically try to rip it to pieces, holding it in place with his two front paws.

Josh carried on over the noise. 'What about your mother?'

Rosa opened her mouth to reply, then clapped a hand over her nose. 'Ugh! Hot, that's disgusting.' Then she went on, 'What's wrong with you today, Josh? This isn't a straight business decision. It must come from the heart. And don't be silly about Mary. I'm sure Queenie and Ned didn't envisage her taking over and she wouldn't want that either. She's quite happy with her few shifts at the Co-op and covering for us here in emergencies. It would be far too much for her anyway, with her bad chest. She even gets out of breath walking the few yards from the Co-op to home and back nowadays.'

Used to his wife's passionate outbursts, Josh put his arm around her. 'OK, calm down. Let's wait until I'm back from New York and maybe I can help you make a proper decision then. It's not as if we have a new house to move into yet, anyway. There's no time limit, is there?'

Rosa's mood changed from red to green in seconds. 'Not for that, no.' Moving Josh's hand back onto her thigh and kissing him gently on the lips, she said seductively, 'I think I'm ovulating.'

Standing up, a now-smirking Josh moved her hand to the hardening bulge in his shorts, saying, 'Quick. Let's go and make some puppies of our own.'

CHAPTER NINE

'One thing! All I ask for is one thing!'

Rosa was greeted by a huffing woman exiting the café door at speed. Her mop of red fluffy hair was covered by a big white sunhat.

'Sorry?' Rosa questioned.

'Oh, it doesn't matter,' the disgruntled one replied haughtily and continued round the beach path towards South Cliffs, her flowery maxi-dress flowing behind her.

Rosa greeted Sara and asked, 'What was that all about?'

Sara said wryly, 'Oh, you haven't met her yet, have you? That was Vegan Vera – well, that's not her real name, it's Bergamot Hamilton-Jones.'

'Bergamot?' Rosa snorted. 'Queen bloody B by the sound of her!'

'Hmm, yes, she is quite a handful. Anyway, she's just moved down from London. Messy divorce, from what I can gather. And already going on at me for not having oat milk or vegan sausage rolls. Now I know this is the thing of this day and age, and I am up for saving the planet in many ways, as you know – but food? I offer full-fat milk, meaty sausages from nearby farms, ditto bacon, real fresh butter and thick, crusty white bread. All locally sourced, all delicious.' She shook her head. 'This is a breakfast place, after all, not a bloody health retreat.'

Rosa laughed. 'I do hear you, but–'

'No need to "but", Rosa. I had made a mental note for us to discuss that very topic this morning. I am mindful that we could be missing out on a bigger market and I am also aware that there are a lot of people who have allergies these days. When I was a kid in the Sixties, we used to eat dirt! Where have all these allergies come from? I remember just a few kids having eczema and asthma, but that was about it. Maybe we should start selling mud pies too, who knows?'

'I reckon you're just resisting so that Piers Morgan comes to visit us and congratulates us on sticking to our principles. He was ranting on about veganism again on breakfast TV just this morning.'

'Oh Rosa, you do make me laugh. But don't you dare tell Alec about my Marmite crush on that man. You see, I reckon Piersy baby would be putty in my hands once I'd given him a large portion of our famous Cockleberry Clotted Cream Victoria Sandwich, don't you?'

'Yes, all of a sudden it would be Alec who?' They both collapsed in laughter.

Rosa tied her apron behind her neck. Despite it being early, a couple of families were already in – probably from the campsite at the top of the hill, she thought. The sea was millpond-calm and the early August sun just poking through.

'I can't believe how quickly the beach has been cleared,' she remarked, beginning to stock up the fridge with Devon yoghurts and bottles of locally made fruit drinks.

'I know,' Sara agreed. 'That's teamwork for you. Another big truck came down early this morning to take away the piles of recycling.'

At that moment a couple of the guys from Sea & Save came in, Nate being one of them. Today his long dark hair was tied back in a neat ponytail. He still looked familiar to Rosa. She hoped that she hadn't slept with him on one of the drunken nights in her past, but then remembered with a feeling of relief that the only guys she'd had sexual relations with down here were Lucas Hannafore and Joe Fox.

'Get me a coffee, please, mate. I've left my wallet at home,' Nate said casually to his colleague as he headed off to the toilet.

The other fellow, who was in his early sixties, grumbled, 'These ruddy newbies – they expect it all.'

Newbie? Rosa was sure Nate had said he had worked for them for two years. The young man was back within seconds. 'Did you ask them?' he pestered the older man.

'Give me a chance, lad.' His companion was busy paying for the drinks.

'Ask what?' Rosa enquired brightly.

Nate took a slurp from his sugar-laden coffee and put it back down on the counter. 'Well, as you know, we had lots of casualties from the storm, so many in fact that we haven't got enough space back at the wildlife centre to put them all. We wondered if you knew anyone around here who might offer to be a temporary hospital.'

'There's nowhere suitable here, I'm afraid,' Sara told him.

'I've got a walled back-yard area,' Rosa said thoughtfully, 'but I've also got him.' She pointed down to Hot who, exhausted from a run on the beach, was asleep in his café basket at the side of the counter.

'It's just two gulls, we have them in cages in the van.' Nate became slightly animated. 'There's no problem with your little dog, but if you can keep him away from them that would be best. All you need do is talk to them and feed and water them.

They do get a bit feisty being penned in, but they should be right as rain in a couple of weeks or so. The vet has given them a good going-over and their wings just need to heal before we can set them free. The charity will pay you for the food if you take them.'

'I…er…' Rosa thought she should maybe speak to Josh first before she added yet another task to her To Do list.

'I'm staying at the Ship until we are done,' the lad continued, 'so I can always pop in and help, if need be.'

The older guy nodded along to Nate's words, then said to Rosa: 'Why not come and have a quick look at them, young lady?'

'Well?' Sara asked as Rosa reappeared a couple of minutes later, looking guilty.

'Of course I'm having them – you know what a sucker I am. They look so vulnerable. I will get Josh to help me put a rack up outside so that Hot and any other visiting hounds won't bother them.'

'That's great. And knowing you, Rosa, they will obviously need names.'

'Already chosen.' Rosa grinned. 'Flotsam and Jetsam.'

CHAPTER TEN

Rosa was just standing on the opposite side of the road, checking how the Corner Shop window display looked from the outside, when she noticed Nate walking up the hill towards her. He was quite short, but his muscly frame gave him proportion and there was something attractive about him. Rosa often thought that about people, men and women alike. A person could have the most beautiful face, but if they had no charisma or sex-appeal, they would not seem beautiful at all.

'Hey. Just thought I'd pop in and see how the gulls are doing?'

'Aw, that's kind. They are noisy buggers, but I have seen an improvement, definitely,' Rosa told him.

'They are lucky to be in the care of such a brave and generous lady.' Nate paused. 'As stated in the *Gazette*.'

'Ah, that. Look, it was nothing.'

'Not to the family of that kid you saved it wasn't, I'm sure.' He followed Rosa across the road and into the shop. 'So, this is the famous Corner Shop you are giving away, is it?' He looked around at the packed shelves. 'Are you mad?'

'I was lucky enough to inherit this place from my great-grandfather. It has brought me fortune and real happiness, and so I am standing by my part of the deal that I pass it on to somebody who truly deserves it. I want it to carry on being a shop and being of the same benefit to the locals and tourists of Cockleberry Bay.'

'So how do you plan to find this "right person" then?' Nate made inverted commas with his fingers.

'I'm not sure,' Rosa said truthfully. 'I'm hoping the universe might guide me.'

'You believe in all that baloney then?'

'Well, I do believe in the Law of Attraction, yes: the simple belief that positive or negative thoughts bring positive or negative experiences into a person's life. My mother is very spiritual.'

'Mary Cobb – that's your mum, isn't it?'

'You know a lot about me, don't you?' Rosa was puzzled.

'Let's just say that woman called Edie who makes my breakfast at the pub likes to talk.' He paused. 'And about everyone down here – not just you, it seems.'

'Ha, yes. Edie Rogers, Chief Stoker of the Cockleberry Bay Gossip Train, strikes again.'

'So how long has your mum lived here?' Nate asked.

'All her life, apart from a stint in London twenty-odd years ago, I think.'

'You think?'

'I haven't known her long enough to get the whole story,' Rosa said quietly.

'How exciting – a long-lost family tale.'

'I'm surprised Edie hasn't told you all about that, too.' Rosa started tidying the shop counter. 'You're still staying at the Ship, then?' she asked.

'Yes, just for a couple more days. I'm in the boxroom and Sheila is only charging me for food and drink, not lodgings. As, in her words, we are in effect "cleaning up her garden".'

'That's kind, although that room is so tiny.' Rosa could remember it well. 'I stayed in the pub for a few days myself when I first moved down from London.'

'It's fine by me. Do I look like someone who's used to five-star luxury?' Nate pointed to his scruffy hair and sand-stained shorts and gave her the familiar smile that made Rosa feel a little unsettled.

'Where do you plan to go afterwards?' she asked. 'Back to the north coast? That's where you're from, I think.'

There was a huge squawk from the back yard. Nate put his hand on Rosa's shoulder. 'Shall we go and see those birds?'

'Yes, come through.' Rosa led the way into the back kitchen and out through the door into the yard, closing it behind her to keep Hot out. 'Working for the charity must be such a rewarding job though,' she said. 'And two years at it, that's dedication. Although the older guy with you in the café said you were a newbie.'

'Oh, er – a newbie to this beach, he probably meant,' Nate said swiftly. 'Here they are. Hello, boys.' Flotsam and Jetsam came to the front of their cages, crying in defiance at still being locked up, and flapping their now mended wings furiously. Pete had reminded him to double-check for a full wing-span, and that the charity leg bands around their legs were not too tight. After watching them in their respective cages for a minute, he was happy. 'Right, let's set them free.'

'Really? That's great. Despite the noise, I will be a little sad to let them go.'

'This shop set *you* free, didn't it, Rosa?' Nate said. 'I can tell just by the look on your face. Free from the rat race, the bullshit we call life. Lucky you.'

'Yes, I do thank my lucky stars every day. But I also believe we make our own luck, Nate. I could have got the shop, just ticked it over, cheated by secretly selling it to someone who wanted it rather than deserved it. But no. I wanted to make a success of it in my own right. Wanted to make my family proud for giving me this chance.' Rosa looked up and suddenly thought how apt it was that Tina had so sweetly named one of those stars after her, stars which she had so often looked up to and wished on so many times during her lost and unhappy past.

Nate opened both cage doors at the same time and with a united screech of relief, the big birds spread their mended wings and flew up to the balcony, before soaring off, high above the rooftops and down towards the cliffs and the beautiful sea.

'There they go,' Rosa said, watching them. 'But like I said, where are you off to, now the beach clear-up is nearly over?'

Without answering, Nate pulled his phone out of his pocket, saying hastily, 'Er, sorry to be rude, Rosa, but Pete needs me down the front. I told him I was only going to be five minutes.'

Rosa let him out of the back gate then went inside the shop and shut the door behind her. Nate seemed to know an awful lot more about her than she did about him, she thought. On reflection, she didn't even know his last name. And what a funny thing to lie about – how long you had worked somewhere... Oh well. Maybe she had just heard him incorrectly. But why was he so hesitant in answering her questions about the future?

There was something about him that made her feel uneasy. Maybe, like her mother, she had been gifted with some kind of sixth sense – but if so, right at this moment, that sense wasn't making any sense at all.

CHAPTER ELEVEN

'Oh Rosa, sadness is but a wall between two gardens. Josh will be back in no time and if I were you, duck, I would grab the opportunity to take a trip to New York before you have nippers of your own running around your feet.' Mary hugged her daughter to her ample chest.

They were in the kitchen at Seaspray Cottage, Mary's home that she had formerly shared with Rosa's great-grandmother Queenie.

'I miss him,' Rosa lamented.

'He hasn't even been gone a week yet,' Mary pointed out patiently.

'I know, but we haven't been apart for ages – and now I think about it, we still haven't been on that honeymoon he promised and we've been married a year now. At least he waited until after our first anniversary to go.'

'Think back to a few months ago when you were in a terrible place. Josh went off to London and you didn't even know if he was ever going to come back to you.'

'Thanks for reminding me, Mother.' Rosa's mind flashed back to her drunken night with Lucas when she couldn't remember whether they had had sex or not. Instead of running out on her, the emotionally mature Josh had made sure that she received all the support she needed – and then came back to her when she was ready to move forward with their relationship.

'You are right though, time will fly,' Rosa conceded. 'Yes, it's only September but I have Christmas forward-planning to arrange for both the shop and the café. So I will be very busy. And there's Titch's wedding to help her with too.'

'That's the spirit, girl.'

'Josh is in New York with his friend Carlton, you know. Goodness knows what the two of them will get up to.' Carlton was a great single mate of Josh's; Rosa had met him a few times and liked him.

Mary leaned towards her. 'You are to go home and make sure the Peridot stone I gave you stays near, all right? You were getting so much better with this jealousy lark.'

'I just don't want anything to go wrong,' Rosa said, close to tears. 'I feel properly happy for the first time in my life.'

'You know what Kahlil Gibran would say on the matter, don't you?' Mary smiled, causing the same reaction in her daughter.

'No, but do tell. Not that I could stop you!'

'That love and doubt are not on speaking terms.'

'OK, your favourite prophet did pretty good with that quote. In fact, Sara was just saying a similar thing about her and Alec the other day. But I'm still scared, that it might all end.'

'Well, if you keep putting that out to the universe, then it might. Stay positive, and life will bring you joy. How beautiful to find a heart that loves you, without asking you for anything else, only to know that you are happy. You're lucky, my girl. Love found you.' Mary's voice tailed off.

Rosa sensed an underlying sadness in her mother's words. They had never spoken about her previous relationships – or who Rosa's father was, for that matter. All Rosa knew was that she had been the result of a one-night stand when Mary was in the dark and painful grip of her alcoholism. Mary had done everything to care for her but one night, under the influence of drink, she had dropped her baby daughter, causing the cut on the tiny girl's cheek, which subsequently became a scar in the shape of a bolt of lightning. That scar was a reminder to them both of Rosa's tough start in life, for from that day forward she had been taken away from her mother and brought up in care.

At that moment, Merlin mad cat came screeching through the cat flap and started munching noisily at his crunchies. Mary reached into her apron pocket and took a large puff on her inhaler. After silently counting to ten, she released her breath and looked at the clock. 'Time for me to go up to get changed for work, love.'

Titch was serving a customer when Rosa arrived back at the Corner Shop. In his basket, Hot raised an ear, then after being tickled behind that ear, he dug himself in under his blanket again and went back to sleep, lying on top of the squirrel rag.

Rosa went to the back kitchen and put the kettle on. She hated the empty feeling she got when Josh wasn't near her. Realising she was maybe getting overly reliant on him again she pulled her shoulders back and let her mother's words soak in. She had to believe that Josh loved her, but after suffering so much loneliness and rejection as a child, she carried deep scars within and it was hard to stay present and correct sometimes. Giving up alcohol had helped with this though, massively. Her mind and emotions were on far more of an even keel now. And if she did feel nagging doubts rising, she could quite easily talk herself down from them. Alec had been and still was her rock for when she needed to talk things through. Maybe she should see him soon, Rosa thought, before this empty feeling started to engulf her.

She went through to the shop carrying two mugs of tea and the biscuit tin.

'I've been dying to talk to you,' Titch said. 'Quick, sit here.' She patted the empty stool behind the counter then reached for her mobile. 'Look! You are only on the bloody *Daily Mail Online*.'

Rosa nearly splattered her tea everywhere. 'What the…? Let me look.' The headline read: *Cockleberry Bay Resident to Give Shop Away for Free*. There were several pictures of her and the shop, taken by Scott on that summer day.

'How bizarre that they've only just picked up the story,' Rosa said. 'It was in the *Gazette* in July.'

'Maybe it's a slow news week.' Titch munched on a custard cream. 'Look at you being famous. There's a good side to it though, as now everyone will know about the shop and that will surely boost sales. And I guess you will want to give the flat away with the shop, won't you?'

Rosa put her hand on her friend's. 'Sorry for not discussing this openly with you before. I should have done when the story appeared in the paper, back in the summer. The thing is, I'm kind of not sure about it. Part of me knows it's time to let it go, but this place is so ingrained in me that another part of me wants to keep it. But Josh tells me it's not viable for our future plans. The way I dealt with that was, I decided to put a ten-year proviso on it, as I would hate someone to buy it just to make a fast buck.'

Titch took a deep breath and held her tongue. Overhearing what Josh had said about her inability to run the shop had really upset her. She had discussed it with Ritchie who said to take no notice – that Josh was a stuck-up mummy's boy and that it was her friendship with Rosa that counted. If truth be told, what Josh had said about her was right, but what she lacked in academic qualification, Titch knew she made up for in common sense, which in her eyes was three-quarters of the battle – in everything in life. And with her husband-to-be's ability to look at a bag of potatoes and know exactly how many chips you could get out of it, she knew there would never be a problem on the financial side of things.

Aware how huge a decision this was for her friend, instead of speaking her thoughts aloud and causing Rosa to feel guilty, she was the bigger person and simply said, 'That's the trouble when hearts are worn on sleeves, isn't it, Rose? We sometimes lose sight of the overall picture.'

'Yes, but I also feel a bit funny because it will mean letting go of something that is mine. After that, everything I have will be shared with Josh. I want to feel secure, Titch. I've never had a home of my own before.'

'Rose, he loves you, mate – he loves you so bloody much. Men don't take on the kids thing lightly. That's why I'm so blessed with Ritchie too; he's taking on someone else's child, as well as me. Now, that is commitment.'

'I do hear you. And we have been on a massive shag-fest for the last few weeks. There is every chance I could be pregnant, I reckon.' Rosa took a slurp of tea. 'Would you want it though? The shop, I mean. I thought you were all set to take over the chippie with Ritchie.'

Titch's voice softened. 'You need to follow your heart, Rose. You always have, and it knows things that your mind can't explain.'

'But?'

'Hush.' Titch put her finger to her friend's lips. 'No more about it, now.'

'OK.' Rosa obediently drank her tea. 'Have you heard from

Theo's dad lately?'

'Yes. Because of Theo's illness, Ben is in regular touch and is coming down to stay with his dad for Christmas.'

'Big Ben, eh?' Rosa laughed.

Titch couldn't suppress her laughter either. 'Such an apt nickname for my last conquest of wild debauchery. It's hard to believe I will be a respectable married woman like you soon.'

'Yeah. Who'd have thought it.' Rosa giggled again. 'I keep forgetting that Alec is Theo's grandad too. Sara hates it when I call her Grandma.' She rooted around in the biscuit tin and helped herself to a fig roll. 'Theo's fine now though, isn't he?'

'Yes, but with the bowel condition he's got, there is a chance it can flare up again. It's just such a relief that Ben has the same blood group.'

Rosa remembered with a shudder the stressful hospital dash with little Theo when he had been under her care.

'Ben's coming to the wedding too,' Titch went on, 'with his girlfriend. Ritchie is so laid back, he's fine about it. In fact, they are both going to mind Theo for us in the evening.'

'That's very grown up.'

'Ben is Theo's father, Rose. He's going to be in all our lives forever, so it's the way forward. We were not in love, we were just strangers having sex on a drunken stag night, so there will never be any animosity. And he's going to be a bloody doctor too, so the maintenance will always be good.'

Rosa tutted. 'You're a tinker and a survivor, Ms Whittaker.'

Titch grinned. 'Takes one to know one, Mrs Smith.'

CHAPTER TWELVE

Rosa sat on the side of the bath waiting for the white plastic stick of the pregnancy test to show her fate. Josh had arranged to FaceTime her shortly, so she thought it was the perfect time to do it. Her boobs had been feeling a bit sore and she had had a few tummy twinges, so she was almost certain that this was it. She turned the stick face down as she almost couldn't bear to know either way. Counting the last sixty seconds in her head, she braced herself and turned the test over.

The words NOT PREGNANT shouted back at her. Amazed at how quickly tears stung her eyes, she stood up. In her promiscuous teenage years, getting pregnant would have been the worst thing in the world to happen to her. It was ironic really, all those times she was so relieved that she wasn't pregnant and this one time, when it was something she really did want, it was negative. Maybe she had tried the test too early? Popping the stick back in the empty box, the moment of hope was dashed when she felt the familiar sensation of period blood trickling down into her pants. Sitting on the toilet, she rested her head on the wall. Sensing her distress, Hot trotted in and plonked himself down across both of her socked feet.

'Hey, you.'

Rosa attempted a smile at the sight of her handsome husband smiling back at her down the iPad screen. Then on seeing her expression his face dropped. 'What's the matter, beautiful girl?'

'I'm not pregnant.'

'Oh, sweetheart. It's OK, please don't be sad. You surely want me around to be able to moan to when it does happen – and just think of all the practising we can do.'

'It's just a bit disappointing, that's all. How's it going, anyway?'

'All good. Me and Carlton are sharing this swish apartment. Here, let me give you a little tour.' He whizzed the camera around so she could see his surroundings.

'Nice. Project going OK?'

Josh knew that wasn't really what his slightly insecure wife wanted to hear. 'Yeah. Work's good but we've only been out once. We've got such a tight deadline that we are going to be knackered most of the time. So, it's same shit, different day, really. We just happen to be in New York.'

'New York, so terrible for you, isn't it?' Rosa smirked at him.

'I want to squeeze that pretty little face of yours,' Josh laughed. 'It is so different to being down in the Bay. I miss the peace, to be honest. I never thought I'd say that after living in and loving London for so long. I won't miss hearing sirens when I'm home, I can tell you that. How's our Hot?'

At the mention of his name, the little hound's ears pricked up. Rosa lifted him and waved a paw down the phone.

'Bless him! I miss you both so much. Do you fancy coming over soon? I'm allowed to put one flight on the company and it would be such fun.'

'The way I feel today, I just want to crawl into bed with a hot water bottle.'

'Bless you, darling. I wish I was there to take care of you.'

'I'm being a baby, it's fine. I do miss you though. Sundays are the worst. Let me speak to Titch about my coming over, but it's not so easy now she's got Theo to look after, and Mary doesn't like to do more than a few hours on her own. Plus, I've got Sara and the café to think about too. And Jacob's pulling his hair out with the puppies so I don't want to burden him with Hot.'

'OK, OK, sweet girl. No stress. If it's not possible I will come home for a weekend. I finish up mid-December anyway, which is not that far away. Better go. I popped back in my lunch-break to have some privacy. Love you both.' He waved and blew her a kiss.

Rosa fingered her wedding ring and with true doggy intuition, Hot put his paw on his mistress's foot and looked up at her. 'Come on, Mr Sausage,' she sighed, 'let's take you for a walk and go and get us both some dinner.'

Saying 'Mr Sausage' made Rosa think of Lucas – aka Luke to her. Luke was what he had called himself when they had first met; when he was on a find-out mission for his mother at the Corner Shop. It was Luke who had immediately nicknamed Hot 'Mr Sausage', making her laugh. She wondered why he hadn't been down to the Bay to see Sheila for so long. Yes, his mother, Sheila Hannafore, landlady of the Ship Inn, was a tricky character – but it just seemed odd that Luke hadn't been seen since before last Christmas. That was the time when she had drunkenly thrown herself at him – the night she had been convinced that Josh was having an affair. It was months ago now, coming up to a year soon, and there'd been no sign of him since. Yet Luke had taken great pride in telling her that he never missed a summer or Christmas down in the Bay.

Rosa asked herself how she would feel about him if she did see him. There was undoubtedly a spark of passion between them, but this had been ignited carnally just once. Single at the time, Rosa had only been in the Bay for a matter of days and was feeling out of her depth in the shop and its shabby, cold and neglected first-floor flat. Luke had deceived her, and she really should have had nothing more to do with him but, just as she had done with so many other men before Luke, she gave herself to him, driven by loneliness, pure lust and the need for human touch – in any form.

In marrying Josh, she had made the choice between security and risky freedom. Lucas was handsome, with a twinkle in his eye and the gift of the gab, but Josh was steady and dependable, good-looking and reliable. And after the turmoil that she had faced throughout her life, Rosa realised that 'reliable' was all right. It had taken a long time and many chats with Alec to accept that life was boring sometimes, it couldn't always be fireworks, parties, hedonistic happenings. She had come from a life in which drama and conflict were the norm – it was all she had known. But she had come to understand now that the day-to-day routine of life had to occur, and that monotony and monogamy were fine – *if* your head was in the right place.

She hadn't regretted sleeping with Lucas. He had lit the fire within her when she had needed it; satisfied a craving – almost like the drag of a cigarette, or the first sip of a crisp cold glass of wine on a hot day. But then Josh had come along and filled her life completely.

This didn't stop Rosa from wanting to know if the handsome plumber was OK. She still had his number but was sensible enough to be aware that she had to let go of everything to do with him. Her respect for herself and Josh was too high for her to go down that road again. Lucas Hannafore being out of sight and almost out of mind was, without doubt, a good thing.

CHAPTER THIRTEEN

Mary was standing on a stepladder outside Seaspray Cottage pruning back the ivy plant that ran rampant over her wall. She stopped when she heard the familiar steps of her daughter walking up the hill, put the clippers she was using in her apron pocket and started climbing down shakily.

'Careful, Mother, that doesn't look too safe,' Rosa called out. Hot started sniffing around, then cocked his tiny leg against the ladder.

'Hot Dog, no!' Mary tutted. Then: 'You got a minute, Rosa?'

'Just a few as I'm meeting Ralph at the garage at twelve. He's taking us to Jacob and Raff's Polhampton place for Sunday lunch and I don't want to keep him waiting.' Despite many pleas for more taxi drivers in town, Ralph Weeks was still the one and only, very busy Lone Ranger.

'That's nice. I just got a juicy joint of beef topside in case you wanted to come to me, but I can freeze it for next week, if you like?'

'You should have said earlier but that would be lovely, thank you.' Hot scampered through the open door in search of Merlin, who was sleeping peacefully on Queenie's old chair. On sensing the playful hound, he reared up and hissed, and fled through the kitchen to the cat-flap there.

'Sit down.' Mary washed her hands in the kitchen sink and dried them, then with her daughter sat opposite her at the table, she reached for Rosa's right hand and began to study the palm. So accustomed was Rosa to her mother doing this to her, that she just sat back and relaxed.

'When is Josh back, did you say?'

'Mid-December. Haven't got a date yet.'

'Are you seeing him before that?'

'I don't know, to be honest, and I haven't told him yet but I'm thinking not. There's a lot going on, what with Titch's wedding and everything else.'

'Don't be scared, daughter,' Mary whispered.

'Mother! Stop going weird on me.'

'I wouldn't want to fly for the first time on my own either.' Rosa, with her closeted childhood and inability to keep a job down, let alone ever save enough for a holiday, had never been abroad. Mary suddenly took a sharp intake of breath, saying, 'Don't go this time. And you tell him to hurry up back, eh?' She paused and her face assumed a look of fear. 'But not until after the fireworks. You've got grandchildren to make – and that's important. But it can wait a few weeks.'

'Mary, what can you see?' Rosa's voice was firm. 'Do you mean after the fireworks night here?' Cockleberry Bay had a legendary annual fireworks display.

Mary lifted Rosa's hand to her face and pushed it hard against her cheek. 'Yes, child,' she hissed. 'Tell your secret to the wind, but don't blame it for telling the trees.'

'Ow. That hurt.' Rosa screwed her face up. 'Stop it, please. And what's that supposed to mean?'

'What happened to that Nate fella who released the gulls the other day?' her mother replied with a question.

68

'Last time I saw him, he mentioned that he was liking the south coast more than the north but I–'

Before Rosa could continue saying that she didn't know what he was doing, Mary cut her short. 'Bloody newspapers,' she grunted, then took on the frail voice of an ailing Queenie: 'Trust your instincts, Rosa, and nothing or no one else.'

'I miss Queenie,' Rosa said without thought. Visions of her wise, white-haired great-grandmother with her weather-beaten, furrowed face and sharp tongue came to the fore.

'She is always with us, child.' A teaspoon clattered to the floor from the kitchen worktop. Mary yawned. 'Always with us.'

CHAPTER FOURTEEN

'*Ciao bella.*' Raff greeted Rosa with three kisses. 'So, I have cooked the roast lamb for you today with all her trimmings. Jacob has even made fresh mint sauce from the garden.' He threw a little piece of meat fat onto the kitchen tiles for Hot to gobble up.

Rosa loved coming to the boys' Polhampton house. It was built high on a hill with the most stunning views of Polhampton Sands below. The couple would quite often entertain, and when they weren't working at the pub on a Sunday, made sure that all the main Sunday papers were put out on a table in the large conservatory overlooking the sea. There would always be sweet and savoury snacks to nibble, and any drink you could mention would be served at a moment's notice. Nowadays, Rosa's preferred drink for occasions like these was either Diet Coke or tonic water.

Her relationship with alcohol had never been a good one. With her mother being an alcoholic, she had often wondered if it was a genetic thing which caused her to love wine so much, but after having many chats with Alec, also a reformed alcoholic, she had begun to understand it a lot more. She would drink to cover her pain, to not have to be present in the world.

To enjoy the veil of unconsciousness, even for a short time. And boy, was she a terrible drunk. But again, she worked out that every person with deep-rooted issues made a bad drunk because it allowed for all the pain, suffering and discontent to come to the fore and be voiced.

The old Rosa's motto was 'only regret the things you don't do', but sober now, there were a few things that she certainly did regret doing. Namely, getting drunk up West Cliffs, then putting her life at risk by falling; she had also put her beloved little companion Hot Dog in danger on several occasions when she was too drunk to know what she was doing.

Her thoughts were interrupted when there was a sudden commotion coming from the hall. She could hear different tones and volumes of barking, plus the sound of Jacob scolding every one of his canine charges, who dutifully followed him into the kitchen and started jumping up at Rosa's legs. In rapture on beholding so many playmates all in the same place and at the same time, including the Duchess with their new pups, Hot proceeded to run around barking madly too.

Jacob put his hand to his forehead and faked collapsing against the kitchen worktop. 'Five of them, Rosa. Five! They are driving me mad.'

Rosa reached down and picked up one of the dachshund puppies. He fitted neatly into her hand. 'I think I may internally combust with love,' she said, tickling the adorable little fellow under his brown chin, then she snuggled him close to her chest. 'He is just so beautiful.' She looked down at the other little fella scratching at her shoe. 'They both are. Have you got names for them yet? I know you said you were waiting for the owners to christen them, but–'

'Uno and Due – One and Two in Italian – for now,' Raff broke in. He was busy taking the roast potatoes out of the oven and basting them. Then, without looking up, he carried on: 'He moan and he moan and he moan. But he loves them all too much, I see.'

'I know that. His bark is worse than his bite,' Rosa joked as she put the little pup down.

'I am here, you know.' Jacob picked up a scalding potato from the sizzling baking tray; a glare from his husband causing him to drop it back in quickly with a sharp 'ouch.'

'So, have you spoken to Titch yet?' Rosa asked. 'The pups must be ready to leave their mum surely by now?'

'She's ignoring my calls, the little bitch.' Jacob licked his fingers.

Rosa laughed, then made a face. 'Oh no. I remember now.'

'Don't tell me she doesn't want one of them!' Jacob groaned. 'Yes, you're right, I do love them all, but this is crazy shit. Is there a male equivalent of Mad Cat Lady with dogs?'

Raff shut the oven door. '*Sì*! You *are* the crazy man with the dogs. But I'm not giving you away.' He whipped Jacob's bottom with the oven gloves.

'She did mention that it might be too much, what with Theo and now planning the wedding,' Rosa admitted. 'Sorry, I forgot to tell you.'

'Well, I'll just have to put an advert in the paper – or maybe Vicki can help.'

'Vicki can help with what?' The voice belonged to their friend, the local vet Vicki Cliss. 'The door was ajar; you didn't hear me knock for all the barking.' She kissed all of them on the cheek as the dogs tore off towards the conservatory, play-fighting as they went.

'Where's Stuart and the kids? I peeled enough potatoes for a small army.' Raff was now rolling pastry for his apple-pie dessert.

'They are on their way. I drove up, but they are so full of energy Stuart said he'd walk up the hill from the beach to try and wear them out a bit. I didn't think you'd be able to cope with five dogs, two unruly kids and umm…' She opened her coat and rubbed her tummy '…and two more little wishes.'

'Oh, that's wonderful news!' Jacob rushed to kiss her on the cheek.

'*Bravissimo*.' Raff wiped his hands on his apron and did the same.

Rosa felt tears welling in her eyes. Partly remembering the awful time earlier in the year when Vicki had lost her little baby boy right here on their friends' bathroom floor. And selfishly too, because she realised more than ever that having children of her own was high on her agenda.

'That's such lovely news,' she said quietly. 'When are you due?'

'Beginning of April.' Ever intuitive, Vicki took off her coat. 'I have approximately ten minutes before those boys of mine get up that hill, so come on, Rosa, let's have a drink in the conservatory before they arrive.' Vicki winked at the equally knowing Jacob who rounded up the dogs from the conservatory and went outside with them to greet the children.

'How are you doing then, Rosa? It's lovely to see you.'

'Fine – I'm fine, and so happy you're pregnant again. It was so awful that day here.' Rosa shuddered. 'Even I get flashbacks, so goodness knows how it has affected you.'

'This has kind of blocked that out now. Twins too.' Vicki beamed. 'I can't believe how blessed I feel.'

'So, are there twins in either of your families then?'

'Surprisingly, no, not that we know of anyway. On my To Do list is a family tree, but I'm too busy growing our own at the moment.' Vicki put her hand on Rosa's arm. 'But it's not all about me. It's OK not to be fine, you know. I remember feeling so blue when we started trying again after losing Fred and the test kept saying no.'

'Aw, you named him.'

'Yes. Just because we never met him as a baby, that doesn't mean his little soul is not around us, moving us on, sharing our lives.'

Tears started to roll down Rosa's cheeks. 'I just got really excited thinking I was pregnant this month and then there it was, the red patch of failure.'

'Not failure at all, simply proof that you are a woman and that everything is working just as it should. You've only recently started trying and you are both young. It will be fine. Producing little miracles isn't always going to be easy.'

'Look at Titch,' Rosa sighed. 'She only had to smile at Ben and Theo arrived.'

Vicki soothed, 'OK, there are some exceptions, I know, but try to relax, not worry too much and just have as much sex as you can.'

'Chance would be a fine thing. Josh got a great opportunity to work in New York, and that's where he is now. He'll be back before Christmas though.'

'That's just weeks away. You have plenty of time. It's OK.'

Rosa blew her nose and felt almost immediately better. Vicki was the kind of person you believed; if she said something was going to be all right, then it would be.

The vet went on, 'I'm just so happy that you made the decision to start a family. It is magical.'

'You know that I struggled with whether I thought I'd be a good mum or not and you really helped me with that.' Rosa pulled back her sleeve to reveal the rose quartz bracelet that Vicki had gifted her as a thank you for helping her through her miscarriage tragedy. 'The stone of fertility. It worked for you, so it has to be my turn next.'

'Exactly.' Vicki put her hand on her friend's arm. 'I could never have got through that day without you, you know.'

Before Rosa could reply, the six dogs, now followed by Vicki and Stuart's two sons, dressed up and whooping like Red Indians, came bounding towards the huge window overlooking Polhampton Sands.

'This *is* the reality of it though,' Vicki laughed, protecting her growing bump with her hand.

'I'm ready for reality,' Rosa said, then, nicking one of the boys' feathered headdresses, she plonked it on her head and began running and whooping around the room as part of the chaos.

CHAPTER FIFTEEN

Rosa shivered as she walked down towards the beach and the café. A magnificent late-autumn sunrise was just coming up where the sky met the sea. She was meeting Sara to discuss winter opening times, as, although they had a great local clientele, even that did dwindle on weekdays during the winter months. The clocks would fall back soon so it would be getting darker earlier.

'I should have worn a hat,' she said aloud to Hot, who was already running ahead on his lead at the excitement of chasing seagulls. Josh had been so clever to rename the café, ROSA'S – as it was half hers and half Sara's. And it still gave her a warm fuzzy feeling when she walked down the hill to see the sign and realise that another dream of hers had become a reality. She could never have imagined this happening even two years ago. And now not only did she have a shop, she also had the café. It really was 'pinch me' stuff.

Yes, Rosa thought, she had inherited the derelict shop to turn around, and turn it around she had, through her own merit and sheer hard work. She had always hoped that the locals would come to feel the same love and affection for her and the shop as they had had for her great-grandfather Ned and his wife

Dorothea. Poor Dorothea, who was unable to have children and who, tragically, on finding out about her husband's affair, took her life by leaping from the very cliffs in front of her. It was Rosa's very own great-grandmother Queenie, Ned's secret lover, who had given birth to Rosa's grandmother Maria, Mary's mum. Rosa had never known about her family tree on her mother's side until she had come to Cockleberry Bay and begun to unravel the mysteries of her past. It was weird to think that if Queenie and Ned had never fallen in love, then she wouldn't even be here.

The lights of the café were already on and the windows slightly steamy. Rosa could see Sara, getting busy laying tables. She was such a great lady and she, too, had worked hard to keep the café running as a little goldmine, just as old Harry Trevan had done before her.

Despite the early hour, Vegan Vera was sitting quietly in the corner seat with a book open on the table. Sara murmured in Rosa's ear that her stroppy customer had almost shown some emotion earlier when she had told her about the soy yoghurts they were now stocking. Rosa looked over and saw that the woman had one in front of her, with fresh raspberries on top, and was spooning it hungrily into her lipsticked mouth, in between sips from a large soy latte. Rosa realised that she had never seen Vegan Vera with a smile on her face. She had tried to make polite conversation with her a few times, but to no avail. The red-headed Bergamot was, in fact, rather an enigma.

Rosa went over to see if she wanted anything else. 'Good book?' she asked pleasantly. Then, glancing down, she spotted an official-looking letter lying between the open pages.

Without looking up, Bergamot replied abruptly, 'Book's great, fucking letter not so much.'

Rosa tried not to laugh. Hearing swear words in a posh voice had always amused her for some reason.

'Bastard husband – or soon to be ex-husband. I really thought that my leaving London and renting down here would make him see sense, but no, he's still shagging the cocking housekeeper. She's got an arse the size of Belgravia too!' Angrily, the woman crumpled the letter up and threw it into her large designer handbag.

Rosa tried to get a word in, but to no avail.

'I never realised the pre-nup would stand, but his solicitor seems to think it bloody does,' Bergamot rambled on. 'It looks like I may have to go back to work at this rate. Me – having to work!' She gobbled a mouthful of yoghurt and then stabbed at the bottom of the pot with her spoon as if her husband was down there, fornicating with the help.

'Oh dear,' Rosa mustered, trying to keep a straight face. 'How terrible for you.'

The disgruntled forty-something drained her coffee and grumbled, 'I'd better get back on the dating sites, I suppose.' As she got up and pushed her chair back, she let out a noisy fart. 'Oopsee,' she said, showing no sign of embarrassment. 'One of the perils of saving the planet.' She reached for her bag. 'See you later – Rosa, isn't it?'

'Yes. Er, yes, see you soon, V…I mean, Bergamot.'

Sara, who had been listening in, was doubled up with laughter when Rosa reached the counter and put Vegan Vera's measly 20p tip into the ceramic burlesque dancer money box that held a sign saying *Nice Tips*.

'I wonder if they ever have a firm stool?' Sara remarked.

'What? Who?' Rosa began to unload one of the dishwashers.

'Vegans,' Sara whispered, although the café was empty now, also causing Rosa to laugh out loud.

Then she tried to be serious. 'All things aside, I do think we need to start offering a couple more vegan options. And well done on the different milks. I tried the oat one and it tastes OK – in porridge, anyway.'

'Yes. I thought I'd make a start after what we discussed previously. We are a tourist industry, after all, and the customer is always right.'

'Does that include Vegan Vera? No, definitely not. I wonder what dating site she'll be looking at,' Rosa mused.

'Gold-diggers dot com, I should imagine,' Sara said and they high-fived.

'What's so funny?' Titch manoeuvred the baby stroller towards the counter. 'Actually, I'll tell you what's not funny. A teething baby. "Oh coo, coo, look at his lovely toothy-pegs coming through," says the childless chuffing stranger in the Co-op.' Titch sighed. 'There is nothing funny or lovely about a ruddy teething baby. I thought by now he would have a full set of gnashers, but no, still they keep popping through. He'll have a set like that Rylan Clark-Neal at this rate.' She pulled off her coat and went to sit at a window table.

Sara made an *oops*-type face at Rosa. 'Large black coffee coming up, girl.'

Hot, who had been contentedly chewing a raggedy soft dog-toy, had got up and trotted over, and was now circling around the push-chair, sniffing and wagging his tiny tail. He didn't bark, but eventually sat down, guarding the pram and its contents.

Rosa went over, kissed her friend on the cheek and peered into the pram. 'Oh look, he's sleeping like a baby now.'

'Ha bloody ha, Rose, yes, he is and probably will for the next two hours, so actually I'm not sure why I've not gone back to bed too. Oh yes, I'm starving, as I've been awake since bloody four a.m., that's why. And I can't get into the kitchen at the bungalow as Mum is fussing around in there. Can I have a bacon roll, please? With loads of butter and ketchup?'

'You sound as if you need it, girl,' Rosa told her.

Titch then smiled. 'That's better – and *breathe*… I just needed to get that off my chest, Rose – sorry. Ritchie is on a double shift at the chip shop later today, so I've left him to lie in. The poor sod, he usually gets my morning rant.'

'You must both be knackered from Theo's first-birthday celebrations too. That was such a happy party you had at your mum's. And that cake Ritchie made was lovely. He is such a keeper.'

'I know. A whole year has gone by since my little treasure flew out of me on to the Corner Shop floor. It seems like five minutes ago, but also five years ago. So much has happened in that time. I can't believe I am going to be Mrs Patricia Rogers soon. It's madness.'

Sara brought over Titch's mug of black coffee and a tea for Rosa.

'Are you sure you're still OK to man the shop as planned?' Rosa asked Titch. 'I just need to sort some stuff with Sara this morning.'

'Of course I am. Apart from needing to get out of the house, I've also come down to show you both a couple of,' she hesitated, 'er…*things*.'

'OK, what's that then?'

Titch reached past the curious Hot and gently pulled a blanket back in the compartment under the stroller. There, curled up together and sleeping soundly in a compact carrying crate were the Duchess's two little dachshund puppies.

Rosa bit her lip. 'But I thought–'

'I thought, too, but when I went to tell Jacob I couldn't have one of them, I fell so in love that I then couldn't split them up, so now I have both of them. The two brothers.'

'Will you be able to cope?'

'You know me, Rose, I moan but I'm a doer, I can sort anything out. The puppies adore Mum too; her wheelchair is like an adventure playground and their favourite sleeping place is on her lap or tucked down the side of her. It's put a big smile on her face, and she says she is more than happy to mind them and feed them when I'm working. Ritchie loves them too, and likes taking them for tiny walks around the block. Not too far, and he has to go slowly, but they absolutely love sniffing all the new smells. We have to keep them away from your mum's cottage though, in case Merlin comes out and has them for breakfast.'

Sara approached carrying a plate containing a delicious-smelling bacon roll. She said wistfully, 'I now have puppy envy.'

'I didn't think to ask you if you wanted one,' Rosa said, and bent down to stroke Hot and keep him from waking all three of the sleeping babies.

'Not at the moment. But who knows, now we are living together – and if Brown doesn't mind. Maybe that's the next step for us. Alec and I both have matching walking jackets already.'

'Aw.' Rosa took a slurp of tea then turned to Titch. 'Dare I ask if you have names for the puppies yet?' She smiled inwardly, thinking if Jacob were here, he would be squeezing his buttocks tightly together in dreadful anticipation.

'Well, as they were born during the storm, we were thinking maybe Banger and Flash – ooh, that's a bit like Bangers and Mash.' Titch couldn't keep a straight face. 'We then thought that maybe we should follow the Duchess and give them lengthy pedigree names too.'

'Despite Hot being from unknown heritage though, of course,' Rosa laughed.

'And I know how much it will wind Jacob up.' Titch took a huge bite of her bacon roll.

'Remember they are stuck with these names forever, the poor little mites,' Rosa warned her. Sara nodded in agreement as she motioned a group of three construction workers who had just walked in, to a window seat.

'But then we thought, me and Ritch, that since we're not pedigree or fancy ourselves, our furry offspring should not be given posh names.' She pointed down to the pushchair and then made the noise of a fanfare while pretending to blow a fake trumpet. 'I would like to introduce you to Mr Sav Eloy, and the tinier little cutie is Mr Chip Olata, Mr Chips for short. So, please meet Saveloy and Mr Chips. What do you reckon?'

'I reckon that you should tell Jacob when he's sitting down, but it's bloody genius, and so apt, dear friend.' Rosa stood up. Sara was shaking with laughter as she took the food order behind them. All the sudden commotion caused Theo to start crying and the puppies to poke their little heads up in their tiny carrying crate, much to Hot's delight who started to bark loudly at his infants.

Titch put her hand to her head. 'It will all be OK,' she reassured herself positively. 'Here.' She handed Rosa a fiver for her breakfast, which Rosa promptly gave back.

'I'll get that.'

'Thanks, Rose. Could you just put the rest of that roll in a bag for me – and get Hot's lead too. I will take them all to the shop now. I'll get Theo fed and back to Mum, put the sausages out in your back yard for five minutes and then be a dutiful shop assistant from eight-thirty, as always.' She took a huge noisy breath.

'Are you sure?' Rosa's voice was caring as she gently stroked the puppies through the bars of their little carry crate.

'The only thing I'm sure of, mate, is that I must be slightly crazy.'

Rosa was just helping Titch out of the café with her laden pushchair, when Nate appeared in the doorway.

'Hey Rosa.'

'Hi. What brings you down to our neck of the woods again?'

'Your pretty face, of course.'

'Hah, flattery will get you nowhere. I'm a married woman.'

Nate grinned. 'I've moved into a mate's house, South Cliffs end.' He pointed loosely up the beach. 'I'm looking for some work actually, if you know of any?'

'So, you're not at Sea & Save any more then?'

'Let's get in the warm, shall we?' Nate ushered Rosa inside and shut the door behind them. 'So, do you know of any work?'

'Nothing here now, but…' For some reason Rosa was slightly captivated by this man. 'I've been harping on about painting the front of the Corner Shop for ages. It needs doing properly as I just did it roughly when I moved in and I want it to be in the best condition when I pass it on. Painting is probably not your thing at all, but–'

'No, no, that's perfect,' Nate said immediately, allowing Rosa to fully understand what the expression 'biting your hand off' meant. He was obviously desperate for a job. 'I can start sanding it down tomorrow, if that suits.' He paused. 'I mean, it makes sense before any more bad weather comes in during the winter. And I'd really like to help you out, Rosa, especially after you helped with the gulls, for nothing and all that. Do you have paint?'

'I do, actually, in the back shed, and Ritchie has got some ladders that will reach. I had budgeted just £250: is that OK?'

'Cash?'

'Yes, cash.'

Nate kissed her on the cheek. 'It's a deal.' He then added cheekily, 'You couldn't just sub me a tenner, could you, so I can get some breakfast?' Then on seeing somebody about to open the café door, he darted to the toilet.

'Rosa, just the lady.' The friendly, ruddy face of Pete from Sea & Save lit up with a huge smile on seeing her. 'We are done here now – bit proud of our efforts, though I say it myself. We saved at least one hundred birds, we did – all safe, well and back in their natural environments again.'

He followed Rosa as she made her way back behind the counter.

'That's truly amazing. Well done you,' she said. 'What can I get you? On the house, obviously.'

'That's very kind, luvvie, but Anthea, that's my wife, she's in the car and it's market day in Polhampton so I'm not going to stop. I just wondered if I could give you this for the counter.' He held up a green plastic charity box with the now familiar Sea & Save logo on it. 'We're hoping that we could fill it quite quickly now the residents know how we've helped clean up their beach. Would you mind having it on your counter?'

'No, of course not. And do you know what? I will put all my tips in there too from now on.'

'And mine,' Sara shouted through.

'Aw, you're a pair of lovely ladies, you are. There's a number on the back if it gets full, but we usually come around and empty them every couple of months anyway. Right, better get out there before my beloved starts moaning.'

As soon as the door shut behind Pete, Nate appeared from the toilet.

'You were a long time,' Rosa said.

Nate made a face and rubbed his tummy. 'Bit of an upset.'

'Oh dear. Better make sure you're not up the top of that ladder when you get caught short, won't you?' Laughing at her own wit, Rosa joined Sara in the kitchen.

'Nice idea to do this for the charity,' Sara said.

'Yes. I've always supported the lifeboats, especially after they rescued me and Hot, but this is just as important.' Rosa thought for a moment, then exclaimed, 'That's it! Genius!'

'What is?' Sara looked baffled.

Rosa was completely animated. 'This has just given me the best idea of how I can pass the shop on fairly *and* in a way that would have made great-grandfather Ned and great-grandmother Queenie proud. *Yesss!*'

CHAPTER SIXTEEN

Rosa did a double-take at the front of her mother's home as she walked up the hill towards the Lobster Pot: she had never seen Seaspray Cottage looking so colourful. Rosa had promised Jacob that she would take Ugly, Pongo and the Duchess on the beach this morning while he and Raff decorated the pub for Halloween.

With so much going on with the café and the shop, preparing Halloween decorations and goodies for the half-term influx of visitors, she had surprised herself with how well she was coping despite Josh being away. She hadn't even needed to go and see Alec for a counselling-type chat. Technology enabled her and Josh to message, talk and see each other every day, so she could feel his warmth through the screen. Sub-consciously heeding Mary's suggestion that Josh should come back *after* the fireworks, Rosa had suggested to her husband that it made more sense and would save money if he just worked through and came back when the contract was over.

Mary was dead right about Rosa not wanting to go to an airport and fly on her own for the very first time. It all seemed a bit daunting. Josh had, of course, totally understood and promised that in the New Year they would go on their much talked-about belated honeymoon to somewhere special, like the Maldives. Where, in his words, they could 'endlessly fornicate in complete peace, quiet and paradise'. Rosa looked forward to that idea. With no Hot, shop, café or external forces to sidetrack them, it could be a time of blissful coitus.

Hot pulled on his lead towards the direction of Mary's front door. The woman opened it wearing her old green dressing gown, and yawning.

'It's not like you not to be up and dressed, Mother,' Rosa said. 'Are you all right?'

Without saying a word, Mary beckoned them into the kitchen and put the kettle on. Merlin screeched and tore upstairs. Hot had the sense not to follow but to plonk himself down beside the fire, though not before sneakily hoovering up the little bit of wet cat food that was left in his arch enemy's bowl. From the top of the stairs, Merlin heard the bowl rattling on the tiled kitchen floor and he hissed, his tail puffing up with outrage.

'I've just got up, because I was up all night carving that pumpkin and decorating the window,' Mary explained.

'But it's not Halloween for a week.'

'I know, but I'm all set for trick-and-treating now, although the kids sometimes get a bit scared, as when they see my long black hair, they think I could be a witch.' Mary fetched down two mugs. 'I'm doing a tarot reading and maybe a séance at midnight on the actual night, if you fancy joining us? Colette from the shop is coming and Edie Rogers, so far.'

'I'll let you know. The boys are doing a special Halloween menu with live music, so I said, if they need me, I may help them clear up afterwards.'

'OK, duck. Well, I expect they will be busy as the Ship probably isn't doing anything special this year.'

'Why do you say that?'

'Sheila's got cancer. Quite aggressive, so Edie tells me. She still does her cleaning down there and you know how she loves to talk.'

'Oh no. As much as no love is lost between us, that's awful. I didn't think Sheila looked very well when I saw her after the storm. Poor Luke.'

'Yes, and Tom. That's her other son. I don't think you met him when you first came down.'

'I remember her mentioning him.'

'They moved up to Bristol, him and his wife Martha and their kids, a while back. He changed his job, I think.'

'Luke hasn't been down since last Christmas,' Rosa stated.

Mary put her left hand to her heart and placed her right index finger clumsily on Rosa's lips. 'Take care, child. For bonds that are woven in sadness are stronger than the ties of joy and pleasure.'

'Mother!' Rosa pushed Mary's hand away.

Mary quickly turned and started pouring boiling water on top of the tea bags. 'You have got time for a drink, haven't you, Rosa?'

Hearing about Sheila made Rosa suddenly aware that she was always just 'popping in' to her mum's and never spending quality time with her. Especially as they still had so many lost years to catch up on. She pulled her phone out of her bag.

'Yes, of course, I'd love a cuppa. I will text Jacob now to say I'll be with him in an hour. What is Halloween all about, anyway? I've always just thought of it as a lot of commercial rubbish if I'm honest.'

Mary looked horrified. 'Let me tell you all about it.' As Rosa settled back into her chair and took a sip of tea, her mother went on: 'Today, yes, Halloween, is celebrated all around the world with sweets, costumes and trick-or-treaters, but all this

88

began as a celebration for the dead to return to the living world and reconnect with their families.'

'Oh, so that is the spooky connotation then?'

'Well, if you want to look at talking to your loved ones as that, then I guess so, but having that gift, I see it as a beautiful thing.' Putting some sugar into her tea, Mary sat comfortably at the kitchen table and went on, 'Halloween is the night preceding All Hallows Day, which is November the first. This date has long been considered one of the most magical nights of the year – a night on which the "wall" that separates the living from the dead is at its thinnest.'

'Wow, why didn't I know this already? It all makes sense now with the ghosts and the ghouls.' Rosa listened, entranced. 'Go on.'

'So, this night was usually a celebration of being in touch with the spiritual world and many would experience heightened sensitivity around this time.'

'So, what does a carved pumpkin stand for then?'

'Well, a folklore tale states that the jack-o-lantern was originally supposed to help lost souls find their way home. It got its name from an Irish folk tale about a prankster named Jack. Jack was a known troublemaker who was stuck between the world of the living and that of the dead. Legend states that Jack tricked the devil into the trunk of a tree by carving the image of a cross in the tree's trunk. His mischievous ways denied him access to heaven – and the devil was so enraged by being tricked that Jack was also denied access to hell. So he remained a lost soul trapped between two worlds. In Ireland, people would carve turnips and pumpkins and place candles inside on All Hallows Eve to help guide Jack's spirit back home.'

'That's an amazing tale!'

Sensing that Hot was asleep, Merlin sauntered downstairs.

On finding his bowl now empty, just as he'd suspected, he glared at the snoozing dog and headed in a huff out of his cat flap, letting it bang shut behind him.

Rosa laughed. 'That cat! He channels Queenie more and more every day.'

Mary fumbled in her dressing-gown pocket for her inhaler, pulled it out and took a puff. She then took a gulp of tea before resuming, 'Going back to my lesson, Rosa, because the veil between the spirit world is more accessible at that time, the tradition of adorning the house in scary-looking decorations is said to keep any bad spirits away.'

'Ah, I see. It all makes sense now. Is it just the UK and Ireland who do this then?'

'No. Many cultures around the world continue to celebrate All Hallows Eve in a more traditional way by lighting candles and offering food for their loved ones who may return. I see it as a lovely celebration to spare a moment to think of those who have crossed over, and send them love and gratitude to help them move on their way.'

'I love that. I'm so glad we stopped by today. I have received a history lesson too.' Rosa went to wake up Hot.

'Me too.' Mary stood up and tutted. 'Anyhow, look at me still in my night clothes. I must get ready for the day.' Facing her daughter, she put both her hands gently on Rosa's young shoulders and squeezed them lovingly. 'Have a good day, but be aware, my girl. The Jacks of this world…they come in many guises.'

On walking up to the Lobster Pot, Hot once again trotting ahead, Rosa's thoughts turned to Lucas. Surely Sheila had told her family that she was very ill – and if she hadn't been able to get a message to Lucas, then his brother must have tried? And if Lucas did know that his mother was ill, then why wasn't he coming down to see her? Or maybe it was because he couldn't bear to see his mother unwell... So many scenarios, but if Alec was in front of her now, he would tell her not to make a story in her head. He'd say that time would tell – and that 'nobody is ever thinking what you tell yourself they are thinking!' He would also probably say it was none of her business.

It occurred to Rosa that if something was wrong with Mary, she would want to know immediately and certainly wouldn't shoot the messenger, whoever they might be. However, that didn't stop her worrying, in case, despite her deep love for Josh, even talking to Lucas might bring back all the feelings from before. She didn't love Luke, just lusted after him and also cared about him. After all, they had had sex, for goodness sake; that emotional connection had been made and would never be forgotten. She stopped to check her phone and, as she had thought, the handsome plumber was still in her contacts list: he had not been deleted in a drunken rage as she quite often used to do when men crossed her. And then, with fingers hovering over his number, Rosa took a huge intake of breath and pressed it.

CHAPTER SEVENTEEN

Rosa reached for the remote control between the sofa cushions and started to flick through the countless TV channels; not settling on anything she fancied, she turned it off and lay back with her head to one side. She had enjoyed her walk on the beach with all the dogs and now Hot, completely exhausted from chasing and play-fighting with Ugly, Pongo and the Duchess, was also lying flat on his back with his bits on show, snoring in his bed.

It had been a mild September, but the late-October nights were drawing in and the heating was cranked up high. Rosa had been so busy preparing the announcement about the official launch of the Gift of the Corner Shop that she hadn't really had time to miss Josh – until now, that is. She checked her watch: it would be one p.m. in New York – maybe she could catch him in his lunch break. She tried him on FaceTime but there was no connection. The last time he had used Messenger showed three hours ago and she also realised that he hadn't replied to her text from this morning. A sudden and familiar pang of jealousy went through her. Where was he? Why wasn't he picking up?

Her heart started to beat a little faster. She thought back to Alec's words of advice for when she started having irrational thoughts; when her fear of abandonment reared its head – a sad result of her childhood in care and never feeling good enough. She must breathe in and out deeply and slowly to help her think clearly. This was the man who had married her, who wanted her children, who had on countless occasions not just said those three important words but had backed them up with even bigger actions.

At times like this before, she would have reached for a glass of wine, imagined every worst possible scenario, drowned them out with alcohol and either texted in a rage or crashed out and gone to bed early. Tonight, she ran a deep bubble bath.

Just as she had sunk into the hot soapy water, she heard the sound of a FaceTime call coming in on her iPad. She jumped up, sending water and suds everywhere, and ran naked through to the lounge.

'Rosalar!' There he was, her handsome husband. 'Oh my God, look at those pert little breasts. I wasn't expecting that. It's not my birthday, is it?'

'Hello, darling!' Rosa replied. 'It's very dark, I can hardly see you. Where are you? I thought it was lunchtime in New York.' As she spoke, Hot heard a noise downstairs and began barking loudly enough to drown out the ring of the shop's bell and the noise of the shop door opening.

'Aw, I can hear my little sausage and yes, it is lunchtime in New York.' Rosa squealed as the voice of her husband suddenly carried up the stairs. 'But it's not in Cockleberry Bay.'

'Blimey, what are you doing here?' Rosa squealed again as all six-foot two of her handsome other half walked in, put his phone on the side and hugged her tiny, wet, naked body tightly to him.

'Getting back into that deep soapy bath with you and then you can take me to bed or lose me forever.'

Rosa giggled. 'Oh, my god! I love it! *Top Gun*. Just show me the way, honey!'

'I needed that.' Josh kissed his wife tenderly. They were both radiating with the glow that only a long session of passionate lovemaking could bring.

'You mean you got on a plane and came all the way back to England just to shag me senseless?'

'Rosa, do you have to be so crude?' Hot came scampering into the bedroom, whining for Josh to pick him up and put him on the bed so he could settle down near his beloved humans.

'Actually, yes I do. You bring out the harlot in me. And I love it.' She caressed Josh's cheek and gave a little groan of pleasure. 'It's so lovely to have you here.' She scrabbled her legs at fast speed under the covers, making Hot rock about and look alarmed. 'I bloody miss you.'

'Me too, so that's why I'm here right now. And, as bold as you are, I also thought you might be just a little nervous about the big shop announcement tomorrow. I know how important it is for you to get it right.'

Rosa cuddled into him. 'I said I didn't mind doing it on my own.'

'I know, but I love you, so I'm here to support you, before I go.'

'Before you go?' She sat up. 'So how long are you here for?'

'Just tonight.'

'You're crazy.'

'Not really. I had to come back for an urgent meeting in the City tomorrow afternoon, so work have paid for my flight and, as it's a business flight, I got the chauffeur car to bring me straight here. Simples.'

'I could have met you in London.'

'No, you couldn't. You're being a superstar tomorrow and I wanted to surprise you. Pass me my jacket, can you?' Rosa handed it to him and Josh reached into an inside pocket. 'Here.' He produced a small box.

They both sat up, leaning against their plush grey velvet headboard, and Rosa excitedly opened the jewellery box. Inside was a beautifully simple platinum band with a blue-flecked heart-shaped stone embedded into it.

'I was thinking of getting you an eternity ring, but I wasn't sure if that's supposed to be when we've been married for ages. I know how you like all your mum's spiritual stuff, so I went to a crystal shop in New York and they made this for you.'

Rosa had tears in her eyes. She immediately put it on the index finger of her right hand. 'It's beautiful. I love it.'

Josh then handed her the leaflet that had come with it. 'Here's the blurb, as I know you will want to learn all about the stone. Lapis Lazuli, I've never heard of it myself.'

Rosa began to read aloud. *'One of the most sought-after stones, in use since man's history began. Its deep, celestial blue remains the symbol of royalty and honour, gods and power, spirit and vision. A stone of truth, Lapis encourages honesty of the spirit, and in the spoken and written word. Wear it for all forms of deep communication. Being a stone of truth, while also bringing harmony to your relationship, it is a very powerful stone for faithfulness.'* Rosa made a cooing sound. 'It is perfect. Thank you, Josh.'

Josh kissed his wife on the forehead. 'I will always be true to you, Rosa, I promise.'

Rosa had tears in her eyes. It was as if he knew what she had been thinking earlier. Josh understood so well that despite her learning more about herself, her fears and insecurities were still there; it was just that she had recently found better ways of coping with them.

'Mary says, or probably Kahlil Gibran did – you know how she quotes her beloved prophet for breakfast,' Rosa began.

Josh laughed. 'Go on, tell me the great wisdom.'

'She says that you can't direct the course of love, for love, if it finds you worthy of it, directs your course. It found us, didn't it?' Rosa's voice broke.

'Don't cry, darling.'

'I'm just so happy.' She took his hand and held it to her tummy. 'And soon – imagine creating little ones of us too. If they are even half the person that you are, they will still be great.'

'And if they are half of you, not only will they be magnificent, but probably quite unruly too.' Josh smirked.

'Oi.' Rosa mock-swiped him.

Hot, who had fallen asleep at the bottom of the bed, woke, opened his jaw as wide as it would go in an enormous shuddering yawn, then snapped it shut and came running up the duvet to busily lick away the tracks of Rosa's tears.

'And yes, we will still love you the same, Mr Sausage.' Josh ruffled the lively little fellow's coat then made a face. 'Even if your doggy breath does stink.'

CHAPTER EIGHTEEN

Rosa was both excited and slightly nervous to see the Cockleberry Bay church hall so abuzz with activity. The Outside Broadcast van from the *South Cliffs Today* radio station brought the enormity of what she was doing to the fore. Sara's friend Wendy was managing the café for an hour so that Sara, ably assisted by Nate, who had insisted on coming along, could serve coffee and tea to the radio and newspaper staff, plus to the abundance of locals. The latter had come along, intrigued to see what was happening with the shop that had been in a lot of their lives forever. There were also a few strangers from out of town. Among them could be one of the lucky bidders, Rosa thought, but this was the exciting thing about the way she was doing this: nobody would know right away who was the lucky recipient of not only the wonderful business opportunity she was offering, but also the building in which it was housed.

Rosa saw Bart Trent, the vicar, chatting to everyone animatedly and then she spotted tall, gangly Ritchie walking slowly around the hall rocking Theo in his arms. Titch was in her element flirting with the cute young sound man at the plinth they had set up for Rosa and the radio presenter to talk from. Rosa had originally thought that she might just be able to make a decision from among the people she loved and knew, but with Titch not showing a great deal of interest and nobody else putting their hand up, by doing it this way, at least a lot of people in the local community would also really benefit.

Jacob and Raff were taking a couple of days' holiday before the Halloween and fireworks rush and Mary, who shied away from crowds at the best of times, was able to look after Hot. With those three not here, it made it even more special that Josh had made the effort to come back to her, Rosa thought. He would have to rush off at eleven to get back to London, but it meant the world to her for him to be involved.

'Rosa hi, I'm Kelly Daly, editor of the local rag.'

Kelly Daly must be in her late fifties, Rosa guessed. She was dressed in tight blue jeans and black thigh-high boots, and sported a sharply angled maroon bob hairstyle. Her top lip had the crinkly look caused by years of smoking; the red bobbly cowl-neck sweater she was wearing matched her slightly bloodshot eyes. Rosa noticed the distinct smell of fresh cigarette smoke on her.

'Oh, so you're the one to blame for getting me on the *Daily Mail Online*, I guess?' Rosa said.

'Guilty as charged. Good little story for us to get out to the real world.' Kelly grinned, revealing teeth slightly yellowed by nicotine. 'We're loving what you are doing here and we can get another great scoop to the nationals as a follow-up, I reckon.'

Rosa smiled. 'I dare say that's a good thing, although I'm not really sure what can of worms this will open. I'm amazed at the turn-out, to be frank.'

'A small community breeds nosiness though, doesn't it, Rosa?'

'It breeds an amazing sense of camaraderie, actually.' Rosa was getting wiser to the spinning of a journalist's words. 'Scott not coming then?'

'Yes. He had some copy to file before he came down but he should be here any minute, I hope. He'll be writing the story.'

As the news and weather was coming to an end, Rosa pulled the yellow headphones down over her ears and with a big thumbs-up from Josh she heard the producer saying in her ears, 'So, Rosa, we are just running with one song and then Barry will come straight to you.'

Rosa had to grin and bear the fact that she was being interviewed by the *South Cliffs Today* main presenter, Barry Savage himself. In the past, this man had tried to get information out of her but she had always managed to keep her mouth shut. This time, though, she would be using him and the airwaves for her own benefit – and for the benefit of many others too.

With his beige-and-white-checked three-piece suit, which was stretched to capacity over his large stomach, Barry Savage was still the image of Mr Toad of Toad Hall, Rosa thought. She also hoped that he had been to the dry cleaners with the suit, as it seemed to be his broadcasting outfit of choice on the last two occasions that she had met him.

'So, that was the Red Hot Chili Peppers with "Give It Away" – and that is exactly what our next guest, Rosa Smith, is doing. She is giving away the Corner Shop in Cockleberry Bay, which she currently owns and is successfully running as a pet supplies store. This has obviously caused so much interest in the local community that we are doing a live broadcast direct from Cockleberry Bay village hall. So, let me start by welcoming you, Rosa, and by asking, why on earth are you doing this?'

Rosa swallowed and looked over to Josh who gave her an encouraging wink. 'My great-grandparents left me the shop in their will. I think they were worried I might just come down here and sell it off, so they made that legally impossible. You see, the shop had been such a mainstay in the community that they felt they owed it to the residents to keep it running as a local shop and not let it be taken over as a small branch of a big chain, just as Trehalligan's the newsagents was, by the Co-op.' Rosa opened up a piece of paper she was holding. 'In order for everyone to be clear, I would like to read out exactly what my great-grandfather stated in his last will and testament.'

'Go ahead.' Barry ran his hands through his greasy-looking, greying hair.

'*One proviso of my gift to you is that you must NEVER sell the Corner Shop in Cockleberry Bay. When you feel the time is right, it can only be passed on to someone you feel really deserves it, and only then.*'

'But both your great-grandparents are dead, aren't they?' Barry said. 'If you sold it off you could make a fortune, and,' he guffawed, 'unless they came back to haunt you, they would never know.'

There was both a gasp and a slight ripple of laughter from the live audience. Rosa thought of Queenie, her outspoken great-grandmother, who would no doubt make her life a misery from the other side if she ever dared to do such a thing, and smiled wryly.

'Some of us, Barry, have morals. I am very blessed that the business has done so well and enabled me to move forward with a new one – the café I run with Sara Jenkins in Cockleberry Bay. But life isn't all about money, you know.'

'Oh, isn't it? One could argue that you probably wouldn't be doing this if you hadn't secured yourself a rich husband who could buy your share in the café now known as ROSA'S.'

Rosa wasn't quite sure how she managed not to rise to the bait. Kelly and Scott were sniggering in the corner, she saw, no doubt thinking of how they could use all this wonderful content in the *South Cliffs Gazette*.

'One could also argue, Barry,' Rosa replied coolly, 'that some people find it so hard to believe that a twenty-something girl from East London could have single-handedly created a successful business that they are just a teensy bit jealous, couldn't one?'

'OK, OK, Rosa.' The rotund presenter was slightly ruffled himself now. 'Why don't you explain to all the lovely people in the room and our morning listeners just how they can be the lucky recipients of the shop and flat – that's right, isn't it? There is a two-bedroom flat above the shop that comes with this gem of an opportunity too?'

'Yes, that's correct.'

There was another little gasp from the audience, as most had assumed it was just the shop that was being given away and not such a substantial investment.

Rosa looked again towards Josh, who blew her a kiss. Sara nodded vigorously in support, and even Nate mouthed, 'Go on, girl.'

Rosa stood tall and addressed everyone there.

'I thought long and hard about how to do this fairly. I also want to make my great-grandparents proud of me.' She took a moment before going on. 'It is often said that something good can come out of a tragedy. And the idea of exactly how to do this fairly, and do right by everyone involved, came to me following the destruction caused by the recent storm. Seeing the compassionate dedication and sheer hard work with which Sea & Save managed to rebuild our beach and save our wildlife led me to recognise that there are so many wonderful local charities out there that don't get the funding they need. So, if you are passionate about taking over my business – and passion is the key word here – these are the very simple steps you need to follow.' Rosa turned to Barry. 'Is it OK for me to go ahead?'

'Yes, yes, I'm as intrigued as everybody else. I might even go for it myself.' As Barry laughed, his stomach rose and fell. There was absolute silence in the hall. You could have heard a pin drop.

Rosa held up her right index finger, on which Josh's beautiful ring fitted so well. The lapis lazuli heart shone out, helping her to speak with sincerity and truth.

'These are the simple steps you need to take in order to be in with a chance of acquiring my business.' She paused for effect. 'I want somebody sharp to take over from me, not someone who needs to be spoon-fed instructions. So, please listen carefully. However, if you do miss something, the steps will be printed in this week's *South Cliffs Gazette*. What's more, the newspaper has kindly agreed to donate one thousand pounds to Sea & Save in exchange for having the exclusivity of this story. So, thank you to them for that.' Rosa smiled towards Scott and Kelly.

'That's my girl,' Josh said under his breath, as Bergamot flounced in and shut the church-hall door noisily behind her.

'OK, here we go. Step One: take the brightest coloured envelope you can find and address it to *Ned's Gift, The Corner Shop in Cockleberry Bay, Main Street, Cockleberry Bay, Devon.* Step Two,' Rosa carried on, holding her fingers up, then, realising that nobody on the radio could see her, she quickly put them down again. 'On one sheet of paper, I want you to tell me the local charity you would like to donate to, a brief reason why you have chosen them, and finally, the amount you would like to donate to them when the ballot is closed.'

'Intriguing, Rosa, very intriguing,' Barry interrupted. 'So, is there a number three?' He was already counting numbers himself – the number of listeners he would be gaining if he announced the winner on air.

'Yes, there is. Number three is, in fact, the most important. In a paragraph or two I would like you to state what exactly it would mean to you to run the Corner Shop in Cockleberry Bay and what you are intending to sell when you take it on.'

'Wow, that's exciting stuff! And how will this work, timewise?'

'I would like all envelopes to be posted or hand-delivered to me by the last day of November. I will then shortlist the best two, who would then go head-to-head in a meeting like this again, where the lucky contenders will present to us exactly what they are proposing. I will be discussing this with my husband, but I shall be making the final decision.'

'Actually, saying that, you didn't mention adding a name and contact number to the form?'

'I was just coming to that.' Rosa smiled falsely at the annoying presenter.

'These entries are to be anonymous. I would just like you to make up a name and put it on the back of the envelope and on the top of the piece of paper. Please also add your best contact number. If I know you, please organise a number I won't recognise. The name you choose must relate to anything Christmassy. This way it will be a fair shot for everyone, and I won't be swayed as to whether I know who you are or not.'

'So, for example, Santa Claus,' Barry interjected with a big boastful grin.

'Exactly. Thank you, Barry.'

'And when will this head-to-head contest take place?'

'Christmas Eve, of course,' Rosa told him. 'The Corner Shop in Cockleberry Bay will be the most wonderful Christmas gift for the most deserving person.'

'And the charity money that people propose – do they still have to donate if they are not chosen?'

'Yes, of course. They must pay up on Christmas Eve. I think

this gives the whole thing a wonderful local-charity feel. So, just as dear, compassionate Ned would have wished, not only will somebody deserving re-inherit the shop, but lots of other local people will benefit from the charity money too.'

There was a collective 'ah' from the audience as Rosa carried on. 'Moving forward, my intention is to set up a charity called Ned's Gift, that will encompass all the charities that are included in the letters. And from then on there will be collection points in any local businesses who would like to participate.'

'That really is amazing, Rosa – so generous in so many ways.' Barry actually sounded sincere, and Rosa's face reddened as applause erupted around the hall and lasted for a good few seconds.

'I know you said you didn't want to do a recap, but I am going to quickly run through what you said earlier. Is that OK?'

'That's fine, Barry, just go for it.'

'So…to everybody listening: you need a coloured envelope and a piece of paper. Write a Christmas name and a phone number on the envelope and paper. State a local charity and amount you are willing to donate, followed by your reason for wanting the shop and what you are going to sell. And then just mark it *Ned's Gift* and get it to the Corner Shop in Cockleberry Bay. Easy! And folks, remember the ten-year block on selling the property, won't you? So act responsibly. So that just leaves me to thank Rosa Smith for coming in and offering this amazing gift, and for me to play this track. Here we have the gorgeous Mariah Carey with "All I Want For Christmas Is You" – *and* the Corner Shop in Cockleberry Bay, of course. Ho ho ho!'

Barry took off his headphones. 'Love this, love everything about it.' He motioned his producer over. 'We've got to cover the decision-making and, of course, have Rosa on Christmas Eve announcing the winner. Let's make it happen, people.'

Josh rushed over to Rosa and gave her a massive hug. 'I didn't think I could love you more. You were right. It *is* genius! The whole thing is genius. I love you madly, Rosa Smith, but I've got to go. I'll call you as soon as I land back in New York.' He then lifted her hand and kissed the stone of the new ring he had given her. 'Always yours, you know that.' As he raced out of the door, Rosa felt warm inside.

Mary appeared with Hot on his lead. 'We stood at the back and listened,' she told her daughter. 'I couldn't not. Ned and Queenie would have been so proud of what you are doing, as are we, aren't we, Mr Sausage?'

Hot barked his approval, then promptly cocked his leg up against the sound engineer's rucksack.

CHAPTER NINETEEN

All Hallows Eve brought with it a beautiful sunny and crisp autumn day. Titch had agreed to work in the Corner Shop every day because it was half-term and the café had been absolutely heaving all week with the influx of visitors. Sara had been doing some superb baking, which sold as fast as she produced the ghostly, spidery fairy cakes and witch biscuits. They had also sold alcohol-free Creepy Cocktails which they were serving to the kids from a dry-iced smoking cauldron on the front counter. Rosa had based herself there and was enjoying the buzz of everything that was going on.

After successfully painting the outside of the shop and proving his worth to Rosa, Nate had been employed by ROSA'S for the half-term week to run 'Spooky Café Cave Tours' for kids and their parents. The event included a pre-tour snack of pumpkin soup and bat-shaped sandwiches, plus a Halloween gift bag. The tour itself was a ghost-inspired walk along the front of the caves at the bottom end of South Cliffs, where Nate had set up some wailing-type music and various cut-outs and flappy things that rustled. Rosa's initial feelings of wariness towards him had faded as he was really bending over backwards to make the tours a success. What's more, he had also taken on the morning cleaning duties at the café, much to Sara and Rosa's delight.

What was pleasing Rosa even more was that her period was three days late and her boobs felt more sore than usual. Well done Josh for his unannounced visit at exactly the right time! Also, this was proof that her mother's warnings – i.e. telling Josh not to come back *before* the fireworks, didn't always need to be heeded. Rosa had decided to wait until now, when she was three days late, not just one, to do the test. Following some kind of crazy logic, she felt that not knowing for a while was far less disappointing than knowing for sure that she wasn't pregnant.

The final tour was ready to set off. Rosa stepped outside the café to help Nate switch on all the head-torches. As she waved the noisy lot off up the beach path, she looked across to the Ship Inn. The big pub was in darkness, apart from one light on upstairs and an orange glow downstairs. It was obviously still not open to the public. Rosa felt a sudden pang of sadness for Sheila. Nobody deserved to be lonely or in pain, whatever trouble they might have caused. Sheila's crime, if you looked at it in its simplest form, was that she was a lioness of a mother. Her involvement in the hit-and-run incident that had occurred during Rosa's first days in the Bay was due to a mother's love; quite a drastic way to try to get rid of Lucas's girlfriend at the time, just because Sheila didn't like her, Rosa thought. Her subsequent paying off of Titch when Sheila thought the young girl was pregnant with her son's child was just because she wanted the best for him. Misguided love maybe, but her malevolence had come from a good place in the landlady's own eyes.

That was the trouble with life sometimes, Rosa thought. There were ups and downs and disagreements with people. But what it all boiled down to, whether you were rich man, poor man, beggar or thief, was that, fundamentally, all you wanted to do was live in comfort with the people you loved around you. And the fact was that, whoever you were in life, you still lived and died the same way as everyone else. We were all human beings. If only everyone could co-exist in peace and harmony in a world where wealth could be shared around a bit, so poverty was not such an issue.

With the departure of the excitable Halloween tour, the café had quietened slightly, and with a strong gut feeling drawing her over to the pub, Rosa wrapped a couple of witchy cakes in a serviette and told Sara that she wouldn't be long.

Shivering as she walked across the beach, she pulled her coat around her and lit her way with the torch from her phone. She could have done with one of the head-torches they'd borrowed for the tour. The waves lapped their soothing lament and a lone seagull gave its familiar cry. With no moon or stars lighting her way, and without the pub lights on, it really was very dark.

This time last year had been a completely different scenario, Rosa recalled. The Ship Inn had just been completely refurbished and a big opening night Halloween party had been thrown. Live music had been blaring and everyone, having been told to WEAR to SCARE, was dressed up as ghouls, ghosts or witches. This was the very party to which she and Titch had pitched up drunk, despite Josh's insistence that Rosa mustn't go; the very party where Lucas had tried to kiss her, and she had turned her head so that his lips landed on her cheek.

Rosa tentatively made her way around to the back door of the pub and pressed the intercom buzzer. Nate had been telling her way too many spooky stories earlier, so when the wind blew an empty crisp bag up over the car park she jumped back and gave a cry of fear. She pushed the buzzer again, hoping that with the orange glow coming from downstairs, Sheila might still be up and about. The wind had started to strengthen now, so trying the buzzer a third and last time, Rosa pressed her ear to it in case she could hear Sheila reply. Nothing. She then pushed open the letter box to check if she could see anything, but it wasn't what she saw, it was what she could hear that caused her alarm. *'Help! Help me! Please, somebody help me.'*

Rosa was just about to phone Sara, but on trying the handle, she found that the back door into the pub kitchen was unlocked. Entering in haste, fumbling for light switches, Rosa called out: 'Sheila! Sheila? Where are you?' Now she was inside, Rosa was sure she could hear the lyrical melody of James Arthur's new single coming from upstairs. As soon as she switched the lights on, however, the music stopped and she thought she must have imagined it.

'Down here.' The publican's voice was barely audible. 'In the cellar.'

Rosa shot behind the bar, then trod carefully down the steep cellar steps. There at the bottom, lying in an awkward heap, was Sheila Hannafore, a shadow of the bold and feisty character that Rosa once knew. Her white hair was stained with fresh blood; her face was gaunt and etched with both illness and fear.

Rosa got down to her level. 'Oh my God, Sheila, I'm calling an ambulance now.'

Sheila held out her bony hand to Rosa and said weakly, with a lone tear running down her left cheek, 'I didn't think it would be you who came to my rescue.'

Rosa felt tears stinging her own eyes. 'Well, it is, and I will do everything I can to help you.'

'Please don't call an ambulance, love. This wasn't an accident, see. And I don't want to get anyone into any trouble. Just sit here a minute.'

'Oh Sheila, I can't leave you like this. Lucas would kill me.'

Rosa got through to the emergency services quickly. 'An hour, really?' she objected. 'The lady has cancer and a head wound. This is serious. Please come as quickly as you can.' Ending the call, she asked softly, 'Where are you hurting?'

'My back.'

Sheila was slightly delirious now; her eyes were closed and blood was running from the wound in her head. Rosa took off her scarf and did the best she could to stem the flow. Trying not to panic, she then placed her hand gently on the ailing woman's clammy forehead.

'Tell my boys it was an accident, won't you? Promise?'

Rosa took Sheila's hand. Her head was moving agitatedly from side to side.

'Try and keep still, Sheila. We'll get you to hospital where you'll be sorted.'

The injured woman then let out a terrible groan. 'Bloody cancer! Nobody tells you how painful it is.' She started to cry.

'Have you got any painkillers?' Rosa asked. 'I can go and get them.'

'I've had enough of those already. Plenty. Don't leave me, please don't leave me.'

Rosa squeezed her hand. 'I'm here.'

Sheila's tears flowed faster. 'I've been a terrible mother,' she sobbed. 'I didn't intend to do bad things.'

'No, you haven't. I spoke to Lucas,' Rosa lied. 'He didn't mean to stay away so long. He's just been so busy, and he had problems with his phone and problems with his love-life. You know what men are like. He said that he was going to be coming down soon. He didn't even realise that so much time had passed.'

A smile spread over the woman's dry lips as Rosa promised, 'He loves you, Sheila. He loves you very much.'

'I think he loves you more,' Sheila managed.

Not knowing how to respond, Rosa was glad to spot some glass bottles of water within reach. She opened one up and poured some on a tissue to dampen Sheila's dry lips. She didn't give her any to drink in case she had to have an operation.

'Thank you,' the woman whispered. Then, 'I didn't want to worry Tom and the girls either; they have their own lives to lead. Can't be looking after a silly old woman down by the sea.'

Rosa felt remorse for lying to her – but what else could she say to explain Lucas's lack of attendance? She then had a terrible thought. Luke had stopped coming down immediately after the conversation they had had about him moving on with his life. Maybe it was her fault he wasn't here. She had to call him – right now. Looking at Sheila, she didn't think his mother had long to live, and he was in London, at least four hours away. Why, oh why could he not have picked up or called back when she had left the message for him the other day?

'Tell them it was an accident, that I tripped and fell, won't you?' Sheila repeated, her voice getting weaker. 'I don't want them to have to go through anything else.' Her eyes flickered open and shut. 'The will is in the back safe. They will get their money. Tell them, Rosa, tell them.'

'Sheila, Sheila, stay with me. Please – the ambulance will soon be here.'

Seeing a shadowy figure coming down the cellar steps, Rosa screamed a full-lunged scream. Then, on seeing who it was, she simply exclaimed, 'Luke! Thank God you're here.'

'Well done for leaving the back door wide open, bird. I left my bloody key at home. Have you called for an ambulance?'

Rosa was sure she had shut it so just replied with a stressed, 'Yes. It's on its way.'

Luke went down to Sheila's level. 'Oh Mum! What have you done?' His voice broke. 'Where's Tom?'

Rosa saw a glimmer of light flash back into the now open eyes of Sheila and she, too, felt a rush of relief, knowing it had been the right thing to call Lucas before.

'My boy, my boy, you came! Call Tom for me, call him, please.'

Lucas's eyes had the look of a frightened horse. Gently, Rosa moved out of the way so that he could get close to his mother. Then, with Lucas on the phone to Tom, Sheila put her arm up and gripped Rosa's hand as hard as she could muster.

'Thank you, kid,' she said breathlessly. 'Whatever happened, I respected you. You're one of life's survivors and I admire that. Look after my boy...' Her head flopped to the side.

Rosa clasped two hands around hers. 'Fight, Sheila, fight, because you're a survivor too. Lucas is here now, and Tom is on his way. Your boys will both be with you.'

'Will you keep my secret?' Sheila said in a threadlike voice.

Rosa put her mouth close to Sheila's ear and whispered, 'I promise that they'll think it was an accident.' Then moving away and in a slightly louder voice: 'Just hang on in there, you're not going anywhere.'

Just as Lucas looked to Rosa in despair, they heard the sound of an ambulance siren.

'I'd better go up and show the paramedics the way in.' Kissing her own hand and pressing it gently on to Lucas's forehead, Rosa ran carefully up the cellar steps and began to silently cry.

CHAPTER TWENTY

'So, run that by me again?' The Managing Director of Costsmart Supermarkets noticed a dirty mark on his desk phone and started rubbing it off with his finger. 'I've got the newspaper in front of me now.'

The voice on the other end of the phone replied: 'I put in the bid for you as an independent purchaser. We make up some schmaltzy words, pick a charity involving animals and suggest a big donation – and if we also say we want to keep it as a pet store or similar, I reckon she will buy that.'

'This all sounds great, but this Rosa Smith tart is no fool and she will know that we are a small but growing independent supermarket chain and she'll tell us where to go.'

'No, you've misunderstood me. What happens is that I take it on from the start when it's all signed, sealed and delivered – *then* you buy it straight off me, for the amount I mentioned earlier. Plus you donate the charity money – although you can probably get away with not doing so, because I know that silly girl wouldn't dream that anyone would not fulfil their promise.' The caller sniggered derisively. 'It's a win, win.'

'Now we're talking business.' The Costsmart man blew out a big noisy breath. 'The locals won't like it, mind.'

'The locals will just have to get used to it. It's the holidaymakers who bring in most of the money down here anyway, and you can just add some more bespoke farm-shop-type produce, so that you are not competing directly with the Co-op.'

'I knew I met you in that bar for a reason.' The supermarket boss went to take a sip of his coffee, but finding it cold, he put down his cup. 'You didn't mention that you'd run shops before though.'

'That's not the requirement, is it? But I've taken a few calculated risks in my time.'

'OK. I need to do a bit of research and have a think. Let's meet in a couple of weeks. Sorry, remind me, what was your name again?'

'Let's just say Frosty the Snowman from now on, shall we?' said the voice.

The supermarket manager laughed superciliously, then hung up.

CHAPTER TWENTY ONE

'Bloody hell, Mother, you scared the life out of me,' Rosa squeaked. Mary had opened the front door of Seaspray Cottage in a tall witch's hat, covered in fake cobwebs.

'I thought you were a late trick or treater, that's all,' Mary said, as Rosa went through to the kitchen and sat herself down at the table.

'You're very pale, daughter. What's the matter?' Mary thought the girl looked shattered.

'Sheila's dead.' The words unleashed a torrent of tears.

'*What*? How?' Mary sat down next to Rosa. 'I knew she was ill, but this all seems very sudden.'

Rosa blubbered her way through the sorry tale. 'And…I know that we never really got on, but at the end of the day, I just saw a frail human being needing help. And now I feel guilty that I was so mean to her before.' At this moment, Rosa felt for some reason that she must keep Sheila's secret, as she had promised. Even from her mother.

'Oh, Rosa. She hadn't exactly been good to you, either. You just were there for that woman in her hour of need.'

'I phoned Lucas a few days ago and told him that she was ill – I felt I should. Felt if it was you who was ill and I didn't know, well, I would want to be aware of it. I know that Josh wouldn't approve but, Mum, I had to.' The word 'Mum' suddenly floated off her lips with ease. Before now, it had seemed too soft, too real, too intimate.

Hearing the word, Mary felt as if someone had just stroked her heart with a feather. 'Josh is emotionally intelligent, Rosa, he would understand in this instance. He also knows that you are the kindest soul and I am more than proud to call you my daughter.'

'And,' Rosa wept again, 'I love you so much, Mum, and I mean that.'

Mary sucked in her emotion in one huge gulp of air. She ruffled Rosa's unruly curls. 'And I love you too, missy, to the moon and back and with stars swirling around us.'

Rosa smiled through her tears. 'That much, eh?' Mary took another deep breath and nodded as Rosa continued. 'Poor Lucas and Tom, they were obviously distraught. They felt so guilty, too, about not seeing her sooner, but she hadn't let them know that she was so ill. Tom told me he saw her a month ago and she just said she had the flu.'

'Then that was her decision and her own doing, Rosa. It is what she wanted. People will do what they want to do, however much you can tell them otherwise. We both know that from our own past mishaps with drinking and the like.' Mary paused, then added with a naughty smile, 'It's quite apt for Sheila Hannafore to pass over on Halloween though. She'll be coming back to haunt us forever now.'

Rosa managed another smile as Mary handed her some kitchen roll. Even Merlin was sitting quietly upright in Queenie's armchair. The fire was offering a comforting glow and warmth. 'Are her boys staying at the pub tonight, then?' Mary asked.

'I don't know. Lucas messaged me from the hospital to say

that despite every attempt to revive her, she had passed. He said that he would probably stay at his auntie's in Exeter with Tom, but wasn't sure. Are you still having your séance tonight?'

'No. Edie has got a bad cold and cancelled – well, that's what she told me – and Colette chickened out. Why? Do you want to do it with me?'

'No, I don't. Not now. That reminds me, I must text the boys to say I can't help them clear up. I can't face it.' Rosa reached for her phone. 'I do feel Queenie is with me a lot of the time, anyway.'

Mary put her hand on her daughter's shoulder. 'I think she'd be delighted that she was going to be a great-great-grandmother too, don't you?'

'Mum?'

'You've just got the look. I know. Have you done a test yet?'

'I was waiting. The longer I don't come on, the more likely it is I am.'

Mary kissed the top of her daughter's head. 'You will do what you want to do too, my darling. And whatever that is, I will always be one hundred per cent behind you.'

CHAPTER TWENTY TWO

With Titch up to her eyes in baby teeth, puppies and wedding preparations, Rosa had told her to have a day at home to sort herself out. All the goings-on at the pub last night had got in the way of Rosa doing a pregnancy test, but was that still necessary? This morning she had woken up feeling slightly sick and with a sensation in her tummy that she had never felt before, so she was certain that something was happening down there. Unless it was due to the sheer number of ghoulish iced cakes that she had consumed in the café the day before.

She'd not heard anything from Lucas, but then why would she? Rosa thought. He'd have a lot on his plate, with a death to register and a funeral to arrange. Chief village gossip Edie Rogers, mother of Titch's fiancé Ritchie, had reported that Luke and his brother Tom had managed to book rooms in a hotel in Polhampton, so she assumed they were still there.

Rosa was just cleaning the back kitchen when the shop bell rang.

'I'll be with you in a minute!' she shouted through to the front. Hot poked his nose out from under his blanket to see who was there, then settled back down in his basket in the corner. Wiping her hands on a towel, Rosa came through and greeted the sun-kissed surfer dude.

'I should have been cross with you, Scott Wilde, for telling the world that ownership of my shop is open to any bugger who wants it. But thankfully, that led to me having a serious think about how I could pass it on in a way that suited both my family and the community.'

'Have you had many envelopes in yet?'

'Not one. I guess people are considering their actions, or maybe there isn't anyone out there who wants to take it on. Who knows?'

Scott laughed. 'For one so streetwise, I don't believe you see that happening. A free shop in this beautiful setting?'

'It's a massive decision if you are moving down here, and still a risk. I think people buy people, if you know what I mean. Somebody could take on this place and keep it running as it is, but they may not have the same impact as the delectable me, Hot and Titch greeting customers.' Rosa smirked.

'Look at you bigging yourself up, but yes, it's not just the dog treats I'd be after if you weren't already hitched.' Rosa tutted at the cocky reporter as he went on cheekily, 'If I wasn't so ambitious about becoming a name in the media world, I might even consider making a play for it myself.' He winked and clicked his tongue.

'Have you not got work to do, Mr Wilde, by name and nature?'

'Later I have, but for now I've got a date with a new señorita. I'm meeting her at the café, or should I say, *your* café in ten minutes.'

'So – to what do I owe this pleasure?'

'Oh, I was just checking in to say hello to the little Rich Bitch of the Bay and to see what was going on with the shop sale – not a lot, by the sound of it. C'est la vie.'

'You'll be the first to know – not.'

'I know you don't mean that. Watch out for charlatans, eh, though, Rosa. You never know who's waiting in the wings to schmooze you without you being aware.'

'Scott, with my background, I'd like to think I'd know if someone was trying to bamboozle me.'

'That's quite a word for a Monday. Even with my exemplary writing skills I'm not sure I know how to spell it. Have a good day, pal.'

Rosa became thoughtful as Scott sauntered off down the street. He didn't miss a trick, and reminded her of Joe Fox with his duplicitous ways. How love had blinkered her then, but things had changed. Yes, without doubt she loved the Corner Shop and all it stood for, but she had vowed she would never be blind-sided like that ever again, in any aspect of her life.

CHAPTER TWENTY THREE

Rosa had taken a lot of care preparing for a FaceTime call with Josh that evening. She had borrowed a baby sleepsuit off Titch and spent ages sticking felt letters she had got from the craft shop in Polhampton on to it. It then took another age and more dog treats than were good for him, for Hot to be convinced that wearing such a thing around his bits was all in a greater cause. Fortunately, she had already relayed the sad tale of Sheila's death by text message to Josh, so that she didn't have to use precious call time with him on that sorry subject now.

'You OK, wifey? Sorry about the noise, I'm walking to Midtown Manhattan for a meeting. Rosa, what have you been up to? You look a bit shifty.'

'Shifty? I think not. How else do I look?'

'Er, gorgeous, as usual. What's going on with you, Rosalar? You're being very strange.'

She disappeared off the screen for a second to hoist up a miserable-looking Hot. As a New York fire-engine siren blasted across the airwaves, making Rosa feel like she was immersed in some Hollywood movie, she held up the now struggling dachshund in his babygrow, which announced in multi-coloured letters WHO'S THE DADDY? Rosa had assumed that this would be a fun and wondrous moment in their lives: one which every mother-to-be dreams of when she announces her big news. However, she hadn't reckoned with a dachshund's digestion. The number of dog treats made a sudden and unwelcome reappearance as, with one huge, gulping retch, Hot proceeded to sick them up all over Rosa's jeans and the iPad screen.

Josh was utterly bemused. Through the chaos of barking and noises of distress from Rosa, he said, 'Bloody hell, Rosa, what's happening – and why is Hot wearing that get-up? Hang on, don't tell me – I need to cross the road.' And on reaching the other side: 'What did it say? I saw the words…' Josh stopped and tried to work it out. 'As in I'm Hot's daddy? Or…' His voice rose an octave. 'Rosa, are you telling me what I think you are telling me?'

'Yes, yes,' Rosa gagged, 'but I've also got Hot's smelly sick literally all over me so I'm going to have to sort this and I will call you back straightaway, I promise.'

'No, don't go. You'll have to get used to more than that all over you in nine months' time. I love you so much, darling girl. When are you due? How are you feeling? And have you had any envelopes for the shop yet? I want to know it all!'

'Josh, I've got to go. Ew, this stink.' She gagged again. 'Call me after your meeting. I'll still be up, and we can have a proper chat then. I love you, Boo.'

'Love you more and I take it I *am* the daddy?' Another siren drowned out Josh's laughter.

Feeling guilty for having subjected her beloved hound to such an ordeal, and rather glad he could only bark, not talk, so as not to report her to the RSPCA, she fussed Hot and gave him a bowl of fresh water. Then, wiping the lumps of sick off her jeans with a tea towel she went through to the lounge to open the balcony door for him, and to breathe in some fresh air. As she did so she noticed the security light coming on in the yard: somebody was entering through the back gate. There were only a few people who knew how to get in that way – and one of them was Lucas Hannafore.

Rosa shivered with the cold and slight trepidation as to what the handsome plumber might want. If he had taken advantage of her drunken state less than a year ago, then the question of: 'who's the daddy?' really could have been debatable!

CHAPTER TWENTY FOUR

'You smell like a battered sausage,' Titch whispered, as Ritchie, tired from his evening shift at the chip shop, appeared in the spare bedroom of her mum's bungalow and kissed her on the cheek.

'And how lovely to see you too, Tinkerbell,' Ritchie smiled.

'I honestly think all of my muscles have seized and I could well wet myself on standing, but I have had complete peace for two hours. I know I should have put him in his cot, but...'

Ritchie gently unravelled the sleeping child from his mother's arms and, making soothing noises as he went, he tiptoed off to put little Theo down in his cot. Bringing a cup of tea back through for them both, he sat opposite Titch and stretched out his long, gangly limbs.

'Your mum's in bed early then?' he asked.

'Yes, thank goodness. It's full-on soaps on TV tonight and you know how loud she has to have it. I so can't wait until we can get our own place.' The puppies carried on gently snoring either side of her legs.

'Soon, it will be soon. Our savings pot is growing now. Let's get married first and then in January, well, it's my aim to get us out of here and into our own home.'

'It's such a shame re Rosa's flat.' Titch stroked the sleeping puppies gently.

'Yes, but it is what it is. I felt a bit bad saying that Josh was stuck-up the other day, but nobody upsets my girl like that and Rosa has got to do what she feels is right. It's up to her.'

'Am I really that useless? I'm sure I could run the shop, you know.'

Ritchie jumped up. 'Come here.' He gently pulled Titch up by her hands and hugged her into him as tight as he could without suffocating her. 'You, my gorgeous fiancée, are not useless at all. You could run that shop blindfolded. And the joy that you and that little man of ours gives me is insurmountable. You've given me a future that I could never have dreamed of, living down here. And if all five of us had to move into a tent on the beach, I'd still be the happiest man alive.'

'You big softie you.' Titch reached up to kiss him on the lips. 'Let's go to bed, it's about time we loved each other properly. But do me a favour, Ritchie. Shower first – you stink.'

'Ta-dah! I present to you one large, clean sausage ready for battering,' Ritchie announced on entering the bedroom, one hand in the air, the other holding a red flannel over the huge erection he was going to reveal, like a waiter presenting a dish.

He let out a soft laugh. For there was his wife-to-be, butt naked aside one stocking and her sexiest bra, spread-eagled across the bed, face down and snoring, with a baby dachshund on either side of her head.

As he went to gently pull the duvet up over her, he noticed that by her hand was a silver envelope, covered in gold stars. It wasn't stuck down or addressed to anyone, and a piece of paper was poking out. With his ardour now fading and his curiosity getting the better of him, Ritchie pulled on his dressing gown and headed off to make himself another cup of tea. Seated at the kitchen table, he started to read his fiancée's neat handwriting. She had outlined various bullet points.

- *Name (To be confirmed)*
- *Charity – Sea & Save and £50 – or maybe that should be more? (will think of something I know she'd like here)*

When he got to a bullet point entitled *Why you should gift the shop to me* Ritchie put his hand to his heart. It wasn't a finished version, as there were crossings out and random words dotted about, but there was enough for him to get the gist and realise that his wife-to-be was just the most incredible woman. Being not only smart, funny, cute, quirky and a wonderful mother, he realised too, on reading this, just how incredibly generous she was, and kind in spirit.

CHAPTER TWENTY FIVE

Lucas sat on Rosa's sofa holding the can of beer he had brought with him. His eyes were red from crying; his body and soul exhausted with the shock and disbelief that only the grief of losing a loved one can bring. Rosa could see how hard he was trying to hold it together. As soon as she said the words, 'All right, geezer?' it was as if their cockney bond allowed him to let go and he began to sob like a baby.

She went to the bathroom to get him some loo roll to wipe his streaming eyes. Every time he tried to speak, off he'd go again. Hot just sat and stared at him, and as if feeling the young man's pain, he began to make funny little whining noises. Rosa wasn't sure whether to hug Lucas or not. In the end she decided on not; just sat beside him on the sofa with her hand on his shoulder. Taking the can of beer from him, she eventually spoke.

'Getting drunk isn't going to help, you know.'

Lucas reared up. 'Look at Miss Sobriety here. And who are you to fucking judge?' He gave a disgusted exclamation. 'And what's that stink in here?'

'Hot was sick – and whoa there, mister, I was only trying to help.'

This wasn't the time to tell Lucas of her decision not to drink, nor of her pregnancy. Rosa actually felt secretly pleased that she now had a valid excuse not to drink without having to explain herself. It was amazing how many people found it a problem that she didn't drink any more.

Lucas shut his eyes and rested his head back on the sofa. 'I'm so sorry. I'm thirty years old and an orphan. Rosa, do you have any idea how that feels?'

'Well, if you want an honest answer, I didn't even know who my mum was for twenty odd years. And I still don't know who my dad is or if he's even alive.'

'Trust you to trump me.' Lucas managed a brief smile.

'I'm sorry, this isn't about me. That was heartless.'

'It's just so shit.' Lucas bit his lip. 'It's as if that storm you had down here has come back and ripped out a piece of me. If ever I've felt this bad about anything, who would I have turned to? My mum.' At the word 'mum' he started sobbing again. 'And I can't believe I'm being such a dick in front of you.' He blubbered, 'But I literally feel like I have a pain in my heart.'

Rosa sat next to him on the sofa, tears forming in her own eyes. 'Oh Luke, there's nothing I can say to make you feel better, I know. But I'm so pleased you are getting it out. Grieve, just grieve. Shout, scream, run, whatever it takes. It's so raw but it will get better, it always does, whatever it is.' She paused. 'When Mary was grieving for Queenie, I tried to find ways to comfort her. I found a quote from CS Lewis, which said "No one ever told me that grief felt like fear". She agreed. Said it was like standing at the top of a cliff and looking out to sea but there was no horizon. There was a vast empty hole inside of her, and she had no idea how she was going to fill it. She was in absolute despair, wondering how she could carry on without such a huge part of her life being there ever again.'

Lucas sniffed. 'That's it – it's the forever bit I'm not coping with. I do feel fear because I know I'll never see Mum again – and when I think of that, then I panic. How can I not ever see, hear or touch her again? How can I carry on knowing that she is not there to turn to?'

'Oh Lucas, you will cope, and you'll have to. It's horrific now but this intensity will pass. Think back to your dad passing – you got through that OK.'

'But I had Mum to help me then,' he replied brokenly.

Rosa wasn't sure how she could answer that one. The death of a loved one was without doubt horrendous. And she was grateful she had never had to suffer it to this extreme. She could physically feel Lucas's pain, he was so awash with it.

'I'm bloody skint too,' he went on. 'I've had things on my mind…not been concentrating on work. I really do need to sort myself out.'

'Do you want to borrow some money? I mean like a hundred quid or something?'

'Don't be silly.'

'Here.' Rosa reached for her handbag and handed him some notes. 'Take this. The last thing you need to be worrying about at a time like this is money. At least you can buy some fags or something.'

'Tom's going to lend me some later, it's fine.'

'Please – just take it.'

Rosa being so kind to him was almost too much to bear. Lucas tried to get a grip and not break down again. 'You're such a doll.' He shoved the money in his jeans pocket. 'And that wasn't the reason I came here.'

'For God's sake, Luke, I know that. Us East Enders, we look out for each other, don't we?' Rosa put her hand on his and then on feeling the same spark of lust she had felt when she had very first met him, quickly pulled it away.

At that point, Hot, realising his doggie sympathy was falling on deaf ears, trotted back to his bed in the corner of the lounge and stuck his head under the blanket.

'I'm even boring Mr Sausage.' Lucas attempted another smile, his voice calmer now. 'Look, I'm sorry, Rosa. I just felt compelled to come and see you, to thank you.' He went to get up.

'Will you stop saying sorry! And sit back down, it's fine. I'm just glad that I was there for your mum when she needed someone.'

'And I'm just so grateful that you phoned me and left me that message. I was actually going to come down and face everything at Christmas, so thank God you got in touch as I would have been too late.' He ran a hand across his eyes, muttering, 'This is so shit. It's not fair.'

'Life isn't fair, is it, Luke. I'm lucky that I've only had Queenie die on me. She was so old it was like the passage of time was right with her. I miss her but I also never got to know her that well. Whereas this is your mum, Luke. I don't think the umbilical cord is ever truly cut, whether our mums are alive or dead. This is the hardcore of losses. It's not going to be an easy ride. But I do know that everyone who has lost someone close does bring out the old "time is a healer" cliché.'

She moved closer to the grieving man beside her. 'Come here.' Without thinking of the past between them, with just the sheer power of compassion towards another human being, one who was so broken and lost, Rosa hugged Lucas tightly to her. Melting into her and without conscious thought Lucas lifted his head to kiss her on the lips. Catching the look in his eyes for a split second, she jumped up. Her voice was breathy. 'We can't, not again, Luke. Not ever again.'

Luke jumped up too and headed towards the balcony door. 'I…er…' His face was pained. 'Shit, Rosa. I was going to say I'm sorry again, but I'm not. Time may be a healer, but how long does it take to get over a broken heart? Why do you think I kept away from the Bay for so long? Why?' With that he pulled open the door and tore down the spiral stairs, causing a crumpled envelope to fall out of his back pocket and land on the bottom step.

CHAPTER TWENTY SIX

'So, are you going to come back for fireworks weekend?' Rosa was chopping mushrooms and peppers for an omelette while talking to Josh on FaceTime. The iPad was propped up against the kettle in the kitchen.

'You should be one of those Instagram cooks,' Josh replied instead. 'You look very fetching in that little outfit. In fact, I can't wait to get my hands on you again. Pull it down a bit… yes, that's right. Ooh, being apart from you is killing me, Rosa.'

Rosa did a little shuffle of her naked cleavage right up close to the screen. 'They are getting bigger by the day,' she said proudly, 'now that baby Smith has started growing inside me. I'm loving it!'

Josh sighed. 'Not as much as me. Anyway, put the knife down and pay attention as I've got good news and bad news for you.'

'Hit me with it. Bad first.'

'I'm not going to be back for the fireworks weekend.'

'Oh Josh! You–'

'Your mother will be happy at least.'

'Oh yeah! I had forgotten her heebie-jeebie goings-on around you not coming back until after the fireworks.'

'Don't be annoyed, Rosa, just hear me out. The reason I'm

not coming back is because…the good news is that the project is going to be finished earlier, so I will be home for good on the sixth of December at the very latest. It could even be a week before.'

'Yeah! OK, that's brilliant. I'd rather you were back earlier. You can help me with Christmas stock, as I don't want to lift too much now. Oh great, it also means you'll be here for my three-months scan too. I've been to the doctor and all my appointments and stuff have been set up and I am very healthy, I'll have you know.'

'Great, and yes, please don't do anything silly, like lifting heavy boxes. I know what you're like. Have you told anyone yet?'

'No, I wanted to see if you minded if I did first. It's usually after the scan you tell people, but sod it, all these silly life rules. I want everyone to know.'

'That's so sweet. I don't mind at all. My mum will be beside herself; I know it's not her first grandchild, but she just loves a new baby in the family.'

'Josh?'

'Yes? What's up? The way you said that sounded ominous.'

'You know I helped Sheila, before she died?'

'Yes.'

'Lucas came around to thank me. I just wanted to be honest with you.'

'Rosa, it's OK. Did he stay long?'

'No, about an hour. He was obviously very upset and as I was the first to get to Sheila, he just wanted to find out what she had said.' That wasn't quite true, and saying it, Rosa wondered why, in fact, Luke *hadn't* asked what his mother had been saying. But she was quickly learning that grief is a wild monster. And when in its grip, logical thought went out of the window.

The night of their recent meeting, Rosa had had trouble

getting off to sleep. Thoughts were whirring around her mind about what she should do with regard to Lucas's outburst. Was it really her, Rosa, who had broken his heart? And if so, did she really want to get into a conversation with him now about it? It was then she recalled what Sheila had said about her son loving her. Now that she was so happy and settled with Josh, to Rosa it all seemed too little, too late. Nearly a year later, in the cold, sober light of day, for the first time she began to think about her relationship, if you could call it that, with Lucas Hannafore. There had been an instant attraction and he had always been so cocksure – 'cock' being the operative word – and he had never demonstrated anything more than wanting her purely for sex.

Or *had* he shown more? She had been so drunk on that night last December, when they'd spent time at his client's swish holiday home, that she would probably have done anything he wanted, yet not only had he *not* taken advantage of her but he had also got her home and into bed safely. And afterwards, he had made sure that she knew that nothing had happened between them, so that she wouldn't be worried. Then he had disappeared back to London so that she and Josh could be alone to move forward with their relationship.

She thought back to the feeling she had got when she touched his hand. The heart had a lot to answer for: it was quite clearly the circuit board to the soul. Rosa shook her curls to try and unburden herself from these thoughts and feelings.

Josh remained upbeat. 'Of course. Well, thanks for telling me.'

'Josh, I love you so much. There is nothing between me and Lucas, I want to make that clear.' The thought of him moving in to kiss her and her jumping up suddenly fled through her mind too.

A brief silence, then Josh's tone changed to a brighter one.

'Well, I'd better let you carry on cooking up a storm. Give Hot and Bump a big kiss from me and I will see you all so very soon, my darling girl.'

As Rosa sat slowly eating her omelette, her mind became full of Lucas all over again. She examined her thoughts and found to her relief that her heart was hurting for him *not* because she wanted to be with him, but purely because she couldn't imagine the heavy weight of pain that he was experiencing in losing his mother in such a sudden way. She also held the secret that his mother had deliberately thrown herself down the cellar steps. How desperate must Sheila have been, to try to take her own life like that, Rosa thought. Surely just overdosing on her extra-strong prescribed pain relief would have been far more peaceful.

It was such a sad story. Rosa thought long and hard. If it was her own mother, would she want to know the truth, to learn that her mum had wanted to end her life in such a tragic and painful way? She didn't know the answer to that, nor did she know what to do. It wasn't every day you were asked to keep a secret on a deathbed.

Suddenly, Rosa felt a rush go through her body; she called it her 'spirit feeling'. The hairs on both her arms stood up. The last and only time she had been present at someone's death was Queenie's.

'Of course!' Rosa said aloud, then with the memory of her great-grandmother holding both of her hands in her dying moments, she repeated the very last words that the old woman had said to her.

'*Sometimes in life, if you don't know what to do: do nothing, say nothing and the answer will come to you. You are blessed.*'

Queenie was right, as she had so often been. Rosa would let it lie. Sometimes when a problem seemed so immediate and overwhelming, that really was the best thing to do.

CHAPTER TWENTY SEVEN

Rosa was just walking down to the café when she could feel somebody close behind her.

'Long time no see.' The imposing figure of Alec Burton linked arms with her. 'I'm going to the same place as you, no doubt. Sara left her reading glasses at home. I suppose I could give them to you right now to take down, but any excuse to see her. And Brown needed a walk.' His Labrador licked Rosa's hand.

Rosa laughed. 'You two. It's like love's young dream.'

'Well, they do say you should pay good deeds forward, don't they, and you certainly did that for me with Sara. I couldn't be happier, Rosa, with you playing Cupid for us that day. I will be eternally grateful.'

'Who'd have thought I could do something of note for you, eh?' She was pleased.

'Rosa, what have I said to you before? We are all equal.'

'Well, *I* will be eternally grateful to *you* for helping me get my life back on track. So there!' Rosa said affectionately. 'It wasn't until I was out of it that I realised what a dark place I'd been in. I now look at drinking so differently. It made me sad, it made me depressed and react in ways that I really didn't want to. It was as if it took *me* over.'

'You've done so well and it's great to see you happy, now. How's that tall fella of yours doing in the Big Apple anyway?'

'Good, really good. He's coming back sooner than I thought now, too, so I'm counting the days.'

'That old devil "separation anxiety" not rearing its head this time then?'

'I've had a couple of wobbles and nearly called you, but being sober, I seem to be able to bring myself back down – and with all the mental tools you gave me, I am able to grasp the real picture and just bash the bad thoughts out of my head.'

'That's brilliant. Like I've said, we can't stop anyone from doing something, not if they are hell-bent on doing it. But I do know that Josh loves you so much that you should feel secure in that knowledge.'

'I do, I do.' Rosa paused. 'Alec...'

'Go on, what is it?'

'I'm going to give you a scenario, and can we pretend you are my counsellor just for today so that I can rely on that trust, please?'

Alec stopped, unlinked arms and looked directly at her. 'You can always rely on my trust, you know that.' He had come to realise that he filled a fatherly role for this young woman, that her upbringing still raised feelings she couldn't quite control and understand.

Rosa tried to sound matter-of-fact. 'Can you be so in love with somebody and want to be with them and stay with them and create a family with them, but still have feelings for somebody else at the same time?'

'OK.' Alec was thoughtful for a second. 'Well, my take on it is this. The human capacity to love is boundless, Rosa. You love your family, you love your friends, you love your pets, but there is a distinct difference between love and lust.'

137

'Yeah, I know that.'

'Hear me out though. True love tends to develop slowly, over time, as you get to know someone.'

They reached the beach. Rosa asked, 'Can we just walk along the beach path before we go in the café?' She was reluctant to let Alec go.

'Of course. Come on – I can let Brown off the lead then too.' Alec headed with her in the direction of South Cliffs. The winter waves looked grey and uninviting. Seagulls circled the empty bins and sang a tetchy lament at the lack of tourist treats at their disposal.

'Going back to our discussion,' he added, 'lust, as we know, is usually quite instant and can have a similar effect on the brain as some drugs do – and that's because sexual-attraction hormones are released into the body. And a bit like with drugs or drink, it may all seem like a good idea at the time. But long-term, it isn't sustainable. You know that.'

'Yes, yes I do.'

Alec continued, 'I always say to my clients, "If you are uncertain of anything, before you act on your feelings ask yourself, 'What am I feeling here?' And avoid making far-reaching decisions based on what could just be a passing emotion'".'

'I love Josh so much; I would never hurt him.'

'That's right. If you love somebody that much, you will never intentionally hurt them. And face it, connected sex in a relationship can easily feel as good or even better than a brief encounter with a lustful stranger. And I sure as hell know what I would prefer, every time.' The big man stopped walking and looked at her. 'Think of that urge like having a drink. You know how to say no to that. And a good, trusting friendship with a member of the opposite sex counts for a lot too, doesn't it? Look at us, for instance,' and he grinned.

Rosa smiled and nodded as Alec then announced, 'OK, I need to get these glasses to my girl, so let's head back to the café.'

As they started walking back, he asked, 'Did that help?'

'Yes, it did, and I shall just add the "What am I feeling here?" question to my sanity bank. Do you know what, Dr Burton, you really are quite amazing.' Rosa knew how lucky she was to be surrounded by such good people now. Ned, Queenie and Mary had led her to so much more than just a shop and a future down here. She now had a great network of people who really did care about her too.

'I have my moments.' The big man was laughing as Rosa pushed open the door to the café.

'What are you doing, stealing my man? I saw you walking up the beach path arm-in-arm,' Sara teased Rosa, and without expecting a reply carried on cleaning a table. Her own jealousy days were long gone, thanks to Alec's all-encompassing love.

'I've actually got an announcement to make,' Rosa chirped.

Sara stopped what she was doing. After their recent conversation, Alec was slightly concerned as to what this could be.

'Josh and I are having a baby.' Rosa stamped her feet up and down on the floor in excitement.

'Oh my God!' Sara rushed to her side and hugged her. 'That is just the best news. Oh Rosa.'

Alec turned away and tried to suck up the tears that were forming, but eagle-eyed Rosa never missed a trick. 'So, what exactly are *you* feeling here, Dr Burton?'

'Come here, you.' Sara went to hug him next, and cupped her lover's bum cheeks. Brown barked his approval too.

Knowing how hard it had been for Rosa to get to this strategic point in her life, Alec smiled through his emotions. 'Happy, Rosa. I feel really happy for you both.'

CHAPTER TWENTY EIGHT

Mary was pushing the mini-trolleys together neatly outside the Co-op when Rosa approached with a disgruntled Hot pulling on the lead.

'What's wrong with old misery then?' Mary could tell he was in a grump just from his gait and the way his usually jaunty tail was hanging down.

'He wants to go to the beach,' Rosa explained. 'I've told him we'll go straight down there once I've talked to you, but like most blokes, he's got no patience.'

Mary laughed, pulled a tiny treat from her overall pocket, leaned down, ruffled Hot's ears and let him lick her hand. 'Ooh, that tickles.'

'I'm just checking if you are coming down to the fireworks or not tomorrow night?'

'No, Rosa duck. All that cold night air and smoke are no good for my lungs.' Mary put her hand to her chest. 'I'm very wheezy at the moment.'

'So, you know what my next question to you is then?'

Mary smiled. 'Of course I will look after old Grumpy here. Merlin will just have to put up with it. He usually shoots under my bed anyway at the first hint of a bang, bless him.'

'Aw, thank you. Titch's mum is looking after her human and canine brood and Ritchie is working so it looks like we'll have a bit of a girls' night, which will be fun. We haven't been out just the two of us for ages. In fact, I haven't sorted a hen night yet, so I can take the chance to talk to her about that.'

'Good for you. Any envelopes to mention yet?'

'Yes! I had one this morning, a bright red one from Rudolph the Red-Nosed Reindeer. That did make me smile.'

'And?'

'Oh, I'm not opening them until the deadline. I'm putting them in the safe, tucked away.'

'That's not like you, to be careful and not go rushing into things.'

'Ah, but this is so important that I want to do it properly.'

'I think that is very wise. Any others?'

'Yes. So, we have Pigs in Blankets, and one just in from Frosty the Snowman.'

Mary laughed heartily then began to cough and thump her chest. Eventually she managed: 'It was such a good idea, them not revealing their real names yet. You're doing this all on substance and not perception. You're a clever girl, Rosa.'

'I do my best.' Hot nudged his snout into her ankle and barked. 'OK, OK, hold your horses, you Hound of the Baskervilles. We are going in a minute, I promise.'

'So, are Sara and Alec going to the fireworks?'

'Oh, yes, they will be down there but sadly Jacob and Raff won't this year. With the Ship Inn closed for the time being, the Lobster Pot is fully booked in the restaurant and they will need all hands on deck.'

'I thought you might be planning to open the café up, with all those people down there?'

'Oh, we are opening, but just for hot drinks and toilet use, as we felt it unfair to compete with the charity tent for food. Bless Nate, he's going to run the show with hot chocolate and marshmallows out the front.'

'That's good then. I know how you love your fireworks, duck. Talking of which, Josh isn't coming back for them, is he?' Mary looked at her keenly.

'No, because he's coming back earlier in December now.' She saw a visible shiver go right through Mary's body and said, 'What's wrong, Mum?'

'It's nothing – nothing at all. That's good news. Very good news.'

'He came back before, and he was fine, you know,' Rosa tried to reassure her.

Mary ignored her comment, asking instead, 'No news on Sheila's funeral yet, then?'

'No, but I'm sure you'll find out before anyone else, won't you?' Mary tutted as Rosa added, 'Ritchie did mention that there is to be a post-mortem.'

'Maybe it wasn't an accident, eh, Rosa?'

Rosa grimaced at the way her mother always knew her better than she knew herself. Just then, the restless Hot, who'd been crossing his little legs, cocked a hind one against the trolleys and did a wee. 'Shit, sorry, Mum.'

Mary was amused. 'I'll wash it down, love, don't worry. Now, was there something else you wanted to tell me?'

Rosa put her hand to her mouth to try and hide the huge grin that had appeared.

'Angels be! I knew you were! Oh darling, that is just the best news ever.' Mary, never comfortable with public displays of affection, gave her pregnant daughter a brief hug.

'I am only telling my nearest and dearest, so keep it quiet for a bit if you can, Mum.'

Mary couldn't contain her joy. 'Well, if Titch tells Edie Rogers you might as well give the *Daily Mail online* another story.'

'I know, I know. I'm not even three months yet, but of course I had to tell you.'

Mary reached inside her overall pocket again. 'Here. I already made this up for you; in case you feel sick at all.' She handed Rosa a small brown bottle of liquid.

'Another magic potion, Mama?'

Mary's face didn't move. 'If you feel as nauseous as I felt with you, then you will need this, I tell you. Just a couple of drops on your tongue.'

'Was I a good baby?'

Mary let out a big sigh. Her alcoholism had overridden every rational thought during motherhood; hence Rosa being taken into care. 'I think so, duck.' Tears pricked her eyes at her past failings. 'You were a very well-loved baby, I do know that. I am so proud of you for not drinking, Rosa.'

'We do what we do, as you say.' Rosa managed a smile. 'And I'm sorry, but I think now I'm going through pregnancy and motherhood myself, I kind of want to know everything.' She paused, then blurted out, 'What was my dad like? You've never even told me his name.'

But before Mary could answer, Mr Duncan, the manager of the Cockleberry Co-op, appeared in the doorway. 'Mary, there's a queue four deep at your till.' He curtly acknowledged Rosa with a nod and a raised eyebrow. She just hoped he didn't notice Hot's spreading trickle of wee.

'I'd better go.' Mary kissed Rosa on the cheek. 'Tell young Josh how delighted I am, will you?' And, as Mary started walking to the door, she turned around and said quietly, 'His name was Kit.'

143

A chill November wind whipped around Rosa's face as she made her way back down the narrow streets of Cockleberry Bay with Hot trotting at her side, his ears blown aloft in the gusts. She was annoyed with herself for not putting a hat on before she'd left the shop that morning. Also, and more importantly, hearing those words from her mother's lips earlier had evoked many emotions; one of them was, strangely, fear – but the overriding one was of guilt.

Guilt because several months ago now, she had sneaked into her mother's bedroom and gone through her personal things to find the one bit of paper that Mary had always told her she didn't have: Rosa's birth certificate. Guilt that she had traced the man recorded on it as her father to an address in London and had sent him a letter. Rosa had undertaken this mission on her own: she hadn't even confided in Josh. Deep inside, she knew that if she had asked anyone's advice about trying to find her father, they would have told her to let sleeping dogs lie. But it was her life.

With everything that had been going on, Rosa had put the matter to the back of her mind. And so far, she had had no reply to her letter. But now that she had a little person growing inside her, she felt that she *had* to know about that side of her family. It was important to her and her unborn child. Yes, the heritage of Ned and Queenie made her who she was; however, despite her apparently being the result of a drunken one-night stand, she still had half this man Kit's DNA.

The feelings of guilt she could understand, but what was the fear about? Maybe it was connected to her having discovered that her birth mother wasn't the magnificent person she'd dreamed up in her mind. She'd had to face facts: that we all have flaws, that none of us are perfect. Maybe she was afraid lest her dad let her down. The fact that she hadn't heard back from him confirmed that he didn't care that she was the product of his loins. Another rejection in life would be too much to bear, Rosa thought. She had come so far with her mental health. Maybe she *should* have just let everything lie; been contented with at last knowing her mother's bloodline. Appreciated all she had now and not be constantly looking for answers that might not even be there…

She popped into the café, waved and just mouthed hi to Sara and Nate, who were busy behind the counter. It was great that their shift patterns were working so well, and with Nate as a safe pair of hands it gave Rosa and Sara the chance to take time off when they needed it.

The tide was coming in, but a wide expanse of sandy beach remained. While Hot ran off the lead, sniffing at tiny crabs and leaping up at seaweed moving in the wind, Rosa checked to see if there was any sign of life at the Ship, and whether Luke's plumbing van was in the car park – but nothing. And as much as she wanted to see if he was OK, after the other night, she felt it would be too awkward to talk to him. She just hoped that he was with his brother and family, and that they were working through stuff together.

Feeling a sudden twinge of nausea, she sat down on the wall outside the pub and reached for the little bottle that Mary had just given her. It smelled strongly of ginger. Putting a few drops on her tongue, she gagged slightly but then immediately began to feel better. Mary was indeed a magician of sorts.

Hot came tearing up to Rosa, licked her hand then went scuttling off again to chase a chocolate wrapper that was dancing along the sand in the breeze. Sitting outside the empty pub brought back memories of the awful night of Sheila's so-called accident. With the woman's anguished face imprinted on her mind, Rosa closed her eyes and sent some virtual love to Luke. Mary had taught her that the blue angel light ray represents power, protection, faith, courage and strength – and that if you felt somebody needed this then you were to imagine surrounding them with blue light. She remembered their local spiritualist church in the back streets of the Mile End Road having a blue light over the shabby front door.

Thinking about Luke suddenly made her remember the envelope falling out of his back pocket when he had run out on her the other night. She had been in such a hurry to get her sick-laden jeans off and have a shower that she had just put it in a drawer in the kitchen and completely forgotten about it. He hadn't asked for it, but what if it was important and he didn't feel he could contact her after baring his grieving soul to her the other night? She must dig it out as soon as she got home.

She had assumed that the funeral would be held here in the Bay, so if not before, at least she would see him then to give it to him. It was weird. Before she had been with Sheila in her final hour of need, she wouldn't even have considered going to her funeral, as there was certainly no love lost between them, but now she felt that she wanted to pay her final respects. And to be there for Luke, even if it was just in the capacity of a friend or confidante.

Rosa stood up and pulled her coat collar up tightly to her ears. She whistled for Hot, who, as usual, ignored her first attempt to get him to come. The wind was now rushing around the Bay as the tide pulsed in stronger, causing the swelling murky waves to crash regularly on to the cold wet sand, and the salty spray to sting her eyes. The light was going. Aside from one other dog-walker right down the South Cliffs end, the beach was empty. The glowing lights of the café were a comforting sight, she thought, amid the gloom of the day.

Apart from fireworks night, Rosa wasn't a fan of November. In fact, if she had to depict it as a colour, it would have to be grey. She had had great delight going through all her suggested colours for months with Titch, one quiet rainy day in the shop. With the promise of Christmas and good cheer, thankfully December was a much more appealing orangey-red, then back to a blue January when the snow and frost came in. And then a bright yellow for April as that was when her birthday fell. June was a light mauve and July a summery pink.

With Hot safely leashed, she was just about to leave the beach when she spotted a police car pulling into the car park of the Ship. She recognised DC Clarke in the driving seat; he it was who had tried and failed to find out who had set fire to a bin in the Corner Shop downstairs kitchen earlier in the year. The bearded policeman waved his hand slowly in acknowledgment and then stopped the car, opening the window as he did so.

'Rosa? Just the girl. Will you be free in, say, an hour or so? I need to have a good look around here again, then ask you some questions. I can come to the shop if that's easier for you than coming down to the station.'

'Station? Questions?' Rosa was bemused. 'What for? Why?'

'Well, it appears from the post-mortem that the force with which Sheila Hannafore hit the bottom of the cellar steps, and the serious injuries she sustained, suggest this may not have been an accident. It appears, in fact, that she could have been deliberately pushed.'

CHAPTER TWENTY NINE

Hot was so exhausted after his walk that within ten seconds of eating his dinner, he was flat-out under his favourite smelly blanket in the corner of the lounge. Rosa was glad it was a winter Sunday; that meant the shop could remain closed until tomorrow. In the kitchen, she made a cup of tea and checked her watch. At least she had a bit of time before DC Clarke arrived. The trouble with the policeman, Rosa decided, was that there were so few crimes committed in Cockleberry Bay and the surrounding areas that she reckoned he made things up simply so he could pretend he was Hercule Poirot for a day.

Opening the drawer to get a teaspoon, she caught sight of the crumpled envelope that had fallen out of Lucas's pocket. The words *My Lucas* were scribbled in black biro on the front, and it had been opened. With curiosity overcoming her scruples, Rosa pulled a typed letter out of the envelope.

Snuggling under the mauve velvet throw on the comfy cream sofa, she took a big slurp from her *I love Dachshunds* mug, put it on the side table and began to read.

My dear darling second boy,
*   You will be reading this because I'm not here any more.*

You will also have found my will, thank goodness. Simple. Just an equal split between you and Tom, and you two can decide what happens to the pub. Me and your dad spent many happy years here, but if you'd rather the cash than the business, I totally understand. Mrs Treborick from the wool shop has taken the cats already. I know how your dear nephew is allergic and your life is way too busy for pets.

I hope that my death was a peaceful one and you didn't have to watch by my bedside for weeks on end. The diagnosis of my cancer was terminal when I got my first results. People may say that I was selfish not to seek treatment, but my motive was the opposite: to spare you boys from seeing me suffer. My mum, your gran, as you know, died of cancer too. It was the single most horrific thing that I have ever gone through. The truth is, I never got over it. I was always so sad that you two amazing sons of mine never got to meet her, as she was taken so young. She wasted away in front of us like a little bird. Her heart and soul were as big as any lion's, but the wretched disease took hold of her body and eventually killed her.

We loved you, me and your dad, we loved both of you very much. I'd never admit it openly, but I missed him so much after he died. Silly old sod. Despite our bickering there was a love of sorts there. My yin to his yang, or as he used to say, my rottweiler to his puppy dog. Wore his heart on his sleeve, your dad did. I think that's where you get your soft side from, my boy. My heart was hard and I kept it inside, not on show. Maybe the death of your gran caused that, or maybe I was just scared to show my feelings in case they weren't reciprocated.

Well, I want to show those feelings now though, lad. To say that my love for you is infinite. To urge you to please live

149

on with happiness. There's half of me in you, you know, so keep flying the flag for the Hannafores. Maybe you'll have some little ones of your own, one day. That will be lovely. You tell them that their gran will always be looking down and cheering them on from the side-lines too.

'Wow,' Rosa said aloud, with tears streaming down her face. This was just so personal to Luke, and so not the Sheila Hannafore she had created in her mind, but she felt compelled to read on, however heartbreaking the contents.

I may have seen you since writing this letter, I may not. If I haven't then do not feel guilty. There is an expression 'Listen to the woman when she looks at you, not when she talks to you.' I saw the way Rosa Larkin or Smith or whatever you want to call her used to look at you. I genuinely believe that she loved you as much as you loved her. But life is already written, son, it really is. Affairs of the heart rarely run smooth. I always knew she would break your heart.

'Hardly fair,' Rosa commented and carried on reading.

Rosa is not a bad person. Rosa is a survivor. There is part of the girl that I admire, but don't fall for her charms any more. She's had a troubled upbringing and she will forever struggle with temptation, not because she wants to, but because it's in her. Help her. Set her free to enjoy happiness with that husband of hers, although I think that you may have selflessly done this already. If you can bear it, she will make a far better friend than foe.

I do understand. Unrequited love is the torment from hell! All I will say, my darling son, is that real reciprocated love, when nurtured, never fails.

So, I sign out not with a goodbye, but a 'see you later'. Make every second count, Lucas, my darling. Don't sweat the small stuff and remember, wherever I am, I will be willing you on and loving you and Tom with all my heart, just as I have since the day you left my body and entered my heart.

Yours forever,

Mum X

Rosa's sobs were stifled by a loud knocking on the door and then the familiar voice of DC Clarke shouting through the letterbox downstairs. He was early. Could he not just ring the doorbell, like everyone else?

She sniffed, wiped her eyes with an old tissue she had in her pocket and made her way downstairs.

'Hello, Rosa. Ooh, I couldn't half do with a cuppa. We've run out of teabags down at the station. And a few of those homemade biscuits you had before would go down a treat,' were the portly policeman's first words to her.

Rosa managed a secret grin. If Titch were here, she'd be beside herself. DC Clarke really was the greediest man. On previous visits, when he was investigating a fire started in the back kitchen of the Corner Shop, he had managed to ingest half a tin full of Mary's homemade delights. His lack of a waistline was proof of his sweet tooth.

She led him upstairs to the flat and then went into the kitchen to make him his tea.

'Here.' Rosa handed him a packet of plain digestives.

His face fell. 'None of those nice ones you usually have?'

'No,' Rosa replied indignantly. 'Not today. On your own then?'

'Yes, I've left Collins at the pub.' DC Clarke sat on the smaller sofa opposite Rosa. After an initial spate of barking and sniffing at the policeman's shoes, Hot was now back snoozing, one eye open, guarding his mistress from his dog bed.

'So, the officer on duty on the night of the thirty-first of October this year tells me that you found Mrs Hannafore. Is that correct?'

'Yes. I suddenly thought that I should go over and see Sheila and take her some of our Halloween cakes.'

'Ah yes,' the policeman said reflectively, 'the witchy ones. My granddaughter brought some home for me, and very delicious they were too, thank you. Now, you always thought Sheila Hannafore a bit of a witch herself, didn't you, Rosa?'

'I…er…she wasn't my favourite person, no.'

'So why on a dark October night would you suddenly decide to go and see her out of the blue?'

'She was ill, and I didn't like the thought of her being there in the Ship on her own. And what exactly are you implying here, DC Clarke?' Rosa demanded. 'I was the one who went down those cellar steps, called an ambulance and comforted her while the poor woman was dying.'

'After you pushed her down them, you mean?'

'*What*!' Rosa jumped up, knocking her empty teacup to the floor as she did so. 'Get out of here.' She put her hand to her stomach.

'You can't tell me to get out,' DC Clarke said, amid Hot's barking.

'Oh yes I can. I'm not under arrest, am I?'

DC Clarke was undeterred. 'Forensic tests show that the way she landed didn't constitute that of a normal fall. She could well have been pushed, and as you were the first person on the scene – well, that points to you as a suspect, Rosa.'

'This is absolutely ridiculous.' Rosa felt the beginnings of panic. 'I need to phone Josh.'

'You can phone who you like, but I'm suggesting a solicitor might be more appropriate.' Suddenly realising that he was running away with the situation, the detective's voice softened. 'Look, Rosa. Come to the station around lunchtime tomorrow. Bring somebody with you if you want to, but we do need to officially interview you. This is a serious matter, my girl. You were the first on the scene and a woman died very soon after.'

CHAPTER THIRTY

'Josh, no, honestly, you don't have to fly back, it's fine. I can see if maybe Jacob or Alec will come with me. I suppose I *would* be a suspect – if Sheila was pushed, that is. After all, I was at the scene.'

'No. I'm coming. No way am I having my pregnant wife put under such stress. I need to be there for you.' Josh's voice brightened. 'And on a positive, we can go to the fireworks together.'

'If I'm not in the slammer,' Rosa said, and laughed. 'But I've done nothing wrong, so it should be OK. I will just answer their questions honestly and that's it.'

'Yes, I can see, too, from their point of view how you could be in the frame though, Rosa.' Josh sighed in exasperation. 'Oh, why did you ever have to go and get involved with those bloody Hannafores again? They've caused nothing but trouble in our lives. Anyway, I've got to rush, I can hopefully get a last-minute flight to Bristol and hire a car and I'll get to you as soon as I can.'

'If you're going to shout at me, I'd rather you didn't,' Rosa huffed but Josh had already hung up.

Previously, at times like this she would have reached for a drink, but now she was pregnant she couldn't even if she wanted to. Brisk walking was as good a substitute as any, she had discovered. She needed to clear her head. Turn her phone off. Be alone for a while. She had done nothing wrong, after all. Josh didn't need to hurry back, but it would be amazing to see him. And as he said, he would be there for the fireworks – quite literally!

With her warm, woolly hat pulled right down over her ears, she marched towards the beach. She decided that calling Lucas wasn't a good idea. Surely, he had stuck up for her? Or maybe he had been told not to talk to her? It was obvious to Rosa that what had happened was that Sheila had jumped; maybe the impact would have been different if she had just tripped and fallen.

She would have to tell Lucas the truth of what had happened. It was a case of what would upset him more, his mum trying to take her own life or thinking that Sheila had been pushed. Neither option was very palatable. Then again, it was Rosa's word against Sheila's and there had been no love lost between the two of them, as DC Clarke had so ably pointed out.

Rosa walked right to the sea's edge. It was pitch black beyond the glow from the powerful hand torch she was holding. She was glad that the Christmas lights would soon be on, as Cockleberry Bay had never been graced with street lighting. In fact, it was one of the first things she had noticed when moving here from the busy streets and markets of the East End of London. Here, it was complete darkness and complete silence. At least the beach wall lights would be on tomorrow for the annual fireworks display. Rosa noticed that the white tarpaulin and poles were laid at the edge of the beach wall, ready to put up for the charity food and drink tent in the morning.

Even the moon was shivering behind the November clouds tonight. Rosa breathed in Mother Nature in all her darkened, mysterious glory. She was feeling liberated but also very small, as the crashing waves and biting wind took control of her senses. It was strangely eerie to see both the pub and café in darkness. The Ship Inn had been such a massive hub for the community, attracting locals of all ages and all types. Families, fishermen and singles alike. Since Sheila's husband had died, she had ably kept it running and the place had only just been refurbished, at considerable cost, a year ago. It was poignant to recall how much life and soul had gone on inside its white-painted walls. If the building itself could talk, it would keep the *South Cliffs Gazette* in stories for ever more, Rosa reckoned.

It would be sad to see it closed – tomorrow night especially. Although it was at the very same fireworks display last year that Lucas had told Josh that Rosa had been in the pub against his wishes, and Josh had gone mad at her. This was the start of a very troubled period for the pair. But they had come through it stronger, and now, despite it all, they were going to be parents. With all the goings-on, Rosa hadn't thought much about the new baby's arrival at all. A mum – she was going to be a mum! She could hardly believe it. She would experience that unconditional love, the immensity of which was apparently quite overwhelming.

She thought back to the mother-love conveyed in Sheila's letter. And then, with a sudden jolt, she halted and remembered the beginning of the letter to Lucas. Sheila had said she hoped that she had passed peacefully. If she had intended to take her own life by throwing herself down the cellar steps, no way would that be peaceful. But if it was not planned, why would she then ask Rosa to tell her sons that she had fallen? Maybe somebody did want rid of her, but she was ill anyway, and it would probably only have been a matter of time before she did die. And what on earth could the motive have been?

Making her way back up the beach to the road, Rosa thought back to what Sheila had written about her. That she would always struggle to resist temptation. Cheeky cow. But everything she had written was true. Yes, she did love Josh so much, but with a drink inside her and when she thought that Josh had been cheating, she *had* been tempted by the handsome plumber and his uninhibited charm. Lucas was her temptation. And if he hadn't been decent that night last year and taken her home because she was so out of it, goodness knows where she would be now. Certainly not with Josh – or pregnant with his child, for that matter.

Lucas called to the part of her that wanted to carry on having fun, not settle down, not be an adult. She had never felt good enough for anyone, but luckily, now, with some counselling and becoming teetotal, she did value herself. She could see that Josh did love her dearly and that he was in it for the long haul. She was wise enough to acknowledge that there still was a physical attraction with Luke. However, she also understood that if she acted on it, she would never be happy. Lucas was never going to be her happy ending. He had been and still was one of the massive steps she had to take along her path to emotional fulfilment and happiness. Thank goodness she could control her drinking now. Because the destructive part was still within her – and like the veil between the living and the dead on All Hallows Eve, the thin line between fidelity and temptation would be crossed if she had alcohol inside her.

Taking a deep breath and with the waves crashing behind her, she reached the edge of the beach. As she approached the café, she shone her torch in to see the perfectly set red-and-white tablecloths and spooky candles that were still there from Halloween. She moved her torch away, but a light within the café caught her eye. She looked again: maybe it was a clock on one of the ovens, but no, it was like the blueish light from a mobile phone. On seeing it suddenly move and then go black, she firstly let out a little scared scream and then became angry. They only kept a small float in the till overnight, but how dare anyone break in there, to their precious café. She reached for her keys, shone her torch ahead and boldly opened the door. Suddenly the back-kitchen light was switched on – and this time Rosa did scream loudly.

'Fucking hell, Rosa, you scared the shit out of me.'

'And you, me. What an earth are you doing here at this time of night? You're shivering, Nate. What's going on?'

'I got thrown out of my place.'

'I thought you were staying with a mate.'

'Yeah, umm…well, she was kind of more than a mate and she caught me with Mad Donna from the bookmakers so she's an ex-whatever she was now.'

'Oh, Nate!'

'And I thought if I hooked up with her – Mad Donna, that is – then she might understand and give me a little loan for my gambling debt, but she didn't, so here I am. Cold and bloody skint. And, as I had the café keys, it kind of made sense to come here.'

More lies, Rosa noted. He had clearly said that he was staying with a friend and not a lover before. She also noticed the rolled-up sleeping bag on the floor and the headphones draped around his neck that were belting out that tinny noise they make when they are not in someone's ears.

'What's that you are listening to?'

Nate put one of the headphone buds to Rosa's ear. 'James Arthur. I bloody love this track. It's sic. I've been playing it non-stop since its release.'

A shiver went through Rosa, and it wasn't just because she was cold. 'So, when did you move out of the pub then?'

'You know when – I told you. There are rumours circling that old Ma Hannafore jumped, aren't there, down those steep old steps?'

'Nate, you should have learned by now not to pay any attention to gossip.' Rosa's loyalty to Sheila surprised her, or maybe it was Luke she was protecting. 'So, where are you going to sleep tonight?'

'If you don't mind, I was hoping I could stay here. I wasn't going to take the piss out of you and Sara and put the heating on or anything. And look at the bonus: I'll be here to open up first thing for you.' Nate smiled that familiar smile.

'Nate, this may sound weird, but would I have met you somewhere before?'

'I can't see how. I've only stepped over the Devon border a couple of times.'

'You managed to escape the Devonian accent then?' Rosa queried.

'Er, yeah. My old man, he sent me to public school. They beat it out of me.'

Rosa's compassion took over her common sense. 'Look, Nate, I would say come and stay at mine, but Josh is on his way home, as I've got to go to the police station tomorrow, and it would take too much explaining.'

'I'm fine here, but what's this about the police? What have you done, you naughty girl?'

'They don't think it was an accident, the whole Sheila thing.'

'Shut the fuck up!' Nate exclaimed. 'What do they think then?'

'I don't want to talk about it. I have to say it does look a bit suspicious that I was the one who found her.'

'Rosa, go on, tell me more. Tell me everything.'

Rosa suddenly had a feeling of nausea go through her and went running to the toilet. She only just got there in time and came out white as a sheet.

'Jesus, I thought it was called morning sickness,' she said weakly, 'not any-time-of-the-bloody-day-or-night sickness.'

Nate came forward to hug her awkwardly. 'You're pregnant! That's so amazing, Rosa. Hey – I'm so made up for you. And you can't be getting stressed now with a little baby on board.'

'Please don't say a word, will you, Nate? I want to tell everyone close to me before my news does the rounds of the Cockleberry Bay gossips.'

'Mum's the word, so to speak.' Nate put a finger to his lips. 'Seriously though, about this police thing – have you got a brief? You can tell them No Comment, you know.' He sighed. 'You've done a lot for me, Rosa, and I'd hate it if you got into any trouble.'

'And you've got far too much experience in all this by the sound of you.' Rosa shook her curls at him and headed out to the big storeroom at the back. 'Here.' She brought through an old Lilo that needed blowing up and a beach towel from one of the cupboards. 'Make yourself as comfortable as you can, put the heating on, help yourself to food and I'll tell Sara to have a lie-in and come down at eight tomorrow so you can open up.'

Nate nodded. 'You can trust me, I promise.'

'And if I'm not locked up in a police cell tomorrow night, we need to get you sorted out with somewhere to live.'

Rosa put her phone torch on and headed out into the dank November night. With a fake smile, Nate waved to her – then, looking across to the black silhouette of the Ship Inn, he slammed the table with his fist.

CHAPTER THIRTY ONE

Mary enjoyed her daily morning ritual of putting the radio on to listen to the local news. Sitting down at the kitchen table with a large mug of milky coffee and two pieces of wholemeal toast – lightly done, with a thick layer of real butter and chunky marmalade – she let out a comfortable sigh, despite her chest feeling tighter than usual. Sensing that fireworks night was almost upon them, even Merlin was happy just to be at home, and was purring loudly in Queenie's old chair by the crackling open fire.

Their peace was broken by a call from Rosa. 'Mother, it's me. I thought I'd better let you know in case anyone else does that I'll be going to the police station later today. They want to interview me about Sheila.'

'Oh, OK duck. Be honest, won't you? About *everything*.'

'Yes, of course. Josh is flying back to Bristol so he can come with me too. He should have landed by now.'

A feeling of dread rushed through Mary, causing her to shiver. 'He's coming back? *Before* the fireworks? What's going on, Rosa? This doesn't sound right to me. You can tell me anything, you know that.'

'It's fine, Mum. Look, I've got to go. I'll pop in and see you later.' Rosa paused. 'Saying that, I haven't heard from Josh yet. I can't believe he didn't even let me know which flight he was on. I just trusted him when he said he'd be able to get here on time.'

When she'd said goodbye, Mary reached for the inhaler in her apron pocket. Her chest was as tight as a drum by now and she couldn't seem to get the air into her lungs. She tried to force the vision of what she had seen the other day out of her head, but it was stuck there: the snow, a plane skidding across the runway. Josh.

Wheezing heavily, she turned to Merlin. 'I told her to tell him to come back *after* the fireworks.' The kitchen light flicked on and off. A spark shot out of the fire onto the black stone hearth.

The *South Cliffs News* reporter carried on doing his job. 'We've just had some breaking news in from the east coast of America.' Mary stopped mid-mouthful. 'Due to the extreme weather conditions at JFK airport in New York...' Holding her piece of toast static in the air then noisily coughing, she managed to say, 'No, no, this can't be happening – not to our Josh.' She repeated, 'I told her – I warned her...' Then, coughing uncontrollably, she started gasping for breath.

Recognising the symptoms of a severe asthma attack, the ailing woman managed to dial 999 and ask for an ambulance. And then sat back in her kitchen chair, exhausted, and passed out.

CHAPTER THIRTY TWO

Rosa was putting clean sheets on the bed, ready for Josh, when her mobile rang. It was Sara. She listened to what Sara had to say, then asked, 'What do you mean, Nate isn't there?'

'I couldn't believe it. There was a queue six-deep waiting outside when I arrived at eight. I've only just been able to give you a ring – I've been rushed off my feet.' Sara sounded very harassed.

'That's really odd. I only spoke to him last night and he said he would definitely open up.' Rosa didn't dare add that all he had to do was wake up and switch everything on.

'The heating was on when I arrived too, which is strange.'

'Shit, I'm sorry, Sara. Can Wendy come down and help, do you think?'

'Don't you worry, I know you've got a lot on your plate today. I just wondered if you'd heard from Nate, that's all. Is Josh back?'

'No – and that's another thing. Josh's phone is switched off and I've no idea what time he's landing. I just hope he will contact me soon as I don't know whether to make my way to the police station on my own or not.'

'He's driving down from the airport, isn't he?'

'Yes – getting a hire car. It's a long journey from New York just to be by my side for a short time.' Then Rosa heard a banging on the shop door and the doorbell being rung. 'Anyway, I'd better go. Titch has just arrived, and it looks like she's forgotten her shop key. I'll phone you later.'

'Oh Rosa, I'm so stressed,' were Titch's first words on barging through the door of the Corner Shop. She looked flushed and upset. Rosa noticed Ritchie was sitting at the wheel of the fish-and-chip van outside, with Theo red-faced and crying in his arms.

'Theo is doing that screaming thing he does when the bowel blockage happens, so we're straight off to Ulchester General. I couldn't get through on your bloody phone.'

'Oh, sorry, Titch. I've been trying Josh constantly, that's why. I should have listened to Mary; I felt in my gut that it was a bad idea, him rushing back for this. Go on, Titch, get moving and don't worry about the shop.'

'Listened to Mary? And what about the Christmas designer coat delivery – it's coming from London this morning, isn't it?'

'It doesn't matter and that's not your worry now. Just let me know how the little man is as soon as you can, right?'

When Titch had gone, Rosa turned the shop sign to Open, sat at the counter, put her head in her hands and let out a massive sigh. 'Oh Hot, what's going on today?'

'Blimey, love, what's up with you?'

Rosa looked up to see a man in a black puffa jacket with a claret and blue scarf round his neck. She wasn't sure if he was fat or whether it was the jacket making him look that way. His hair was cut so short it could pass as stubble. His light eyes owned a distinct twinkle, while his right cheek bore the kind of scar you were too scared to ask about.

Rosa found herself confiding, 'It's just – well, my husband's gone AWOL, my best mate's kid is ill, I need to go and talk to the Old Bill and there's a big Christmas delivery on its way.' She became more businesslike. 'Can I help you before I try and get my head around it all?'

'I feel stressed for you myself now, after hearing that lot. I was looking for a Rosa Smith, but with Ma's description and noticing you are a fellow scar-wearer – although it's a mere blemish to my train track – I think I've found my girl.' The thirty-something held out his hand. 'Danny Green. You saved my little Alfie's life. I had to come and see ya, soon as I could, like.'

'Oh, hello.' Hot started barking as Rosa's mobile rang. She put her hand up to halt the fellow Londoner and mouthed, 'Just a sec.'

Danny nodded and made himself busy looking around the shop. Hearing Rosa gasp he looked over. Her face had gone white and her hand was trembling. He went to her side as she spoke. 'Oh my God, when? OK, yes, sure. Thank you, Colette. Exeter? Yes, I understand, I'm on my way.'

'You OK?' Danny said with concern. 'Not your day, is it?'

'No, it's not. That was Colette from the Co-op. My mum has collapsed. An ambulance is taking her to Exeter.' At that moment, the delivery man rang at the back door with the Christmas order. Tears started to pour down Rosa's face. 'Oh, this is just all too much. I can't cope.'

Danny took control. 'You go, darl. Give me your keys. I'll sort the order and look after the little dog. The delivery just needs taking in and signing for, yeah?'

Rosa nodded shakily. 'Are you sure?' For some reason she felt she could trust Alfie's dad. 'That would be great. Hot, that's my sausage dog, his food is in the little kitchen there. His lead is on the back of the door, and you need to feed him a small bowlful of his special biscuits at twelve.' She jotted down her mobile number, saying, 'Danny, will you ring me so I've got your number? And phone if there are any problems. Thanks!' And she raced upstairs for her coat and bag.

When she came down, Danny was already bringing in the boxes from the supplier and holding the paperwork to check. 'Just go,' he urged her. 'I'll be fine. It's the least I can do for you for saving my boy's life. Now go to your mum. Now!'

'Danny Green, you're a diamond,' Rosa called, albeit a rough one, she added mentally. Then she threw the stranger her keys, and with one hand on her tummy she pelted out of the door, straight into Lucas.

'Jesus, bird, you nearly knocked me clean over.' Then he saw the look on her face. 'What's the matter?'

'It's Mary,' Rosa gulped. 'She's collapsed and I don't know where Josh is and Theo is sick again too, and there's an order coming in and–'

'Blimey. I just saw a blue-lighted ambulance going hell-for-leather at the top of the hill and wondered who it was for.'

'Oh no, why didn't they wait for me? It must be serious.' Rosa could feel herself going into a full-blown panic attack.

'OK, calm down, girl. What can I do to help?'

'The Royal Devon and Exeter Hospital. I need to get there – and fast.'

Merlin jumped down from Queenie's chair, tipped back his head and started prowling around the empty kitchen, wailing. It was as if he was calling out to his mistress to tell her that if she had just finished listening, she would have learned that the only drama was that, due to extreme weather conditions in New York, all planes had been grounded until further notice.

CHAPTER THIRTY THREE

Staring ahead, Lucas Hannafore sped down the fast lane of the M5 in his Mercedes van, Meatloaf's *Greatest Hits* blaring out from the loudspeakers. Rosa, oblivious to the dust, crisp wrappers and empty Coke cans rolling at her feet, decided she'd better phone the Corner Shop. Now that the first panic had subsided, realisation had set in that not only had she left a total stranger in charge of her livelihood, but she had also left her precious hound and best friend, Hot Dog, in his care too.

Rosa reached forward to turn the volume down so that she could make the call. As she did so, Lucas took a deep breath and said, 'Look, about the other night, Rosa.'

Getting a sudden whiff of the sausage roll that Lucas was now scoffing next to her, Rosa felt her stomach rising and an awful feeling of nausea overtake her. Before she had a chance to ask him to pull in and stop, it was too late; she only just managed to open the window in time.

'Oh my God, bird, why didn't you tell me you were going do that?' Lucas was trying bravely to stall his own gag reflex.

Rosa reached for a tissue from her bag and wiped her face. 'At least I managed to miss the window.' She laughed and then began to cry at the same time.

Lucas put his hand across her arm. 'Rosa, please don't cry. It must be the shock. What do you want me to do? Stop at a service station so you can get cleaned up?'

'No, just keep going. Oh Luke, what if she dies?'

'Don't be so dramatic. Look, she's in the best hospital. What actually happened, anyway?'

'It's her COPD again. Around fireworks night it's always worse. She told me that she had got all the emergency drugs handy for when she was going down with a cold so it didn't reach her chest, but only the hospital can help when she has a bad asthma attack like this.'

'I can't believe Colette didn't phone you earlier, so you could go in the ambulance with your mum.'

'Colette did everything she could. She saw the ambulance pull up outside. Apparently they found Mum unconscious.' Rosa checked her phone again. 'Damn, Josh, where are you? Shit! And now my battery has gone!'

'Here. Have a drink of this.' Lucas handed her a bottle of water from his side door compartment. 'We're not too far now. And you can connect this charger to the lighter. How are you feeling now?'

'I'm fine,' Rosa replied weakly, sticking her tongue out and making a yuk-type noise as her nose and throat burned with vomit. Something else to stall her from telling him about her pregnancy.

'Somehow the words Lucas Hannafore and Exeter Cathedral don't seem to go together,' Rosa murmured as she came in and sat down next to the handsome plumber.

'I thought it might be a long wait and something compelled me to come in here,' he replied, equally quietly. 'It gave me a chance to think about Mum.'

As she looked up at the magnificent, stone-structured, vaulted ceiling, tears began to fall silently down Rosa's cheeks. 'God, it's so beautiful here.'

'You can't say God like that when we are in a place like this,' Lucas remonstrated. Then, on noticing Rosa's tears, he put his hand gently on her coat-covered leg. 'What's the score, sweet lady?'

'She's on oxygen, but her breathing is back under control. She's now just very tired.'

'You heard from your old man yet?'

'No, and I can't get hold of Carlton either, to find out what's happening. I'm worried bloody sick about him too now.'

'OK. So, did you see your mum, then?'

'Yes, but she was too weak to talk, just kept patting my hand, and crying. I promised her I'd feed Merlin and make sure the kitchen fire was safe – you know, the usual things.' Rosa yawned. 'I needed the walk here in the fresh air to calm me down. I'll go back and sit with her in a bit.'

'Mothers, eh…' Lucas's voice tailed off. 'Can't live with them, can't live without them.'

'Life isn't very fair, is it, Luke? It always seems to be loving families who lose a parent or a child. I do believe the good die young.'

'My mum wasn't that young.'

'She wasn't that good either.'

'Oi.' They both then laughed nervously.

Rosa continued, 'How are you feeling today?'

'No different from any other day this week. I mean, she's been gone less than a week and I'm numb. Kind of devoid of emotion. Can't really describe it. It'll be good to get the funeral out of the way, I suppose. All me and Tom are doing is talking about her, which is positive in one way, but part of me wants to just forget for a bit and start getting back to normal.'

'Grieving is a process, Luke. You've got to do the time on it, or it will come back and bite you in the arse later in life.'

'Well, give me the fucking rule book then, Rosa, and I'll see what I can do.' Lucas raised his voice. 'I don't think it's quite as easy as that. Step One: cry like a wild animal. I've done that. Now, shall we tick that off and see what Step Two brings?'

Visitors to the sacred building stared in disbelief at the couple's lack of respect.

'I was only trying to help,' Rosa replied quietly. The cathedral was cold; she shivered.

'Well, don't bother. Let's go,' Lucas said gruffly, striding off towards the great wooden doors that led outside.

When they were out in the chilly November air, Rosa put her hand on Lucas's shoulder. On the grass nearby, a man was placing large Remembrance Day poppies on crosses.

'I am so grateful to you for bringing me here,' she said, 'but honestly, do get back if you need to. I can take the train home. It's fine.'

'Get back to where?' Lucas sighed. 'I feel so fucking lost, Rosa.' A lone tear trickled down his right cheek.

'Oh, Lucas.' On reaching for a packet of tissues in her bag, Rosa noticed the letter from Sheila. 'Here, you dropped this the other day.'

'I take it you read it?' Lucas bit his lip.

'No, I – no, I...'

'What is it you always say? You can't kid a kidder. It's fine, I'd have read it too.'

Rosa felt it was the right moment to address the love-shaped elephant in the room. Too many times she had acted like a child and brushed things under the carpet as if they weren't happening. 'Come on, let's go for a coffee, it's freezing out here,' she suggested, then gasped and put her hands to her head. 'Oh no!'

'What now?'

'I was meant to go to the police station today, but with all this going on I totally forgot all about it. PC Poirot will be putting a warrant out for my arrest by now.'

Lucas began to grin, but then he, too, looked a bit concerned. 'You've just reminded me that I had a missed call from him yesterday as well. Me and Tom were busy discussing the funeral – not that we're allowed to set a date yet with a post-mortem going on.'

'What does DC Clarke want, do you reckon? Not that it matters.'

'You already know, Rosa! So, it obviously does matter. It's about Mum's secret, isn't it? I overheard her say it. I'm not stupid.'

CHAPTER THIRTY FOUR

'Can I help you, sir?'

'I hope so.' Jacob smiled at the bear of a chap behind the counter of the Corner Shop. With that twinkle in his eye and a scar fitting for a James Bond villain, Jacob thought he was rather sexy. Hearing the publican's familiar voice, Hot came rushing off his basket and jumped up at Jacob's designer-clad legs, his own little ones scrabbling furiously.

'Danny, isn't it? I'm Jacob, Rosa's friend from the Lobster Pot pub up the hill. She just called me from the hospital in Exeter so I thought I'd pop in and say hi and check that you're doing OK. It's really kind of you to step in like this.'

'It's the least I could do after your mate Rosa saved my son's life. My old dear is called Tina – you might have met her when she was staying in the Bay with my boy.' He smiled to reveal a gold back tooth. 'They'll be down here later for the fireworks. I know they'd love to see Rosa – if she's back, that is.'

'I'm not sure if she will be, in the circumstances.'

'Well, I'm all right to stay for a bit longer if she needs me to.' Danny looked around. 'Bet it's a little goldmine here, isn't it?'

'Er, she does OK, I think. Look, if you're sure you don't mind hanging on for a while here that will be incredibly helpful for

Rosa, especially at this time of year. Thank you, Danny.'

Ding! The shop bell rang, and a fur-coated Bergamot flounced to the back of the shop without acknowledging either man and began looking at the Christmas gift selection that Titch had so beautifully displayed only the day before.

'Cool.' Danny leaned forward and said in a low voice, 'I've seen a safe out the back. Any idea of the code? I shall need to put the takings away in there later.'

'I have no idea. Sorry.'

'OK, I shall come and find ya at the pub after, then, shall I? I'll bring the takings. Don't want to be leaving a load of cash on the premises, eh?'

'It's not like London here. Just leave the notes in the microwave out the back, and it should be fine. I'll take Hot with me now too, so I can keep him amused while the fireworks are going off.' Jacob leaned down to clip on Hot's lead, causing his furry friend to bark his approval at a pending walk. Before he left, Jacob asked, 'So, Danny, where are you staying while you're here?'

'At the caravan park at the top of the hill.'

'OK. Well, look – thanks again on Rosa's behalf.' He handed the stranger a business card. 'Here's my number if you need to ask me anything at all.'

'Nice threads,' Danny said under his breath on clocking Jacob's designer coat and jeans as he walked towards the door.

'Pardon?' Jacob turned around.

'I said, "Have a nice day, mate".'

As Danny was looking around for the light switches, he noticed a dark-haired young man stop outside the shop window and peer in. The fellow's hair was dishevelled, his long parka coat dirty, and he had a rucksack on his back. His anxious grey-eyed stare made the Londoner feel slightly uncomfortable.

Relieved to find the light switches, Danny illuminated the

shop and poked his head out of the door onto the street. The man was still outside.

'You all right, mate?' Danny asked.

'Who are you?'

'Who's asking?'

'I'm looking for Rosa.'

'She ain't here, mate.'

'I can see that. What time is she back? Do you know?' The lad scratched at his greasy hair.

'Dunno, sorry.' Danny had a lot to thank this girl for, and although he knew nothing about her, he certainly wasn't going to be sharing her business with anyone – especially someone who looked like a homeless stray. 'See you then, mate,' he said, beginning to close the door. 'I better get in, got a customer. Who should I say called?'

'Nate. Just say Nate.'

Bergamot was still fingering items on the Christmas shelf but on hearing Danny come back in she turned around and smiled at him. Her long red hair framed her thin pale face and her red lipstick somehow brought out the blue in her eyes. She had undone her faux-fur coat, and her tight, white roll-neck jumper alerted the Londoner to the fact that she was obviously bra-less. He tried hard to keep his eyes at face level.

'Nice to see a new – and may I say handsome – face down in the Bay,' she said in her posh voice. 'I'm internet dating, you see, and there are very few handsome men to be found in this area, as you can imagine.' She picked up a thick church candle from the shelf and held it at the base with both hands.

Danny blinked and cleared his throat. 'Er, well, I've been swiping right in London for a while and it's not that easy there either. I think my scar puts women off. They reckon I'm a gangster.' He smiled somewhat awkwardly.

'A gangster? How divine,' she drawled, her posh accent standing out against Danny's not so posh one. She put the candle down and came to stand within a foot of Danny's bedazzled and now somewhat hungry eyes. 'Lock.' She placed her finger gently on his nose. 'Stock.' Then on to his lips. And then stroked her hand over the shocked man's now firming trouser area. 'And two smoking barrels.' She ran her tongue around her lips.

'Er, I need to…erm…' Danny straightened himself up and took a deep breath. Even in prison he hadn't encountered such a direct approach.

Bergamot made her way to the front of the shop, turned the hanging sign to *Back in 20 minutes* and locked the door. She then led Danny into the back kitchen, roughly pushed him against the cooker and after huskily saying, 'I know exactly what *you* need,' she planted her red lips onto his and began to unzip his trousers.

CHAPTER THIRTY FIVE

Mary managed a smile as Rosa approached her hospital bed in a little side ward off the main ward. She was just about to lean down and kiss her mother's pale cheek when her mobile rang quietly.

'Sorry, Mum – it's Josh, thank God. At last! Josh, where the hell have you been?' she hissed, aware of the two other patients in the small ward.

Hearing that it was Josh, alive and well and speaking on the phone, Mary's eyes had opened wide with relief; any wider and they would have popped out of her head. She held the oxygen mask to her mouth and inhaled deeply several times.

Rosa gave her the thumbs-up and carried on speaking to her husband. 'I love you too... Yes, yes, honestly, I'm fine... Yes, Mum is coming along just fine too. Josh, stay there as planned for now, OK?'

'I told him not to come back before the fireworks,' Mary said agitatedly, pulling her mask back down.

Rosa gently laid her hand on her mother's and helped to replace the mask, saying, 'I won't be a minute, Mum.' She went out into the corridor to finish her conversation in private. On her return, she was glad to see that a nurse had helped Mary to sit up in bed, where she was now drinking some orange juice.

Mary handed her daughter the beaker to put down. 'I've had enough, thanks. Now, what's going on, duck?'

'It's the weather. It's so bad in New York that they've grounded all planes. Josh said he'd messaged and emailed but nothing has come through yet, and for some reason he was unable to call out. It could be something to do with phone signals in the storm, I don't know.'

'I thought his plane had crashed,' Mary said in a weak voice. 'It sent me into a right old state. I saw the bad weather; I saw it all.'

'Hmm. Sometimes that crystal ball of yours needs a good clean, eh? There were no planes even flying out of New York, let alone crashing.'

A tear ran down Mary's cheek. 'I was thinking all sorts, lying here, like your little mite wouldn't have a daddy, just like you didn't.' She swallowed a sob. 'Are you all right anyway?'

'I'm fine, just sick of sick, that's all. Of feeling it and being it.'

'Well, I bet it's a girl then, as that's exactly how I was with you.' Mary reached for a tissue and blew her nose.

Rosa sighed heavily and sat on the chair next to her mother's bed. 'For once I am glad that we couldn't talk earlier. I don't know what I would have done if you'd told me that my husband was potentially in a plane crash and then I'd not been able to get hold of him. So much has been going on that I've been oblivious to the world outside.'

'And what about the police station?'

'I called and PC Poirot was fine. He had already heard about you, as an ambulance call-out is big news in the Bay.' Rosa sighed. 'I shall need to go and see him tomorrow.'

Mary pushed her hair away from her face. 'So, Titch is OK minding the shop and Hot, is she?'

Rosa clapped a hand to her forehead. 'That's something else – I'd better let Danny know what time I'll be back.'

'Danny?'

'Theo had a bad tummy again, so Titch and Ritchie went off to Ulchester General and Danny Green, who is Tina's son – you know, Tina, whose grandson I managed to save? Well, he showed up and said he'd look after the shop.'

'I think I understand.' Mary nodded. 'That's very trusting of you. And that poor girl and baby – not again.'

'I know, and I didn't have a choice about Danny helping so please don't tell me off. If the Christmas delivery hadn't been imminent, I would have just shut up shop, but it was a lot of pallets and I wanted to get to you fast. Somehow, I don't think robbing somebody who has saved your son's life would be on the agenda, do you?'

'Unless he runs a kennels, of course. Then he'd be sorted for free dog food and diamanté leads for years to come,' Mary joked feebly. She looked utterly exhausted.

Giving her mum a kiss on the cheek, Rosa smiled and said, 'Save your energy for getting better, although they do say laughter is the best medicine, don't they? Whoever "they" are.'

Mary took a large, rattling breath. 'OK, I hear you. Now, you get off, love. I'm staying here for tonight and then that handsome Dr Reginald will be back in the morning to see if I'm fit to come home tomorrow. And don't you be worrying about driving me back, I can get hospital transport home.'

'If you're sure, then I will head off. And ring me once you've seen the doctor. I'm sure Jacob will drive up and get you if I ask nicely.'

'I'm sorry to have worried you, duck. I forgot for a second that you're growing a bairn in that little tummy of yours – my grandchild.' Mary beamed.

'I'm fine, honestly, and your ginger potion really helps. Unfortunately, I forgot it today in all the kerfuffle. This little one is a survivor – like me, I reckon. Baby Smith is hanging in there for the duration.'

Mary couldn't suppress a yawn. 'I can't wait to meet the little bundle. And, yes, you get on home. I know how much you love those fireworks, although I doubt if Titch will be with you now. Text me later, won't you? Let me know you're home safe and I want to know how the little 'un is. Oh, and can you feed Merlin, please?'

Rosa stood up, making sure that her mother could reach the water jug and then tidied her bed covers. 'Of course, and before I forget – here, your favourite.' She pulled a large bar of Cadbury's Dairy Milk from her bag.

'Oh, Rosa,' Mary tutted. 'You know how dairy makes me cough.'

Rosa smiled at her mother's occasional lack of graciousness. 'Right, I'd better get home and see what's going on. I wonder what your old mate Kahlil Gibran would have to say about my having to deal with so many things at once.'

Mary looked up to the ceiling and shut her eyes. 'He would probably say, "Most people who ask for advice from others have already resolved to act as it pleases them".' She then opened her eyes and reached for Rosa's hand. 'And please remember what I said at Halloween, Rosa. I may not get everything spot on, but what I do know for sure is that the Jacks of this world come in many guises.' She then shut her eyes again and promptly started snoring.

CHAPTER THIRTY SIX

Ritchie and Titch sat in the consulting room at Ulchester General, awaiting the results of Theo's X-ray. Ritchie's hand was turning white from the force with which his wife-to-be was gripping on to him. He, of course, said nothing.

Ben Burton, Theo's dad and son of Alec Burton, was at the end of his phone waiting for the news. They were all praying that it wasn't the same Volvulus from which the little lad had suffered previously and which had caused his bowel to twist and give him so much pain.

'It will be all right, won't it, Ritch? He's going to be fine, isn't he?' Titch gently stroked Theo's black curls. He had thankfully cried himself to sleep and was now lying peacefully in the carry cot next to them, making little snuffling noises as he breathed.

Ritchie kissed the young girl's forehead. 'Yes, of course it will, darling. They know him now and they sorted him before, didn't they? And Ben's on standby if they did need any more blood, which they won't as they already told us they have a good supply of it, despite it being such a rare group. They are all prepared.' He carefully moved his hand from her vice-like grip and placed it on her knee. 'And look at him. He's not in pain now, is he?'

Titch jumped as the door flew open. The harassed and tired-looking young doctor held out his hand to her. 'Fielding, Dr Fielding. Mrs Whittaker?'

'Er, no, it's Miss, but I'm soon to be Mrs Rogers actually.'

'Mr Whittaker, good afternoon to you.' Ritchie felt no need to correct the blustering doctor again as he continued, 'When did he last have a bowel movement? Theo, I mean, not you.' He looked at Ritchie without so much as a smile.

Titch had to giggle. 'Erm, yesterday afternoon,' she told the doctor, 'so I was wondering–'

Dr Fielding held up a hand and stopped her in her tracks. 'Did you notice anything missing when you tidied up his toys last night?' Ritchie started to laugh as the doctor held up the X-ray to show them. 'If I'm not mistaken, that looks distinctly like a plastic car. A very tiny one, for sure, but most definitely a car. I can't believe he didn't choke on it.'

'Oh my God, I told you to watch him,' Titch began, then added: 'Sorry, Ritchie, I was only saying the other day that you have to have eyes in the back of your bottom when you've got a little toddler.'

'So, it's not Volvulus then?' Ritchie asked.

'It looks more like a Mini than a Volvo to me,' the doctor said drily. 'I've got a young daughter, so don't beat yourself up about it, but at this age you have to watch them like a hawk as they do tend to put everything into their mouths.'

'So, what do we need to do now?' Ritchie wanted to know.

'You don't need to do anything, but keep an eye on his nappy. It shouldn't pain him to pass the toy now that it's moved down. A big poo and he'll be as right as rain.' The doc smiled. 'What a shame that isn't the answer to all our problems.'

With that, Theo let out a long, grumbly fart.

'Looks like the garage doors might be opening sooner than we thought,' Ritchie stated, much to everyone's amusement and Titch's immense relief.

CHAPTER THIRTY SEVEN

Rosa propped the phone on the bedside table as she talked to Josh on Facetime, at the same time pulling on knee-high winter socks. They chatted animatedly.

'You look so cute in those long socks,' Josh said.

'I don't feel cute, just bloody cold. The temperature has really dropped, and the heating's been off up here all day. And they're not quite so sexy over thick tights.' She made a face at him on the screen.

'Well, turn the heating up then, you mustn't be cold. Mind you, it's a good job you're not here. Brr! It's minus five today.' Josh shoved a piece of cake into his mouth. 'I can't believe your mother had me for dead, by the way,' he said, chomping with his mouth full.

'Josh, that's gross!' Rosa blinked at the sight. 'I know, sometimes these premonitions of hers aren't a good thing. This time, it nearly did for her.'

'To be fair, she did get the weather bit right, and several planes *were* skidding along the runway before they decided to close the airport. I'm so sorry if I worried you. And don't be so snooty about the cake, wifey. I've been up since four, so I need some sustenance.'

'It wasn't your fault. The messages you sent all came through together, just as I got back earlier.'

'How did you get to the hospital anyway? Exeter's quite a drive.'

'Don't be cross, but Lucas took me. I was running out of the shop and–'

'Rosa, slow down.'

She felt tears hitting her eyes. 'I'd never hurt you again, I promise.'

'Don't you think I know that – or there wouldn't be a little bubba growing in that beautiful tummy of yours. How is Mr Bump anyway?'

'It could be a Miss Bump. I was thinking about that the other day: shall we find out the sex?'

'That's not until the second scan though, is it?'

'Look at you knowing all these things.' Rose lifted her jumper and flashed her midriff at him. 'No sign of anything yet. But I've been so terribly sick. Every single day and not just in the morning.'

'Oh darling.'

'It's fine, I'm excited now, and hopefully the sickness will go soon.'

'Well, I've been reading that it might not,' Josh said knowledgeably.

'Hmm, thanks for that – *not*, Dr Smith. Let's maybe leave the textbooks alone until we meet him or her, shall we? As I think we'll need the guidance far more then.'

'Talking of babies, how's Theo?'

Rosa started to laugh. 'Basically, he just needed to have a big poo. He'd eaten a tiny plastic car and it got a bit stuck on the way down.'

Josh's shoulders shook. 'That's hilarious, but bloody hell, he was lucky he didn't choke.'

'I know. Titch and Ritch are on super-high alert now. He really is into everything.'

'All the more reason we need to get a house and not have the worry of those steep stairs for when our little one comes along.'

'Yes. I'm excited about moving now. In fact, I'm excited about a lot of things.' Rosa got up from the bed and began hunting for her green wool roll-neck dress. 'Talking of moving, I got another envelope this morning – a blue one labelled *Quality Street.*'

'Another genius name, funny. How many is that now?'

'Only four. I honestly thought they'd be flooding in. That doesn't seem many, considering what's on offer.'

'You said yourself that it's a massive decision, even more of a risk if you don't know the area or clientele. I also think putting a ten-year block on selling it will deter some people, but it gets rid of those wanting to make a fast buck. Hopefully it will be somebody from around here who takes it on. Ned surely would have preferred that. And that way, you're far more likely to get somebody who genuinely wants to make a go of it. It's all good, Rosa. I'm so proud of you.'

'Aw, I agree about Ned and I'm quite proud of myself too, thank you very much.'

Josh was thrilled at just how far his wife had come from her previous issues with low self-esteem and jealousy. 'So, you're not getting on the mulled wine with Titch at the fireworks do tonight then?'

'No, of course not. I'm pregnant with our child, remember. Or I might have,' Rosa said slightly defiantly.

'Just checking,' Josh teased. 'Well, have the best time.'

'I will. I need to pay Danny and thank him for looking after the shop. Tina and their little Alfie are down here too, so it'll be good to see them in much happier circumstances.'

'It was so good of Danny to step up.'

'Yes, it really was.' Rosa let out a breath. 'He saved my bacon at a very fraught time.'

'And, Rosa...you're sure that DC Clarke has calmed down and he's saying it's just a formality now, your interview?'

'Whatever it is, it's all under control, so please don't worry. I'm not guilty of anything other than caring.'

'You are so sweet.' Josh blew a kiss to her. 'OK, I'd better go. I'm bloody knackered, what with all the airport goings-on and then worrying about you and Mary. She is going to get through this, isn't she?'

'Bless you – I bet you are knackered. As for Mary, I believe she's on the mend and I hope she can take things easy for a while.'

'That's good to hear – and Rosa?'

'Yes? What have I done now?'

'Nothing. Just wondered if I'd told you lately that I love you to where the sky touches the sea.'

'You hadn't actually,' Rosa said nonchalantly, her whole being smiling inside and out.

'Well, I do.'

'Oh, bugger off and finish your cake.' Rosa laughed and blew a kiss to her now smirking husband down the screen.

CHAPTER THIRTY EIGHT

With Alec busy in a counselling session, Sara took the opportunity of walking Brown down to the beach before the bangs and whistles of the fireworks commenced. She was disappointed with Nate. She and Rosa had been nothing but good to him – and not only had he let them down this morning, but she hadn't been able to get hold of him to give them a hand with opening up for the fireworks this evening. Instead it was Alec, her rock, who had helped her set everything up for the hot chocolates to be served outside, and despite her insistence that Rosa have a night off after her terrible day, her young partner was having none of it.

Leaning down to make sure that Brown's collar was securely fastened, Sara's torchlight picked up the willowy figure of Bergamot coming out of Rosa's back-yard gate. The vegan one's mop of red hair was looking messier than usual and her faux-fur coat flapped open. Not wanting to make small talk, Sara just smiled and said, 'hi,' as a flushed Bergamot put her head down and hurried past her, heading up the hill.

'Here she is.' Sara gave Rosa a friendly kiss on the cheek. Alec was busy sprinkling chocolate on the top of the steaming milk he had just heated up inside.

'Sorry I'm later than I said I'd be,' Rosa greeted her. 'With Mum not home, I had to check on Merlin and then on Hot, who has been up at the Lobster Pot today. He's having the best time with the Duchess and the pugs; I doubt they'll even hear the bangs.'

'We've left the radio on for Brown and put him in the back room. He slept through the storm, so I shouldn't think he'll even lift an ear.'

'Bless him.' Rosa shivered and pulled her hat down further over her ears.

'How's your mum doing?'

'As good as can be expected. I phoned her on the way down here and she was already nodding off.'

'And Titch and Theo?'

'They're fine.' Rosa's face broke into a smile. 'He had eaten a plastic car.'

'What?' Sara's face began to twitch. 'No! I shouldn't be laughing.'

'You can now because everything is OK. Well, as soon as he's done a poo it will be. Titch and Ritchie are both sat at Titch's mum's waiting for it to emerge. And they don't want to leave him, in case it gets stuck in the garage doors so to speak.'

Alec, who had caught up with the conversation, was now laughing too, fit to burst. 'Kids, eh?'

'Don't, it makes me even more scared about what I'm getting myself into.'

'You'll be a natural, Rosa; you wait and see.' Alec patted her on the arm and went inside to get more cardboard cups.

'Any word from Nate today?' Rosa asked Sara.

'No. I'm a bit annoyed with him to be honest.'

'I hear you, but he's troubled. Money problems, I think. Last night I found him in here, with no agenda other than sleeping on the floor. He promised me that he would open up this morning, so I was as surprised as you when he didn't show.'

'Oh, really? He'd been so reliable up until now. I wonder what's changed all that? And if he's broke, you'd think he'd want to keep working, surely? I just don't get it.'

A penny suddenly dropped as Rosa looked over at the pub. The Ship Inn was in complete darkness apart from the twinkling fairy lights that adorned the wall in front of it. 'Now I understand,' she said to herself.

Sara overheard. 'Everything OK?'

'Oh yes, just thinking aloud,' Rosa prevaricated, for some reason her gut still wanting to protect Nate. 'I meant to bring some cash down for Danny Green. Do you mind if I just whizz back to the shop for ten minutes?'

'We're not busy yet, and I'm sure we can manage on our own. You've got enough on your plate so don't rush and do yourself a damage.' She pointed to Rosa's still-flat belly.

'In or out, this child is going to be coming with me wherever I go,' Rosa said. 'I don't need to slow down.'

'OK, OK. I just care about you, you know. Off you go. See you in a bit.'

Rosa walked against the crowd of people now streaming down the hill to the beach and the imminent firework display. Maybe something *had* happened in the pub that night – something too terrible to contemplate. But what would be the motive? Cash on the premises, maybe? But the pub hadn't been open for a while, so there wouldn't have been much, and Sheila was so ill, anyone could have taken it quite easily without her knowing, and certainly without pushing her down a flight of stairs.

But Sheila had gone on about 'the secret' – what did that

really mean? Was it simply that she had intended to kill herself, or was there something more? Recalling the music that she'd heard when she had arrived in the pub made Rosa cringe. It could be a complete coincidence that Nate liked James Arthur too. Thinking back, had the music stopped when she arrived – or had she been so intent on looking after Sheila that she had imagined that too? Lucas had thanked her for leaving the door open – but she wasn't a hundred per cent sure if she had done that either. Normally she would have closed it behind her. Maybe there had been someone else in the pub? Rosa knew she definitely needed to get her head together for the police interview now. That was for certain.

And, yes! The memories were flooding in now. Nate *had* been staying in the boxroom upstairs at the pub, and had been far from clear about when he had moved out when Rosa had questioned him. There had been so many lies from him, in fact. About how long he had worked at Sea & Save, and the way that the friend's house he had been staying at had suddenly turned into a girlfriend's house. Too many things didn't add up. But despite all this, he had been so clever in schmoozing her that she had not only paid him for painting the shop but had also given him a job at ROSA'S. A job for which he was getting paid – but now, due to his admitted gambling problem, he didn't even have enough money to look after himself. When Rosa had told him that she was seeing the police the next day, he had become particularly animated, and it also seemed weird that last night of all nights, he had decided to up and leave.

Feeling annoyed at so many people barging into her down the narrow streets, she took a side road and went through the back gate into the Corner Shop's courtyard. The bright security light came on. Surprisingly, the back door was not locked. But then again, she hadn't reminded Danny to lock it and the poor bloke couldn't be expected to remember everything, especially as Hot would have needed to be let out and in again for a pee before Jacob collected him. Danny had texted her to say that on Jacob's instruction he had left all notes, totalling a very satisfactory £425, inside a mug in the microwave and that Tina, Alfie and himself were really looking forward to seeing her at the fireworks later.

Putting her bag down on the side in the kitchen, Rosa noticed that all the mugs, even those she had used herself early that morning, had been washed up and were neatly placed on the draining board. There was also a broken one next to a bit of paper, with a note saying, *So sorry, I knocked it off the side.* He might look like a dodgy character, Rosa thought, but at least Danny had manners. And then again, who was she, to judge someone by a scar? Every scar could tell a story, big or small. She was, in fact, rather fond of hers now. It made her unique.

Her phone beeped the signal of a very long text message.

Biggest shit he's ever done and yes, there it was, a tiny blue and now somewhat brown plastic Mini. Sorry, but I'm not coming out. His Lordship is understandably knackered and whingey, Ritch must work and it's not fair on Mum to leave her to cope. Enjoy the bangs, chance would be a fine thing! See you tomorrow. T X

Still smiling from Titch's usual irreverence, Rosa opened the microwave and reached inside for the *I Love Dachshunds* mug that Danny had put in there. The mug was empty. Thinking the cash might have fallen out when he put it in there, she ran her hands around the back, then lifted the glass plate inside – but there was nothing. Going through to the shop, she checked the till; no notes, only coins stared back at her. She noticed that

Danny had even tidied up the counter, bless him.

Locking the back door behind her, Rosa set off down the hill thinking that there had to be a simple explanation.

With a crackle, sizzle and extremely loud bang, the Cockleberry Bay Residents Association Annual Firework Display began, filling the freezing night sky with not only light, colour and joyful explosions, but the obligatory chorus of *oohs* and *aahs*. Screaming children were laughing and running around with sparklers as adults shifted from foot to foot, cupping their mulled wine and hot chocolate as if their lives depended on them.

Standing behind the table outside the café that they had set up for drinks, Rosa looked around her and smiled. The beach was packed full of smiling faces, everyone happy and enjoying themselves. This was what life was about – community and coming together. It was one of the reasons she truly loved Cockleberry Bay.

The last firework wove its colourful dance down to the sea, leaving the distinct smell of sulphur hanging in the air. As Sara and Rosa chinked their cardboard cups in a toast, they were interrupted by two familiar faces running up to them.

'There's our gel,' Tina Green said loudly. 'What you got to say to her, Alfie?'

'Do you sell sweets in your shop too?'

'Oi, that's naughty.' Tina tutted at her grandson. 'He's five today and full of it.'

Rosa walked to the front of the table then crouched down to the little boy's level. 'Happy Birthday, Alfie, and I'm sure I can find you some sweeties here in the café if you'd like them.' She knew there were some chocolate buttons left over from the ones they'd used to decorate some freshly baked cupcakes.

The lad grinned at her. He was so cute it suddenly gave Rosa a surge of love for Bump, who was growing inside her. She hadn't even thought about which sex she would prefer, but a mini-Josh would be mighty sweet.

On reappearing outside with the chocolate buttons in a paper bag and three cupcakes, one each for Alfie's family, Rosa noticed Danny approaching in geezer-like fashion, plastic pint of beer in hand, across from the charity tent.

Alfie grabbed him by the hand and pulled him towards Rosa.

'This is my daddy! He had to go to prison because somebody hurt him, and he told me he'd be safer in prison and I'm happy he doesn't have to go there again.'

Danny and Tina grimaced. Rosa handed the lad the treats while Sara and Alec began clearing everything away.

'You know what, Alfie? I'm very glad he doesn't, too.' Rosa winked at Danny, whose face instantly relaxed.

'And Rosa?'

'Yes, Alfie?'

'Fank you for saving my life.'

Rosa went over to the little boy and gave him a big hug.

'Ew.' He promptly pushed her away. 'I don't hug girls. And Grannie Green, I need a wee.' The two of them disappeared hastily into ROSA'S to use the toilet there.

Danny shrugged when Rosa told him, 'Thanks so much for stepping in, Danny, that meant a lot. It's not often I trust a stranger.'

'Look, love, about the prison thing–'

'That's your business. We've all got a past.'

Danny reminded her so much of some of the boys at the children's homes she'd grown up in. They'd had a hard start in life, but even if they were a bit rough around the edges, that didn't mean they were bad. In fact, growing up as she had done, there wasn't much that fazed or shocked Rosa, which she saw as only a good thing.

'There's something I wanna tell you.' Danny held her arm and looked right into her eyes. 'My ex – that's Alfie's mum, Leah – well, she was a drug addict. Crack cocaine, poor cow.'

Rosa nodded. 'That's tough. I used to drink too much – different addiction, but same motive and outcome. I'm sober now though and – I never thought I'd say this – but I'm enjoying it. I hope Leah can reach this point one day.'

'"Middle finger up to your twisted head" and all that. Damn, I love that James Arthur lyric,' Danny added. 'I could listen all day to "Finally Feel Good".'

'Another one,' Rosa said to herself.

'What?'

'Another one who's listening to James Arthur.'

'Yeah, well. His new album is really good.'

'So, she's better now then, is she? Leah, I mean.'

'Yeah. She's doing good. She's gone back to stay with her mum who lives out in the countryside in Wales, so it's easier for her to recover, you know.' He paused. 'I loved her, Rosa, but it's gone now. Too many demons. For both of us.' Then his face lit up. 'But she gave me our Alfie, so I will always hold a candle for her. It's been bloody hard. Thank God for my old mum.'

'*The deeper that sorrow carves into your being, the more joy you can contain.*'

'What you on about?'

'Oh, it's something my mum said: she likes to quote from the prophet, Kahlil Gibran.'

'That's too deep for me. Blimey, I think I'll stick to song lyrics.'

Rosa smiled. Grannie Green, on noticing the couple deep in chat, tactfully walked towards the charity tent with Alfie. She fancied a cuppa.

'Talking of carving, that's how I got this.' Danny pointed to the deep red line on his cheek. 'Leah had managed to get the money together to pay her dealer everything she owed. I went with her; he was still a complete wanker to her, so I gave him a piece of my mind. He had a blade. As well as doing a bit of signwriting on my face, he also had a shit-hot lawyer. Turned out the dealer looked squeaky clean, and it was me who ended up doing the stint in bird, until my appeal quashed it. I'm only just out. You know something, Rosa? I want me and Alfie out of city life. In fact, somewhere down here would suit me and the boy perfectly.'

'Yes, it would. It's quiet, mind, compared to the Big Smoke. What do you do for work?'

'I work for C&V – you know, the big hardware outlet? That's why doing a bit of shop work for you today didn't bother me.' He grinned. 'In fact, I bloody loved it.'

'You're still there then?'

'Yes, thankfully they took me straight back – C&V, that is. I may have got a record now but I'm no criminal, Rosa. Just a bloke brought up by a single parent, who is now a single parent himself, and from a tough background. I'm a bloody hard worker too and my employers knew that, which was such a blessing.'

'I take it you know I am gifting the shop to somebody I feel deserves it, don't you?'

'Er, yeah. My old woman did mention it. Unbelievable.' Then: 'We are a bit like kindred spirits, you and me, I reckon.'

A brief silence ensued, then Rosa piped up, 'While we are talking shop, where did you leave the cash? I got your message, but it wasn't in the mug in the microwave. Well, the mug was there but no money. The back door wasn't locked either. I wanted to pay you out of it.'

'You're having a giraffe, aren't ya?' Danny put his hand to his head. 'Honestly, that cash was in there when I left, but fuck me – sorry, Rosa – I meant to lock the back door. Jacob had said that you don't always lock doors down here. I mean, I'm usually paranoid but his comment must have soaked in and I didn't lock it. Shit. The money hadn't fallen out somehow, had it?'

'No, I checked.'

'Oh no!' Danny clapped a hand to his head again. Then: 'Wait – listen. There was some shifty-looking fella hanging around at the front of the shop earlier. Long, dark, messy hair. Looked like a tramp. I didn't trust him at all. I didn't tell him where you were either, Rosa. He asked for you. Said his name was Nate. I'm not one to grass usually, but you saving my Alfie, well, that makes you one of the family.' He added scornfully, 'I know his sort. I've lived among them. He knew you weren't there, too.'

'Ah, OK.'

'You know him, do you?'

Rosa sighed. 'Yes, you're right, I do.' It pained her to think that Nate could be capable of stealing from her. But knowing herself, as she did now, she also accepted that addicts were liars and often desperate. However, despite all this, the thought of the money being stolen hadn't even crossed her mind.

In fact, she was quite relieved that Nate had been looking for her. Rosa felt a certain affinity with him – another stray to fill her own deep-rooted insecurities. Also, she was desperate to talk to him about the other night. She assumed he had no credit on his phone, or he would have replied to her message. Titch used to be like that all the time when she was skint too. The same now-blossoming-and-happy Titch, whom Rosa had rescued from the beach bench all those months ago, when the younger girl had found herself pregnant and with nowhere to turn.

'Look, I'm so sorry, Rosa. Is there anything I can do? I don't want paying for starters and that's a given. I could kick myself. For fuck's sake!'

'Don't be silly, it may turn up yet. So, think back, can you remember one hundred per cent you putting the cash in the mug in the microwave?'

'Yes, definitely. It was only a few hours ago, and I'm not going senile yet, I don't think.'

Mind you, Danny thought guiltily, the last hour in the back kitchen of the Corner Shop was a bit of a blur. What he did remember very clearly, however, was that posh tart, whose name he didn't even ask for, swiping her arm across to clear the worktop and smashing a mug as she did so. He hadn't had sex for months, so he wasn't turning it down when offered on a plate like that. In fact, it was the best sex he'd ever had – and it had been a long time coming. She had insisted he take his socks off too. Kinky cow. He still couldn't believe that it had happened; none of his mates would believe it. Her voice was so plummy too. Made it all the funnier.

At that moment Alfie came charging back to them, holding a pebble up in his hand. 'Daddy, Grannie Green says we can throw some stones in the sea!' he shouted excitedly. 'We got lots of flat ones, and they are in Grannie's bag.'

Tina Green came puffing up behind the young lad and Danny noticed how tired his mother looked.

'No throwing in the dark, Alfie, but tomorrow for sure. Come on, my old darlin',' he said to his mum, 'let's get you back to the campsite. Rosa, we're here for the weekend, so we'll come and see you on our way to the beach tomorrow. If you're about, that is?'

Danny put a sulking Alfie on his shoulders, linked arms with his mother and as they started walking up the hill, the deep-thinking ex-con let out a massive sigh.

'That doesn't sound too good, son. Everything OK?'

'Yeah, Ma, yeah. It will be.'

Alec waited while Sara locked up the café.

'I enjoyed that,' he said. 'The fireworks and the hustle and bustle of being on the front line of serving.'

'I've done bugger all, sorry.' Rosa bit her lip.

'Good,' Alec replied kindly. 'I'm under strict instructions from Josh for you to take it easy anyway.'

Sara appeared outside. 'It was worth opening though; we've taken a tidy penny.'

'Great! But let's not leave money in the safe any more,' Rosa said hurriedly. 'I think one of us should take it home to bank on a Friday from now onwards. Let's just leave the float.'

'OK, but I've never had a break-in here before. You know what this place is like.'

'Yes, but it looks like I may have had the day's takings stolen from the shop earlier. I don't want to discuss it now, if you don't mind, as my head is all over the place and I'm tired. I might be wrong – I hope I am.'

'Ah, right. Are you sure you're feeling all right though?' Alec was concerned.

'I'm fine, honestly.'

'And don't forget you've got that snazzy CCTV system.'

'Oh yes – you're right!' Worried for their safety after a fire was started deliberately in the shop, Josh had gone security-crazy and insisted they install the best equipment on the market. It was so discreet and well-hidden that Rosa had forgotten it was there.

Just as they started to head up the hill, a stranger approached them. He was a very upright, white-haired man in his mid-fifties, wearing a long black coat and sucking on an ornate marble pipe. He could have stepped straight out of a horror film, with his debonair good looks and somewhat spooky appearance.

'Excuse me and sorry to bother you folks but I missed the show, did I?' His voice was soft, almost hypnotic.

'Yes, the annual excitement for Cockleberry Bay is over,' Alec said in a dead-pan voice.

'Damn. I was looking for someone too. He always did love the fireworks, you see. I thought it would be a definite.'

'Oh, what is his name? We may know him, as this is a small place,' Rosa replied politely.

'It's Nathaniel, Nathaniel Webb.'

'Er, we do know a Nate,' Sara chipped in.

'Webb, you say?' Rosa suddenly felt sick.

'That's him, he always did like to shorten it, much to his mother's dismay.' He then looked directly at Rosa. 'He's got curly dark brown locks, just like yours, in fact.' He stared at Rosa for what felt like a minute, but was probably only seconds.

For some strange reason Rosa, again, instinctively wanted to protect the long-haired loner. She said, 'I don't have his number, but he quite often comes into my shop. Should I take your number, and then when I see him, I can ask him to call you, maybe?'

'Great idea. Here's my card.'

Rosa looked at it. *Christopher Webb, Webb & Sons, Funeral Directors.*

'Ah, I see. You must be family then?' Rosa's voice shook slightly.

'You're a bright spark, aren't you, young lady?' The silver fox tapped the contents of his pipe into his palm, then, looking at her intently again, said, 'Yes. Nathaniel is my son.'

CHAPTER THIRTY NINE

Lucas had insisted that he sat in with Rosa while she was being interviewed by DC Clarke. Knowing full well that she wouldn't be capable of pushing anyone down a flight of stairs, he was here to protect her, as well as learn why the police were insinuating such things.

'If she's tried to murder my old woman, I want to hear it straight up,' he imparted with a completely straight face, much to Rosa's annoyance.

'That's enough now, son. You're not on *CSI*. Sit quietly or sit outside, please.'

Did this man not have any kind of empathy? Rosa thought. Poor Lucas hadn't even buried his mother yet, and here was Poirot having a go at him.

The DC sniffed, then added, 'Rosa, you've gone very pale.'

With that the pregnant girl, splaying her fingers over her mouth and forming the muffled sounds of 'Where's the Ladies?' ran as fast as she could to the door. As light suddenly dawned, a big lump of emotion filled Luke's throat like a stone. He coughed loudly in an attempt to shift it without bursting into tears.

DC Clarke, oblivious as ever, busied himself with the reams of paperwork in front of him, while the blonde young woman police officer tried hard not to look the handsome plumber in his tight indigo jeans and black hoody up and down.

'How are you feeling?' The detective smiled kindly on Rosa's return, as she held a tissue to her mouth.

'Dodgy burger last night, I reckon. I'm so sorry.' She sat down. The WPC handed her a fresh glass of water and gave her a friendly, knowing nod.

'Are you sure you want to carry on, Rosa?' Luke put his arm gently on hers.

'Yeah, let's just get this over and done with, shall we?'

DC Clarke tapped a pencil annoyingly against his phone. 'Very well, we'll make a start.' He took a mouthful of coffee and smacked his lips. 'So, Rosa Smith of the Corner Shop in Cockleberry Bay, I want you to tell me your movements from the very beginning to the very end of October the thirty-first of this year.'

CHAPTER FORTY

The small, ancient church with its stained-glass windows was packed right to the last pew. Sheila Hannafore may have made a few enemies, but her pub had been the main drinking-hole for centuries and a local haunt for most of the mourners here today. The formidable woman had certainly known how to run a tight Ship! And that was blatantly obvious from the turnout today.

Rosa was so happy that her mum had agreed to accompany her, as she didn't think she could have faced it on her own. Mary hadn't had a proper chance to catch up with her daughter yet, as the hospital had decided to keep her in longer than expected. Her breathing did seem much better than before though, so as much as it had irked her to be away from home, she had been grateful for the intervention.

Tom Hannafore stood up, his eyes red from crying. Although Tom stood taller and dressed older than Lucas, you could tell they were brothers. Peering through the mourners to the front of the church, Rosa could see half of Lucas, and that his arm was linked into that of a woman. Rosa could only assume it was an auntie, as she had the same bright white hair as his mother had had.

Lucas had been worryingly quiet, almost mute on the way back from the police station the other day. Not surprising really, on discovering that his mother had tried to take her own life to make his and his brother's lives easier. But at least the 'secret' was out now. And thankfully, while they were sitting there, DC Clarke had relayed the confirmation from the pathologist that the deceased's injuries could have been caused by an intentional jump and not a push, which was something the police hadn't even considered. They just knew it couldn't have been an accident.

Rosa's great-grandmother Queenie's words echoed in her head, asking: 'Is it necessary? Is it kind?' A moral dilemma arose as to whether Rosa should mention that she had heard music in the pub, thereby insinuating that someone else had been there at the time of Sheila's fall. After thinking long and hard, she had concluded that revealing this information would not benefit anyone, especially Lucas. And thinking of her pregnant self, not her and the child either.

Anyway, if Nate *had* been at the scene, then surely Sheila would have said something. Rosa's judgement of people – excluding that creep, Joe Fox – had always been spot on, so it was that same judgement which had allowed her to make the final decision. She would say nothing further. Nate Webb was a vagabond, not a murderer. And whatever else had gone on within the walls of the Ship Inn that night could now be buried along with its feisty landlady.

Tom Hannafore cleared his throat and tugged at his black tie before beginning to speak. 'I'd firstly like to thank you all for coming. It means a lot to my family to see such a big group of friendly faces. To all of you, Sheila Hannafore was Good Old Sheila from the Ship Inn, a fine publican as I know most of you would agree.' 'Hear hear!' reverberated around the still church.

His voice softened. 'But to me and Lucas, well, she was our mum.' He took a deep breath. 'We may not all be blessed with fortune, but what every single one of us does share is both time,' he paused for effect, 'and love. So, before we all head down to the Ship, where we would like to give Sheila a good send-off, please listen and take in these beautiful words from the poet Henry Van Dyke.'

Holding back her own tears, Rosa grasped her mother's hand as Tom bravely began his short recital.

'Time is too slow for those who wait
Too swift for those who fear
Too long for those who grieve
Too short for those who rejoice
But for those who love,
    Time is an eternity.'

He held an imaginary glass upwards and catching Luke's eye, finished with, 'Cheers, mum, gran, cousin, sister. Sheila, we will love you forever.'

CHAPTER FORTY ONE

Titch was sitting up waiting for Ritchie to come home to her mum's bungalow from his evening shift at the chippie. As soon as she heard the key in the door, she went through to the kitchen and put the kettle on.

'Hello, my fishy fiancé, smelling gorgeous as usual.' She rushed up to him and stood on tiptoe to kiss him.

'How's my beautiful girl this evening – and am I to assume that our little man behaved himself?'

'I'm fine, ta, and your son was remarkably asleep by seven-thirty too. So, I got to watch some of the TV that I've been wanting to catch up on. Do you fancy a drink, something to eat?' Titch offered.

'I could do with a beer actually.' Ritchie stuck his face in the fridge and fished out a cold can. 'I've been on with Mum tonight; she's driven me mad. She's so bossy – it's her way or the highway. I'll be glad when they retire to be honest. We can run it our way, then.'

'I've been meaning to ask you,' Titch added, looking a bit guilty. 'Have you seen an envelope anywhere? I had it that night I crashed out, but I can't for the life of me remember where I put it.'

'You mean this one?' Ritchie pulled it from behind some bills that were stacked in a rack on the side. 'I meant to talk to you about it and I forgot too. Life is so bloody busy.' He took a long pull of beer and sighed with the relief of taking the weight off his long legs. 'I hope you don't mind but it was open with no writing on the front, so I nosily pulled it out and read it.'

'I've got nothing to hide from you, my darling, so of course it's fine.' Titch made herself a cup of tea and sat down next to her husband at the kitchen table.

'What you've written is beautiful, from the heart. You so deserve to be gifted that shop, Titch.'

'That's the thing – I started writing it and well, I don't see any point. Josh really knocked my confidence that day. Maybe he's right and I'm not good enough to take it on. I would fail and I don't want that for our little family. Plus, we will have the chip shop business eventually, so I think I should let it lie.'

'You've already said you prefer serving at the Corner Shop to working in the fish-and-chip shop.'

'Yes, but I said that rashly before you told me that it was your family business and was being passed down to you/us when we are married. I will, of course, do everything to support you,' Titch said loyally. 'We're a team, remember. And I don't want to muck things up for any of us.'

'The shop would be so much easier to manage with a baby than working late nights.' Ritchie smiled and kissed his pretty fiancée gently on the lips. 'And if we are going to have some babies of our own, then you need to be happy and I don't want you working all the time if you don't have to. Especially not at night.'

'I don't know.' Titch sighed and sipped her tea.

'All I'm saying is that you shouldn't let that one comment from Josh stop you from following your dream, because, on reading between the lines, I believe that's exactly what running the shop would be for you – a dream come true. You love that place. You love Rosa. It just makes sense. And talking of sense, you have common sense in spades. You know all about the ordering, the stocktaking, and if you get stuck, I can sort the figures. I'm good at all that shit – I've had to be from a young age working where I do.'

Ritchie drained his beer. 'I believe in you, Titch Whittaker. And there's less than two weeks now to get it to Rosa. So, in my opinion you need to finish what you started.'

'I'll see.' Titch stuffed the envelope back behind the bills.

Realising nothing more needed to be said on the matter tonight, Ritchie stood up. 'Talking of finishing what we started, or tried to start that night, this sausage is in desperate need of a fine old battering.' He took Titch's hand and put it down the front of his joggers.

'It's a good job my mother wears earplugs.' Titch laughed. 'But come on, you rude boy, you're right – it's about time we had some fun.'

CHAPTER FORTY TWO

On seeing Luke standing by his mother's graveside, Rosa halted uncertainly. She was taking Hot on his early-morning walk and didn't expect anyone to be here at this hour. She had come to see what people had written on the mountain of flowers that were propped against the raised mound of earth. Despite her non-religious beliefs, she not only loved a church but, weirdly, had always found graveyards fascinating. Had even started getting ideas for baby names from the headstones.

Mary and she had agreed that attending the wake wasn't the right thing to do. 'We've paid our respects, duck, and that is enough,' Mary had said firmly. Rosa could tell that Josh was secretly pleased with her decision. She also knew that with Luke's emotions running so high with her, it would be much kinder to step back and leave him to deal with everything to do with his family in his own way.

It was too late to turn around. Casually, she walked down the path towards the grieving man, doing her best to act as if she always took this route, trying to stop Hot peeing against gravestones as she did so. The cemetery was on higher ground and made for a breath-taking view of the bay. Winter sun was poking its head through, and even the gulls sounded more cheerful than usual with their constant mewing. Spotting a white dove sitting on a raised crypt near the edge of the wall, Rosa thought there were worse places one could wish to rest for eternity.

She was almost on top of Lucas before he spoke to her, his voice breaking. 'Why didn't you tell me straightaway, Rosa?'

How silly was she to think that he would never mention something so massive?

'Oh Luke, I wanted to but also I didn't want to hurt you any further. You'd just lost your mum and then to hear that she had thrown herself down the cellar steps deliberately, well...'

His voice was now barely audible. 'I meant about you being pregnant.'

Rosa inwardly cringed. She'd rather talk with him about his mother than confront the great big baby-shaped elephant in the room now.

Since that day in the police station, when Rosa had been sick and the penny had dropped, Lucas had felt as if his insides were burning. When he had met the pretty brunette, she had been single, and he wasn't. When she was in a relationship, his hopes were still quite high that she might dump Josh for one of her own kind. Even after she was married he had kept a faint hope going – but pregnant? No, he knew now that the chances of ever being with Rosa Smith, formerly Larkin, were completely over – and the realisation of this hurt. It hurt a lot.

'Oh! Well, I haven't told everyone yet. I'm not even three months, Luke,' she replied, trying to make light of it but feeling his pain so strongly it compelled her to hold her arms out to him.

'No. *No*, Rosa! Just leave me alone. I came here for some peace.' He turned away from her, then swung himself back round. 'What is wrong with me? Common sense tells me you're married, and I know I can't be with you.' Then, not knowing what to do with the emotions that were searing through his veins, he set off and started walking towards the cemetery gates.

Letting Hot off the lead and praying he would behave in this sacred place, Rosa ran after the troubled man. Holding both of his arms tightly, she said, 'Look at me. You're going through hell but *I'm* not the problem. It just seems as if I am because you are hurting so much about your mum. I will always be here for you as a friend. I really like you, Luke. And if I'm being totally honest, and if it helps, well, I fancy you too.'

'Then why can't we be together?' he burst out. 'Isn't that what a relationship is? Friendship and lust?'

Rosa closed her eyes for a second. 'Oh Luke. I am in love with Josh. Life's all about timing, and well…it was just off for both of us.' She tried to sound upbeat. 'Now we can have everything without the complication that a real relationship brings, can't we? Friendship, fun, a bit of banter – some harmless flirting?'

Lucas put both hands over his face as if that would make all his pain disappear. He then looked directly at her and said bitterly, 'You just don't get it, do you?' He pulled away. 'Everything, you say? Are you really that deluded, Rosa? We can't have *anything*, not now.'

'I'm so sorry, Luke.' Hot appeared now, barking at both their feet. 'So sorry.'

As he strode out of the gates and down the street towards the bay, Lucas looked back and shouted hoarsely, 'And if I can't have you – what's the fucking point!'

CHAPTER FORTY THREE

'How much do you reckon a fifty-voice soul choir would be for the reception?'

Titch was sitting at the Corner Shop counter flicking through a wedding magazine that she'd stolen from the doctor's surgery.

Rosa came through from the back kitchen with mugs of tea and a plate containing some of the Co-op's Triple Chocolate Cookies, as recommended by Mary.

'You crack me up, Titch Whittaker. We can only seat thirty in the café. Where would we put them all?' Then, on placing the tray down by the till, Rosa added, 'Saying that, I'm sure me and Sara can step in. We do a mean rendition of "Ave Maria" every time we mop the floor, but I can't guarantee it won't flatten the bubbles in the champagne.'

Titch's expression didn't alter. 'Hmm. Can I take a rain check on that?' She then said randomly, 'Have you thought of any baby names yet?'

'No, I haven't had much chance to think about Mr Bump's name yet, because there's been so much going on.'

Titch shoved a biscuit into her mouth, licked her fingers. '*Mr Bump*, eh?' she said with her mouth full.

'You sound like my mother.' Rosa sighed as she sat down at

the counter next to her friend.

'Would you prefer a boy or a girl then?' Titch carried on looking at her magazine.

'I honestly don't mind. The way I'm feeling, I half hope it's triplets. I'd only have to go through this sickness once then.'

'Be careful what you wish for, Rose.' Titch shook her blonde head. 'Imagine it – three of them, pooping, feeding and crying – all at the same time. Nightmare!'

She shoved yet another biscuit in, mumbling, 'Ooh, these are gorgeous... Listen to the silence,' she added dreamily, wiping her chocolatey hands on a tissue. 'I love Theo to pieces but working here is like being on holiday. Saveloy & Mr Chips are as hard work as having two kids too. They all behave for my mother though – of course they do.' Without drawing breath she rambled on, 'I have to say I quite fancied a mini-me, but when that little munchkin flew out of me on this very floor, I was so glad it was a boy. I think Ritchie is happy too. Saying that, he would love a baby tiger if it came from my loins.'

They both laughed at the word 'loins'.

'And I'm sure he will want to create a little Rogers someday too,' Rosa said.

Titch put her hands over her ears and sang, '*Lalalalala*, I'm not listening! Hot Dog, make her stop.' But the dachshund took no notice from his basket in the corner. He merely did one of his long, shuddering yawns with his jaws opened the widest they could go, before closing them with a snap.

Rosa laughed. 'Well, even if Hot ignores you, at least Ritchie loves you, and that's a fact.'

'Yes, and it is just the best feeling in the world,' Titch said. 'You know, Rosa, I never thought I'd put away my Fuck-Me boots for any man, let alone a lanky chip-shop worker from Cockleberry Bay.'

'OK, let's get serious,' Rosa said, snaffling a chocolate wafer before her friend ate the lot. 'We had better talk wedding plans, hadn't we? It's only weeks away, after all. You're getting married in the church and then filing down to ROSA'S for the reception, which is to be fish and chips and champagne, right? Correct so far?'

'Correct. We should be down at the café around one, so everyone can just eat when they are hungry. There'll be none of that waiting around for ruddy photos to be taken. Can't bear all that malarkey.' Titch started flicking through the magazine again. 'I would love daffodils on every table though.'

'Daffs? We might struggle this time of year.'

Titch just as quickly changed her mind. 'No, I think if we are going the "fur coat no knickers" route, then we just keep it simple. It's about the people. No one's going to judge me if there are flowers on the tables or not – and if they do, then they are no friends of mine anyway. And if my mother-in-law wants to complain, because Edie complains about everything, we'll let her. She could give us money instead of a fish-and-chip supper, couldn't she?'

'Is there anything else you've always dreamed of having?'

'Apart from my dad or brother to give me away, you mean,' Titch said quietly.

Rosa gave her friend a look full of understanding. 'I can't help you with that, I'm afraid.'

A short silence, then Titch piped up again. 'It was the choir really. You see, I once saw a film where Stevie Wonder's classic, "As", was sung at a wedding. It was just the best, most moving thing ever. Such a track! But the little savings I have left from the Titchy Titch fund of old are for a deposit on a place of our own.'

From those words, Rosa assumed that Titch wouldn't even

be bidding for the shop and flat, and that made her a little sad.

Despite that, Rosa's gut instinct told her she had done the right thing in the way she was conducting the proceedings. Local charities would benefit, and with the ten-year selling proviso, the successful candidate would be somebody who truly wanted to make the business work. That was something else that needed sorting before Christmas. There was so much to do! She was pleased that Josh would be back soon to help share the load. Yes, she was young and energetic, but this pregnancy lark was making her feel more tired than she'd ever felt before in her life.

Ding! At that moment the shop door opened. '*Dong!*' Titch said under her breath at the sight of the man standing there.

'All right, darl? Mum and Alfie are in the car outside. We've come to say goodbye and, well, I wanted to thank you again for saving my little boy's life. Blimey, that sounds so lame, just saying the words.'

'I'll come out with you, hang on.' Rosa went to get her coat. Titch managed a shy hello. Titch was never shy!

'Did the money turn up?' Danny said on Rosa's return.

'Not yet. But it will,' she replied with certainty.

'I still feel it was my fault, so I got paid yesterday and I want you to have this. There's a ton there.' He handed her one hundred pounds in cash.

Rosa pushed it straight back into his hand.

'No way. You did me a massive favour. Nobody got hurt, and I'm just happy my mum's well again. It was just one of those crazy days we all have sometimes.'

Danny gulped. He felt so guilty. If he hadn't been in an after-sex haze, he would have remembered to lock that back door for sure. He was, however, secretly relieved that Rosa had handed the notes back to him. Money was tight, and Rosa had no doubt gathered that already. Even though he sensed that she wouldn't suffer fools or allow a kidder to kid her, she obviously trusted him and wanted to help him and his family. She really was a diamond of a girl. Shame she was married, in fact. Privately, he was more relieved that she hadn't found out about him having sex with a total stranger in her back kitchen than that she might think he'd nicked the money.

Rosa went outside to say her goodbyes. The morning's early sunshine had been replaced with a thin, cold, November drizzle. She waved and blew kisses to Tina and Alfie, who were tucked up under a duvet in the back seat together, ready for the long journey back to London.

As Danny started the engine she walked round to his side of the car and banged on the window for him to open it.

'Random, I know, but did you lose a sock when you were here? It's just, neither Josh nor I support West Ham.' Danny tried to keep his face level. In a hurry to get away from the scene of his sexual crime, he was sure that he had shoved both socks in his coat pocket.

Rosa handed him the screwed-up claret and blue sock. 'You need to get a new pair; this one's got a big hole in it.' Then she winked, leaving a paranoid Danny wondering exactly what on earth she knew.

Titch was putting dog biscuits into the bowl on the counter when a slightly damp but good-humoured Rosa reappeared, saying, 'Don't tell me, Titch – you'd get your Fuck-Me boots re-heeled for him, wouldn't you?'

'Dear friend, I'd even shave my armpits.'

CHAPTER FORTY FOUR

Alec knew that Rosa wouldn't contact him lightly about something so serious, so he immediately packed a small rucksack, put on Brown's lead and headed for the West Cliffs path. He was relieved to reach the familiar bench halfway up to the cliffs and see the hunched figure of Lucas Hannafore sitting on it. Despite him having his coat hood pulled over his head, the young man was shivering, Alec could see.

'All right, chap?' Alec said friendlily.

'I was just going, mate.' Lucas went to stand up.

'Oh, don't move on mine and old Brown's behalf. I call this my thinking bench. Rain or shine, if I need to think, up we come. I've got some coffee if you want to share it?'

Lucas sighed and slumped back on the bench. He knew of Alec because Rosa had mentioned him, but only to say that he was now hooked up with Sara from the café and he was a shrink of some kind. Lucas had never been able to understand people who went to counselling. He thought they were weak, that you should be able to talk though your problems with those closest to you without having to pay for the bloody privilege.

'I feel devoid of thought or feeling at the moment,' he said dully.

'I'm sorry for your loss, lad.' Alec handed him a steaming cardboard cup of coffee. 'It comes as it is, milk and two sugars.'

'Thanks. And thank you about my mum. Yeah, they don't teach about death or how to handle it at school or anywhere, do they?' Lucas cupped his hands around his hot drink.

'Sadly, no. Nor do they teach us how to talk to each other about it, for that matter. We men are the worst at that, yet we often need it the most.'

Silence was one of the main tools Alec used in his work. The two men sat looking out to sea, watching a solitary fishing boat heading into the mist. Brown, sitting dutifully at his master's feet, held the offer of a warm coat for the troubled young man beside him to stroke.

Alec was relieved when it was Lucas who eventually decided to talk. 'My old man is dead too, you know, and with my brother grieving too and, well, with the other person I love, not really being able to talk to her… I don't know who to talk to.'

'Brown's an amazing listener.' Alec put his hand on Lucas's shoulder. 'He hears all my troubles and woes, doesn't argue, doesn't even flap an ear.'

Lucas managed a smile. 'You're lucky.'

'OK,' Alec said softly. 'Hit me with it, if you want to.'

'I don't want to sound like a dick, but I've been having these dark thoughts.'

'Like what?'

'I'm finding it hard to see a future without my mum and that someone else.'

'Go on.'

'The pub – well, it's always been my home. Wherever I've lived, whichever part of the world I've travelled to, I always knew that I could come home. Home to the Ship Inn. And now the lease is up at Christmas on my London flat and I don't know what to do. I've got mates in London, of course, but most of them are married – got kids. And my brother, he's got his own family.'

'So, you've got nieces, nephews?'

'Two nieces, one nephew. They are great kids. They call me Uncle Louie – always have.'

'That's pretty cool.' Alec took a slurp of coffee. 'Kids open our eyes to things, speak the real truth.'

'It's not that I want to top myself.' Hearing these words allowed Alec to instantly relax. The troubled lad went on, 'I'm definitely not brave enough to kamikaze myself over a bloody cliff edge, that's for sure. It's just… I don't know where I want to be, and I can't see a way forward. It's like I don't want to be with me.' Lucas sighed. 'Oh, I don't know what I'm saying. It's just so fucking hard.'

'Yes, it is hard. You've just lost your mother. That's about as tough as it can get, mate. And it's not going to be easy. You've got the whole monster of grief to go through, but go through it you must.'

'Rosa said that too. Clever little bitch.' A light came on in Lucas's eyes, causing Alec to remember back to a conversation he had had with Rosa. It all made sense now.

'She's lovely with it though, eh?' he said.

Another silence ensued until Lucas broke it again. 'We should go. It's freezing up here.' The view from the cliff out to sea was now shrouded with a thick fog.

'I'm having one more coffee, and there's enough for us both – if you like?'

Lucas held his cup out, muttering, 'You can't tell anyone this. Promise me.'

'Trust me,' Alec said strongly.

'I dunno why I'm telling you this, but I love her. Rosa, that

218

is. I wasn't sure how this love thing happened, but one minute I had sex with the girl and then as I got to know her this other feeling caught up on me and now I would do just about anything for her. She completes me. I just adore her and everything she stands for.'

Alec looked thoughtful. His voice was gentle when he said, 'I don't believe that anyone completes anyone else. You've got to be a complete whole yourself to live a full and happy life.'

'All right, quit the shrink-speak.' Lucas was too unhappy to be polite. 'And just tell me this: how do I stop loving her?'

'If I could provide a pill for that, I'd make a fortune. It's like grieving, I'm afraid, there's no easy fix. And whatever I say to you now won't seem like I'm helping, but listen up anyway.'

'Say something though, mate, I can't feel like this any more.'

'Keep out of her way for a bit, do some exercise, maybe focus on some hobbies, keep yourself busy. Even go on a couple of dates, without making any promises. You're a plumber, aren't you?'

'Yeah.'

'Get working then, anything to keep you busy will help with the grief and the heartbreak. And those dark thoughts will come, but that's what they are – just thoughts. Think what you've got to think and then send them on their way. We are all just a series of thoughts really. Fill your head with as many good ones as you can. It might feel like the end of everything now, but no one ever died of a broken heart, you know. We all get over it.'

'OK.' Lucas stood up. 'Thanks, but I really do want to go down now.' The wind had started to get up and even Brown was whining slightly in discomfort.

'Hang on and we'll go down with you.' Alec packed his rucksack. 'What are you going to do with the pub?' he asked as they set off.

'It's bought and paid for, so we could actually keep it. Tom, that's my brother, we haven't even got that far yet, as there's so much to sort out.'

'Whether it stays a pub or becomes a house, it would make a lovely home on the beachfront,' Alec said wisely.

As they reached the bottom of the path, he handed Lucas a business card. 'If ever you want to chat again, man to man, this is my number. I'll leave this phone on twenty-four/seven for you, for two weeks. And even if it's one a.m. and you have any of those dark thoughts you mentioned and can't bat them away yourself, I'll be at the end of that phone, all right? And if I haven't heard from you in that time, I'm thinking that maybe you, me and Brown here, could share another coffee sometime. Preferably not in the rain. If you want to, that is?'

Lucas shook Alec's hand. 'Thanks, mate, thank you so much.'

'And lad – I know that Rosa cares about you. Maybe not in the way you want her to, granted, but she's got your back. I know that much.'

CHAPTER FORTY FIVE

Merlin shot out through the front door of Seaspray Cottage at speed, nearly knocking Rosa over as he did so. Hot started barking as loudly as he could with excitement.

'Whoa, you crazy cat. I have precious cargo on board now,' Rosa told his disappearing back. She pushed open the front door to be greeted by Mary, who was on her hands and knees polishing the fire hearth. Hot, free from his lead, immediately trotted at speed through to the kitchen to see if there were any leftovers in Merlin's cat bowls there for the emptying.

'Oof, you made me jump, duck.' Mary got up slowly and made her way to the kitchen. 'Time for a cup of something?' She was short of breath, but far better than she had been.

'I'm glad to see you looking so much better, Mum. What a relief, eh. Never thought I'd say this, but have you got any herbal teas?'

'Not the bags, but I've got some fresh ginger and lemon. Sit down, and I'll make you something nice. I've just baked a batch of that cinnamon shortbread you love too. I was going to drop some in later, so I'm glad I've seen you now.'

'Your ginger potion is kind of helping me feel less sick, but I'm still like a vomit factory – it comes hurtling out of me with practically no warning. And as well as not fancying caffeine, I keep craving boiled eggs with horseradish. What's all that about?'

'Bless your heart. Remind me when you are due again? I must put it on the calendar.'

'Ninth of July, they think, but I never did keep a proper record of my periods, despite Josh wanting me to start a spreadsheet.' She laughed.

'Well, that's his thing and we love him for it, our Josh. Has he got a date to come home yet?'

Rosa sat at the kitchen table and let out a little sigh. 'Two weeks today, thank goodness. We need to sit down and go through the applications for the shop then.'

'You mean you still haven't looked?'

'Nope. Scott – you know, the journalist from the *Gazette* – he wants to do another article this week to update the masses, put the word out again. Being honest, I'm glad that we only have a handful of entries, since that gives me hope that those who are going for it, are genuine. I think the ten-year embargo on selling the shop on has really helped cut out the timewasters.'

'You look tired.' Mary stirred an extra spoonful of local honey into her daughter's drink and handed it to her. Hot was now under the table chasing titbits of cucumber in a rubber kong that Mary had thrown under there to keep him occupied.

'I am bloody knackered.' Rosa yawned. 'Much as I love both the shop and the café, it will be nice to have just the one business to think about. I'm also really looking forward to moving now too, reaping the rewards of some of mine and Josh's hard work.' Ever intuitive, Rosa clocked her mother's face. 'We won't go far, so you will always be required for baby-sitting duties, don't you worry.'

'You must do what's right for all of you, not for others –

and that's not one of Kahlil's sayings, that's one of mine.' Mary reached over and took her daughter's hand briefly. 'I want you to be happy, darling.'

'I am happy – and how are you doing, anyway? You've not been long home from hospital and look at you, cleaning like a mad thing already.'

'Oh, hush you, child. And sod all this mindfulness meditation stuff they keep going on about. Cleaning is my escape from the madness, Rosa. And, I have to say, whatever Dr Delicious – I mean, Dr Reginald – stuck in my inhaler this time, it's made me feel like a teenager again.' Mary nodded. 'There's life in this old dog yet, I tell you. And when the baby does come, I've decided I don't want to be Grannie this or Nana that. Queenie was always Queenie to me and you, so I just want to be Mary, straight, OK?'

Rosa smiled at her mother and raised her eyes. She still found it hard to believe that Sara was older than her mother. Having lived in the Bay for so many years, Mary was an old-fashioned soul who was happy to dress from charity shops, wore no make-up and hadn't had her extremely long black hair cut in all the time that Rosa had known her. It was quite refreshing that looks weren't the be-all-and-end-all to her. Mary was her own person, that was for sure. Saying that, she had got down to a healthy weight for Rosa's wedding, so she had made some concessions.

There was no denying that Mary's heavy smoking and drinking had taken their toll, but she was doing the right thing by abstaining now, and the mischievous sparkle in her sea-green eyes made her round face pretty, and so similar to Rosa's it was almost like looking in a mirror. Rosa had tried to put make-up on her once, knowing that she would look completely stunning, but Mary had always stopped her. 'Beauty is in the eye of the beholder', she would quote. And follow it up with: 'Not that there is anyone I care to behold, presently.'

'Of course it's all right. Mary it is then. OK, mister,' Rosa bent down to stroke Hot's ears and clip on the lead, 'it's time to go. We've got to relieve Titch and refresh the Christmas gifts this afternoon. I'm looking forward to being in the shop today. It's funny how I'm also looking forward to Christmas so much this year too.'

'You're happy, duck, that's why. Christmas isn't for the faint-hearted or lonely – we all know that.'

'You could be right.' She picked up the shortbread and ginger package that Mary had wrapped for her and said, 'Thanks, that's lovely. I'm glad that DC Clarke won't get his greedy mitts on these. They're much too good for him.'

Mary followed her to the door, then put a hand on her shoulder. Unexpectedly she said, 'A thief is a man or a woman in need; a liar is a man in fear.'

'Kahlil?'

'Kahlil.'

'Goodbye.' Rosa kissed Mary on the cheek and gulped. Her mother might not get everything right, but when she did, it was more than spooky.

CHAPTER FORTY SIX

Rosa yawned. She was very much looking forward to a nice long bath and an early night. Humming along to the sound of 'Santa Baby' sung by the sultry Eartha Kitt, she pulled down the shop blind and started to cash up the till. If the *South Cliffs Today* presenter said it was OK to play Christmas songs in November then it was all right with her too. She really must download a Christmas album and play it in the shop; set the mood for the festive season. She was also going to get a big tin of Quality Street for the counter, as adults and children alike could pick their favourites then. This made her thoughts shift to the envelopes sitting in the safe; one of them had been labelled *Quality Street*, she was certain.

If only she had given Danny the code to the safe, Rosa thought, then all that money wouldn't have been stolen. But as with all life's valuable lessons, that wouldn't have given her the knowledge she had now. Thank heavens for the CCTV that Alec had so brilliantly reminded her about, and for the hole in one of Danny's socks!

The goings-on that the camera had picked up in her back kitchen that day had certainly been an eye-opener, even for somebody as broad-minded as herself. But despite what she had seen through the big hole in Danny's sock, which someone had put over the camera, she had made the monumental decision to keep quiet and not share this with anyone, not even Josh – not yet, anyway. Rosa knew that she had to handle this in the right way at the right time, and ideally without any police involvement. She'd had enough of that lately and she was trying to simplify her life, not create more dramas. She would be guided by that old saying: 'Revenge is a dish best served cold.'

She closed her eyes and suddenly felt the familiar tingle of Queenie by her side. Once again, she heard her say the words: *'Sometimes in life, if you don't know what to do, do nothing, say nothing and the answer will come to you.'*

'I hope so, Queenie. I really do,' Rosa replied aloud.

At that moment, there was a loud knock on the back door which almost made her jump out of her skin. Hot tore across the shop floor, barking loudly. Thinking it could be Luke, she opened the door to a bloody-faced and shivering figure.

'Nate? Is that you? What's happened?' Seeing the lad's blackened eye and split lip made her grimace slightly but the memory of where she'd come from herself, and her less than perfect past, meant she couldn't send him packing. 'Get in here, quick. Come on.'

A bedraggled Nate followed suit as Rosa led the way upstairs, carrying Hot. It was warm and cosy up there. As she pulled an old dressing gown from the airing cupboard, she felt nothing but sympathy for the troubled figure in front of her.

'It might be a bit big but it's warm,' she told Nate. 'Have a shower and you'll feel better. We can talk properly then. Have you got any clean clothes?' Nate shook his head. 'In here?' She pointed to his bag as he nodded. 'OK. I'll get them washed and dried in no time.'

'Thanks so much. It isn't–'

'It never is,' Rosa interrupted. 'Just get in the shower, Nate.' She passed him a big, warm bath towel. 'There's shampoo in there, spare wrapped toothbrushes and shaving stuff as well.'

Rosa checked the freezer then turned the oven on to heat up. Pizza and salad would be quick and easy, as she guessed he was probably starving too. Despite her now being comfortable and, in her words, 'safe', her past life was always circling, and more than anyone she understood the currency of the fist when intelligent conversation and resolution had not been ingrained as a child.

Twenty minutes later, Nate reappeared in the lounge. His injuries looked less severe now that he was clean from blood and dirt. His mop of tangled greasy curls, Rosa noted, was no more.

'You've cut your hair.' She gulped. Then, without thinking, 'You look even more like me now.'

Nate laughed nervously. 'Did it myself, couldn't bear not being able to wash it properly.'

'Sit down.' Rosa pointed to the sofa. Hot had accepted the presence of Nate and was perfectly happy chewing away noisily at a bedraggled headless rabbit dog-toy.

Rosa went to the kitchen and returned with a mini-feast of pizza and coleslaw and Diet Coke. She put the tray down on the coffee table and said, 'Help yourself.' She waited till they'd both eaten before asking, 'So, do you want to tell me what happened?'

'Not before I say I'm so sorry for letting you down at the café after Halloween.' Nate put his empty plate back on the tray.

'Yes, that was really wrong of you. Even a short text would have helped. But I guess you had no credit.'

'I panicked. Look, Rosa, I've done something really bad.'

'Is this connected to your face being smashed up?'

'Oh that? No, I fell.'

'And I'm Mother bloody Teresa. Give me some credit, Nate.'

Nate started to talk quickly. 'OK. I didn't steal your money, Rosa. I know what it looks like – I heard you got your takings nicked the other day. And who the hell was that bloke in the shop with the scar? He thought it was me! I reckon he was just pinning it on me; he looked like someone straight out of *The Godfather*. He punched me so hard, it knocked me over. Told me to hand back the money, but how could I, when I didn't have it. He told me that if I ever troubled you in any way again, he'd make sure it'd be more than a punch I was getting.'

Hearing this, Rosa put her hand to her tummy.

'Shit, I forgot about you being pregnant,' Nate said. 'I'm sorry if I'm stressing you out.'

Rosa grimaced slightly. 'I did just get a little pain, but I've had something similar before. Probably trapped wind, the speed I shoved that food in. I was hungry.' She burped. Rosa found it so easy to be herself around this man.

'Do you want a cup of tea – would that help?' Nate asked. 'Here, put your legs up.' He threw her the blanket that was on the sofa.

'Nate, calm down. Like I said, it's probably wind.' Then Rosa added softly, 'And I trust you didn't take the money. But will you stop saying sorry and tell me what you've done that's so bad.' She braced herself for the worst. Despite nothing really fazing her, if he had pushed Sheila down the cellar steps, she wasn't quite sure how she would deal with that kind of revelation.

As if he'd read her mind, Nate mumbled, 'I didn't push that woman, if that's what you think.'

Rosa tried to get comfortable. She twisted her legs around so she was lying on the sofa and resting her head on her favourite dachshund cushion.

'So, you *were* at the pub that night, then? I knew it.'

'You know everything.' Nate sighed. 'After I lost my wages at the betting shop, and upset Mad Donna too – well, I had nowhere to go, as I told you. I still had the key for the pub, I knew that the cleaning lady had a day off and that poor old Sheila was so ill she would never venture to the back of the pub where the boxroom was. And as she was moving so slowly, I could hear her in advance and keep out of her way easily by coming in and out of the back door.'

Nate drained his glass of Diet Coke. 'However, that night when I sneaked in, I found her sitting behind the bar in a terrible state. She said that she'd taken loads of tablets and wanted to end it all. I sat with her, Rosa – I did, I swear. We talked about her whole life, her sons. It was so moving. It was so sad. I said that I should call an ambulance. She insisted I didn't.' Nate looked at Rosa, his face twisted with distress. 'I honoured her wishes. When an hour had passed, she became a bit delirious and went to the top of the cellar steps. She asked if I could push her down them – hard. Finish her off properly. I obviously refused. She then said she was going to do it herself. I don't know where she got the strength from, but when I tried to stop her she shoved me away so hard I lost my grip on her, and she then overbalanced and crashed backwards. She landed with such a thump…and the rest you know.'

He swallowed back tears. 'I know I should have stayed with her, that I should have rung an ambulance and tried to save her, but instead I focused on trying to save my own skin. I was so horrified and scared that I might be implicated that I ran upstairs to get my phone, and in scrabbling to pack things away I knocked my wireless speaker which started booming out my music. At that moment you, thankfully, arrived, and I rushed out through the back door of the bar without you seeing me. I knew then you'd ring the ambulance and do what needed doing.'

'Oh Nate. I knew someone was in there. Bless you for talking to her for so long. I bet that meant a lot.'

'She said I reminded her of her younger son. Said he was a little terror at times too.'

'He is that.' Rosa smiled.

Nate was anguished. 'What I really need to know is, would she have lived if I had called the ambulance sooner? Am I responsible for her death?'

'No,' Rosa soothed, and not knowing the answer herself, for his sake she lied. 'She was terminally ill, and it was a bad fall.'

Nate hardly seemed to hear. 'I literally felt sick,' he went on feverishly, 'mainly because when I heard the rumours that she might have been pushed, I knew the police would pin her death on me if they got to know I'd been there. I then felt so terrible because you were involved. The last thing I'd want to do is hurt you, Rosa. I was a coward, as I've said, and ran away – but then realised that I had nowhere to run to, and no money. So I came to see you, to find out what was going on – and that was when matey boy tried to kick the living shit out of me.' He gave a reluctant grin. 'You've got plenty of knights in shining armour, I can tell you that.'

He got off the sofa, knelt beside her and held her hand. 'I need to tell you something else too, and I'm not proud of this either.'

'Bloody hell, Nate, I don't know if I can cope with any more.' Rosa struggled to her feet. 'I'll make us a cup of tea and you can carry on.'

'No, let me do that, it's the least I can do.'

'Check on the tumble drier while you're out there too – see how your clothes are doing. One sugar, please.'

Nate came back with two mugs of tea and sat down again. With Josh being so broad and tall and he being short and slender, he looked comical in Josh's grey-striped oversized dressing-gown. His hair was drying now into tight, dark curls, his grey eyes bloodshot from fatigue and from being punched.

'Before you start, I saw your dad,' Rosa remembered suddenly. 'He came to look for you at the fireworks.'

'Shit, really?' Nate went pale. 'You saw him?'

'Yes.'

'I borrowed someone's phone, said I was in trouble, then realised him coming to fetch me wasn't "standing on my own two feet", as he always professes I should, so I dumped the call.'

'How did he know you were here?'

'I dunno. Maybe he called the number back and asked them – who knows?'

'So, do you have a mum, too?'

'Too many questions, Rosa.'

'It's quite a simple one.'

'They got divorced when I was little. She went off with some right numpty and I never forgave her. I lived with Dad, but I was such a handful, he sent me to boarding school. We lived in London then, but when I was done with school, he decided to move his funeral business to North Devon. People die everywhere, so it's an easy one to set up.' Nate managed a smile. 'I didn't lie about everything, Rosa.'

Rosa shook her head. 'Don't lie to me, ever again.'

'I'm sorry,' Nate replied quietly.

Rosa was still puzzled. 'So you did live in London… Are you absolutely sure we haven't met before?'

'It's a big place, that London.'

Rosa then laughed. 'I got around.' She reached for her bag that was at the end of the sofa and rummaged inside. 'He said to call him – here's his card.'

'It's funny,' Nate told her. 'I may not have seen him for a while,

231

but I know that mobile number off by heart.'

'You get on with him then?' Rosa decided to wean the inevitable out of him little by little.

'He's a good man. Slightly eccentric but his values are all there.'

Hearing that, she said very gently, 'Why don't you go home, then?'

'I will now. It's the other thing, you see – that's why I'm really here.' Nate's face dropped.

'Let me go to the loo and then you tell me more.' Rosa stood up. 'You wouldn't even get this sort of drama on the television all in one evening.' She smiled at the now anxious lad. On her return, her face told a different story too.

'What's the matter?' Nate asked. 'Something's wrong, isn't it?'

'It's going to be all right, but I need to call my mum. God, I wish I'd learned to drive.' Rosa's voice was deliberately controlled and calm.

'What is it?'

'Just a bit of blood. I'm sure it's nothing.' But remembering back to the awful night when she'd had the miscarriage not long after her wedding, a lone tear fell down her cheek.

'That's it: you are *not* losing this baby. And this time, I am ringing for an ambulance straightaway.' Nate's panic was evident.

'It will be quicker to drive. I know – I'll ring Jacob. He can take me. You look after Hot, OK? Here are some spare keys and a fiver. Go and top up your phone so I can reach you, then stay here. I'll be back soon, I'm sure.'

'Oh my God, Rosa, you can't lose this baby,' Nate repeated.

'I won't. It's all going to be OK.' Rosa grabbed her phone and keys and threw them into her handbag. Her visitor was now practically hyperventilating. 'Nate, what is wrong with you? Calm down. You're stressing me out now.'

The young man put both hands through his short, curly brown hair and began to cry, saying over and over again, 'You can't lose this baby!'

'Nate, stop this.' Rosa took hold of his wrists. 'You really must get a grip because I have to go.'

'I'm trying to explain.' Nate's battered face looked tortured. 'But it's all coming out wrong. You can't lose this baby, Rosa, because...' Then, in one short sentence he confirmed the enormous truth that Rosa already suspected. 'Because I'm going to be his or her uncle.'

CHAPTER FORTY SEVEN

Sara whistled as she opened up the café. The recent dreary November weather had been replaced by a wonderful sunny and crisp morning. Everyone seemed to smile a bit more when the sun was out, she thought. Even the bread delivery man, whose face often resembled that of a basset hound, managed a hearty hello.

Vegan Vera strutted in and plonked her designer handbag onto a table overlooking the beach, her matching designer purse in her hand.

'Oh hi, Bergamot,' Sara said politely. 'How are you?' The response wasn't quite what she'd expected.

'God, I could kill for some fucking bacon,' the moody redhead grumbled. 'You know how people say "I need a drink" when they are stressed? Well, I need meat. My husband or soon-to-be ex-husband – he just doesn't get it. How am I supposed to survive on the pissing pittance of an allowance he's offering me? How, tell me that, you!'

Sara still winced at her foul language, but was now so used to her boring, consistent rhetoric, she just let it all go over her head.

The angry one was mithering on: 'He's still shagging that fat bitch of a housekeeper too. I hope she's got bloody syphilis.' She blew out a noisy breath. 'Never sign a pre-nup, however they sugar-coat it, darling.'

'Your usual?' Sara went to get the soya milk out of the fridge.

'No. Sod that for a game of soldiers. A double espresso, please – and pronto. I need a caffeine hit.' The posh voice was getting more strident and obstreperous.

'And a bacon sandwich?' Sara questioned tentatively.

'What? Don't be bloody ridiculous!'

Sara bit her tongue, wishing at times like this she could channel Rosa's acerbic and quick wit. Rosa would never have put up with this rudeness, since to her, the customer was always right – but only up to a certain limit. Sara, however, had always just meekly sucked it up and let it go.

'I'll just have Bovril on some brown toast, please,' Bergamot said more calmly, 'but don't tell the fucking planet police it's not vegan, will you, darling?'

As Queen B removed a twenty-pound note from her bag, two others fell to the floor, along with a red business card. The man who'd just walked in bent down behind her to help pick up the money. They almost clanked heads on rising. For one always harping on about being broke, Bergamot seemed to have plenty of cash this morning, Sara thought.

Greg Picket always wore a white, old-school milkman's hat. The ladies loved it. Sara had sourced the excellent products from his farm shop for some years now. His cream-laden 'gold top' milk was always a winner with the older locals and made a delicious milkshake too.

'Oh, hello sailor,' Bergamot said suggestively, clocking the man's weather-beaten but still undeniably handsome face. 'I bet your cream always rises to the top.'

Sara's mouth fell open. Greg winked at her discreetly. He was a happily married man with three kids, but a bit of milkman banter had kept his business going for years and he was always on the look-out for new customers.

'Sign up for my delivery service today, madam, and I will of course endeavour to provide *full* satisfaction.'

Bergamot's pout increased as she wrote her number down on the back of a serviette. 'I'll be seeing you,' she said seductively, her dairy allergy suddenly disappearing without trace.

An hour later, Titch arrived, pushing Theo in his pram, with the puppies in their little crate tucked inside the shopping rack below. She picked up the red business card that Bergamot had dropped earlier. 'Polhampton Paws', she read aloud, then handed it to Sara, who placed it on the shelf under the counter.

'That's weird,' Sara said. 'Alec mentioned them the other day. They are a local dog and cat shelter, I think.'

'Always good to know for when these two start playing up.' Titch pointed at the puppy crate.

'Titch! You don't mean that.' Sara laughed at the youngster's irreverent humour. 'Anyway, what can I do you for, this fine morning?' Walking around the front to peek in the pushchair, she was faced with the rare sight of a sleeping Theo.

'I've just come down to tell you about Rosa, actually.'

'Is she all right? I did wonder, as I texted her earlier and it's not like her not to be up and about.'

'She's fine now but she had a bit of a scare last night.' Titch lowered her voice. 'She had a few spots of blood, but Jacob took her to the hospital, and they scanned her immediately. Everything is fine. Evidently this sometimes happens in early pregnancy.'

'Oh no! Bless her. Has she told Josh?'

'Yes, she spoke to him last night. He is of course now frantic and wants to come back, but you know what she's like. So bloody stoic about everything. We just need to try and keep her stress-free, and I for sure won't be letting her lift anything in the shop from now on.'

'Is she at home?'

'Yes. Mary is with her now. It's her day off from the Co-op so she can open the shop up and I'm in there this afternoon. Can you cope on your own here, Sara?'

'Oh yes. At this time of year it's usually quiet.' Sara sprayed a table with sanitiser and quickly wiped it down. 'I'd planned to be on my own this morning anyway. But it's such a shame that Nate disappeared the way he did. He was a good worker and I liked him. I need to talk to Rosa about advertising for someone else.'

'Good idea. The university students will be breaking up soon, so even if you got someone in here just for the holidays, it would help during the Christmas period.'

'That's a great suggestion – thanks. Right, what can I get you?'

'I'll have a coffee and a sausage sandwich when I come back, please, but while he's asleep, I'm going to put him out the back if you don't mind, so I can run these scamps on the beach for a minute.' The two puppies were now scrabbling around, eager to escape from their crate prison.

As Titch let her tiny canine companions explore the seashore on a double lead, she noticed Lucas's white plumbing van pull into the Ship's car park, closely followed by the distinctive bicycle with a basket on the front belonging to Edie Rogers. She watched from the pub wall as one by one they threw the windows open, upstairs and down. It was a perfect day for airing the place, Titch thought – cold, bright and crisp, with just enough breeze to make a difference.

A lot of time and water had flown under the bridge since

Titch had slept with Lucas and accepted the bribe from Sheila Hannafore to get rid of the baby which she had pretended was his. She had avoided him since, so was quite shocked to see him open the door, and then give her a wave before coming over to join her.

Titch tutted as the ever-inquisitive Mr Chips went rushing towards him and started sniffing his ankles.

'Sorry, he's just a puppy. Into everything and everyone at the moment.'

'You never could keep the boys under control, could you?' Lucas gave her a wry smile.

'How you doing?' Titch said, with care.

'Not bad. Keeping busy. You know.'

At that moment his phone went. Holding his hand up as a goodbye, he strode back to the pub and shut the heavy door behind him.

But Titch *didn't* know. After losing her father and brother at such a young age, the thought of losing her own mother was a constant underlying worry, and for once she felt a massive pang of compassion for Lucas Hannafore and his grieving soul.

CHAPTER FORTY EIGHT

'Josh, it's five in the morning where you are, darling. You'll be knackered all day. Please try and get a couple of hours sleep in.' Rosa's handsome but very tired-looking husband stared back at her on the phone screen.

'I'm just worried about you, Rosa. So, for the last time, are you sure you don't want me to come home today? I will just drop everything; we are nearly done on this project now. Carlton could cope, if he had to.'

'And for the last time, no. I'm fine. It literally was a couple of drops of blood, there is no drama and I promise I will do as I'm told and let other people lift and carry for me. This baby is in here for keeps, I'm telling you. I still feel pregnant and I was sick as a dog again this morning. It's common, what happened, I'm told. I just feel bad I saw the scan before you though.'

'Show me again.' Rosa held up the grey and white picture. 'Aw. That's our baby, that is.' Josh was beaming. 'Look to the right, I'm sure I can see a willy.'

Rosa laughed. 'I don't ever want to see one of those again if it makes me feel this sick.'

Josh laughed back. 'Do you still fancy me?'

'Of course I bloody do.'

'What good taste you have, madam. Oh, and Rosa?'

'Yes, Josh?' Rosa let out a pretend huff.

'I still love you to where the sky touches the sea, you know that.'

'I love you too, you old smoothie, you. Now go away and get a bit more sleep, we can talk later.'

Rosa could hear Mary serving a customer downstairs, Hot was pottering about on the balcony, letting out random barks every time a seagull even dared so much as catch his eye. She checked her phone for the umpteenth time. Nate had been gone when she had arrived back late last night and she couldn't believe he hadn't left her any sort of message, let alone tried to find out how she was. She also wasn't best pleased that he had left Hot, but she had messaged to say she would be back that night, so he obviously realised that the dachshund would be OK.

Not quite sure how she was managing to hold everything together, by herself, and to herself, Rosa lay down on the sofa and shut her eyes. She was so tired, and the recent revelation that Nate Webb was her brother had sent her into a spin. What's more, once it was common knowledge, it would send the whole of the Bay into a spin too – and she didn't feel she was ready to handle that and all the consequences it might bring.

She had an actual brother! That was insane but also incredibly exciting. Well, he would be her half-brother, she guessed, unless Mary had maybe kept something from her. No, Mary would never do that, surely? And anyway, Nate had said that his mother had run off with someone else. Mary couldn't possibly have lied about something so massive as her giving birth to another child and giving them up, could she? Nate and Rosa did look alike, but if they shared a father then that was entirely possible.

Bittersweet – just like the poisonous plant that Alec had once pointed out to her on the West Cliffs path – that's what this whole scenario was. But now, in order to find some semblance of peace, she had to investigate further. Some very BIG conversations needed to be had.

Rosa still couldn't believe that she had been face-to-face with her supposed real-life father. Saying that, it hadn't been until she got home to the Corner Shop that the realisation had hit. The name Christopher Webb wasn't uncommon – she'd quickly found that out, when her initial search for him had begun online. She hadn't gone any further than finding what she thought was an address for him. Naively, or maybe subconsciously, at the time she didn't want to think that he might have other children. However, with Nate definitely being the funeral director's son, and with the similarities of his looks and wild hair to her own, this told her that she must be right in her thinking. Also, the fact that she had felt a weird connection with Nate from the very first time she had met him also made her believe that they were related: a new branch to her expanding family tree.

When she first got hold of the card from Christopher and the penny finally dropped, she had gone numb, but once she got home, she had been violently sick; Rosa wasn't sure if that was because of the baby or at the shock of it all. Christopher Webb's card gave an address in North Devon. So, all the time she had been down here in South Devon, her presumed father had been literally across the other side of the county from her. Surely, Mary couldn't have known this either. If she did, the hurt would be just too great to bear. And obviously this was why Rosa had been so far off the mark in her search for any kind of address. Foolishly, she had looked no further than London, as that was where she knew her conception had occurred. The letter that she had written had asked her dad to contact her – but the letter had been sent to a London address. None of it made sense. If he had received it, all those months ago, why would it have taken him so long to get back in touch? Why would he be down here now – and why would he be looking for his son and not her? So many questions.

It also made her feel even more in awe of her great-grandfather Ned and great-grandmother Queenie for how, against many odds, they had managed to find her. Especially as she wasn't even known as a Cobb among her work colleagues or friends. No, if her mum didn't love her and had given her away, Rosa had decided that she didn't want one of her names. No way. Rosa Larkin was who she wanted to be known as. The one and only.

Larkin – for no other reason than that she had watched old reruns of *The Darling Buds of May* in one of her children's homes. The successful TV show, based on a series of five books written by HE Bates, revolved around a big, brash and beautiful family, the Larkins, who didn't have a care in the world. They lived in an oast-house in the glorious countryside of Kent, spreading joy and happiness in all their dealings. She had so wanted to be part of that family. And in her damaged and deluded eyes, in becoming Rosa Larkin by personal deed poll, she was.

Before she acted on Nate's massive revelation, Rosa knew that, first of all, she had to talk to him properly and find out the truth. There were so many questions that needed answering before she could even think about talking to Mary. Or maybe she should talk to her mother before anyone? But Rosa was half-scared that Mary would make her promise not to do anything. No, Rosa had to follow her gut instincts on this one – and they were telling her to speak with Nate.

With the shop about to be passed on, and her being pregnant, it all really was such bad timing. But as she'd said to Luke, life was all about timing – and that timing didn't always work the way you would have wanted.

She then sat upright and put a hand to her head. It wasn't the voice of Queenie who spoke this time, but that of her clairvoyant mother. 'The Jacks of this world come in many guises.' With her streetwise head on, Rosa came to a sudden dark dawning. For all his faults, she had become rather fond of Nate, and now all she could do was naively pray that the guise he had come in was one of truth – and not of greed and duplicity.

Hot had been curled up in his basket, giving himself a thorough wash. Then, as if sensing his mistress's anguish, he scrabbled up his sofa steps and climbed onto her lap. With his feet digging uncomfortably into her thighs, he reached up and started to cover her face in smelly dog lick.

'Aw, my little munchkin,' she said, stroking his warm body. 'Why is life so bloody complicated, eh?'

CHAPTER FORTY NINE

'So, it's your last chance, lucky listeners,' Barry Savage announced across the radio waves. 'Yes, today is the day to get your coloured envelopes in for the opportunity of a lifetime – to be the proud owners of not only the Corner Shop in Cockleberry Bay but also the flat above it.'

Rosa dropped the Christmas bauble she was holding, smashing it on the tiled floor. She had got up in a sprightly mood, hadn't even felt nauseous, and was keen to decorate the real Christmas tree that Alec had kindly set up in the front window of the shop. She planned to use a selection of festive doggie treats, since they had been a big hit with customers last year, interspersed with some old Christmas baubles that must have belonged to Ned and his wife Dorothea.

Barry Savage continued with his excitable soliloquy. 'It surely will be a Christmas to remember for the lucky winner, folks.' Rosa tutted as she picked up the broken pieces of bauble. 'As with everything,' Barry went on, 'if you're not in it, you can't win it. You can go to our website for further details, but it couldn't be easier. Here's what you have to do. Think of a Christmas name to call yourself, as this is an anonymous competition. Pledge a donation to a local charity of your choice. Then explain *what exactly* it would mean for you to run the Corner Shop in Cockleberry Bay – and what you are intending to sell when you take it on. How simple is that!' He laughed his annoying cackle. 'I will be speaking to Rosa Smith, the owner and, may I say, most generous proprietor of the Corner Shop, later to see just how many envelopes she has had in. Tomorrow, she will make her choice from those submissions.'

Just at that moment, her mobile phone rang. 'Hi, is that Rosa?' said a woman's voice.

'Yep.'

'It's Charlotte Hill here, I'm the intern on the breakfast show *South Cliffs Today*. Barry's just nominated me to ask you to speak about the Corner Shop proviso. Sorry for the short notice, he's always doing this to me.' The young girl's voice was full of stress. 'So, er, can you? I mean, are you OK to speak to him?'

'On the telephone, I can, sure.'

'Phew, that's a relief. Thanks, Rosa. Are you free now?'

'Yes, let's do this.'

'Ok, just stay on the line. This song will finish soon, then we are going to News and Weather, then Barry will come directly to you.'

Rosa wished she'd had a wee before she'd agreed now. That was something she'd found out when she had become pregnant, that her bladder had shrunk to the size of a pea – pee being the key word here.

Not thinking to put her *Back in 20 minutes* sign up, she began to shift from one foot to the other while waiting for Barry to come online.

Ding! The shop doorbell rang. Looking clean and smart, his black eye now a shade of grey and pink, and with no sign of a split lip, was Nate. His short dark curls were shiny and despite his grey, not green eyes, Rosa felt it was like looking in a mirror.

'For you.' He pulled a bouquet of white roses from behind his back.

Rosa pointed to her mobile phone, made some animated facial expression of thanks then whispered, 'I can't talk now.' She then ran to the door to lock them both in and put the *20 minutes* sign up. Nate tiptoed over to the counter as directed and sat quietly, waiting.

When Barry Savage made a grand introduction and further explanation of how the proviso would come into play, the young lad's face broke into a beaming smile. Hot started jumping up at his legs, so he gently lifted him up, gave him a tiny treat from the counter and started to stroke his soft brown ears.

'Hello Barry,' Rosa said through gritted teeth. She would never warm to this man. Their energies collided and that was that.

'So, can you give up a sneaky peek into how many envelopes you've had in, and maybe who they are from? I'm sure the listeners would love to hear.'

'Well, yes, if you want me to, I can. Of course.'

'Great news! Let's just go to a song and we will be right back with you.'

'Thank God, hold this quickly.' Rosa handed Nate the phone then turned to run.

'Rosa, there's something I need to–'

'In a minute,' Rosa hissed. 'When I come back. Put Hot down and make yourself a drink out the back, if you like. I need the loo!'

Privately, Rosa herself was surprised at having received only four entries. She had expected at least ten, but she acknowledged that it was a big undertaking and she hadn't really given anyone much time. Also, the fact that whoever got it couldn't sell it for ten years would definitely put a lot of people off. The music stopped and Barry handed over to her.

'As you can imagine, Barry, I have been inundated with entries,' Rosa lied. 'The Corner Shop is a wonderful little business and Cockleberry Bay just the most idyllic place to live. So, you see, I made a pact with myself not to open the envelopes until decision day, which as you stated is tomorrow. At the moment, I don't have a clue who is entering.' That too was a lie. After an enlightening conversation she had had with Danny last night, she already knew for certain of one person she was bringing to the grand finale. It was just a case now of who else.

Rosa played her part well. 'So, all I can give you now is a little taster of the names on the envelopes. We don't want to give too much away, do we?'

She could tell that Barry would be beside himself at the way she was ably creating a buzz for the audience.

'Oh. No, no, *no*,' he gloated, Mr Toad-like. 'We love a surprise on the breakfast show.'

'And, of course, I am very much looking forward to announcing the winner with you [her third lie] live on Christmas Eve from the Cockleberry Bay Village Hall.'

'Oh, yes, it's going to be amazing. It's all everyone is talking about on all our social media channels,' he gushed. 'The anticipation is driving us mad.'

Nate sat nervously in the back kitchen, fiddling about on his phone, while Hot sniffed around him, angling for a walk.

'So, we have Rudolph the Red-Nosed Reindeer, and there's a Pigs in Blankets.'

'Hahaha. I like those,' Barry interjected.

'And not forgetting Frosty the Snowman, whose entry arrived in a beautiful bright orange envelope. So, brownie points for that too.'

'Well, thanks for that, Rosa, and we can't wait to all be there for the grand finale in just over two weeks' time. And now, listeners, here's the King himself, Elvis Presley, singing "I'll Be Home For Christmas"...'

'I always did find it easier to walk and talk.' Rosa let Hot's lead out to a length where he could run ahead without fear of him going anywhere near the cliffs' edge. It was yet another bright and crisp day. A couple of pleasure boats had even made their way out to sea and gulls were circling and mewing their delight at some much-appreciated winter sunshine.

'Do you also make a habit of closing the shop mid-morning?'

'Only for something this important.' Rosa sat down on what Alec called his 'thinking bench' and patted the place next to her. She pulled her woolly hat down over her ears and dug her gloves out of her pocket.

'Don't you be getting too cold up here though,' Nate said, sitting close to her.

'I won't. Thanks for the roses, by the way.'

'I heard that white roses were a symbol of trust. That's what brothers and sisters should have, right?'

Rosa gulped at the enormity of the situation. All those years she'd been alone in those children's homes, alone in her tortured mind, not even knowing if she had a mother or father left in the world, let alone any siblings. And now here she was in her favourite place in the whole world with a mother, supposed father and half-brother. It was extraordinary, exciting and terrifying all at the same time.

She couldn't bear the suspense any longer. 'Nate, let's stop skirting around the issue, shall we?' she blurted out. 'Just get on and tell me the truth. I want to know everything, warts and all. And if you dare lie to me, well... Just please don't.'

CHAPTER FIFTY

In the rush to help Titch get the puppies walked and fed, and Theo dropped at the nursery they had decided to put him in one day a week, Ritchie had left the house without his clean apron.

Knowing his mum would give him her 'cleanliness is next to godliness' speech, he came hurrying up the hill and through the back door into the bungalow. Greeting Titch's mum, who was sitting in her wheelchair, knitting by the fire, he grabbed the clean apron from the radiator, smiling as he noticed Saveloy and Mr Chips snuggled up on either side of her, sleeping soundly. The radio was buzzing in the background, but it was loud enough for Ritchie to catch the tail-end of Barry Savage talking about the Corner Shop giveaway.

'It's the last day for young Rosa to get entries in,' Mrs Whittaker said, busily knitting a blanket for the puppies. 'I think she's mad giving that shop away. Old Ned and Dottie will be turning in their graves.'

Ritchie didn't have time to explain that Rosa was acting with Ned's blessing; instead he kindly asked Titch's mother if she needed anything done before he left. Thankful that she didn't, he went to the bill rack – to find the silver envelope with the gold stars still sitting exactly where it had been left.

CHAPTER FIFTY ONE

Josh was paying Ralph Weeks for his taxi ride from the station when Lucas came running up the hill, dressed head-to-toe in Nike gear. On seeing the big man, he stopped, took out one of his wireless earbuds and walked over to the car.

Lucas stood up straight and took a deep breath. 'Welcome home, mate. She's desperate to see you, you know.'

Josh, slightly thrown by this greeting, just mumbled, 'Er, thanks.' Then, remembering what had happened and despite not having had any time for Sheila, he offered, 'Sorry to hear about your mum.'

His dislike of Lucas Hannafore had slightly waned since 'the incident' last year when Rosa didn't know if she'd slept with the plumber or not. Lucas had been man enough to tell Josh that despite him fancying Rosa, nothing had gone on. Josh recognised that this had taken guts – and showed respect for Rosa too.

It was Hot barking that alerted Rosa to Josh's arrival. Hurtling through the Corner Shop front door, she jumped into his arms, forcefully throwing both legs and arms around her husband.

'Oh my God, I am SO happy to see you. You're early – why didn't you call me?' She showered his head with kisses.

'I wanted to surprise you.'

Lucas looked on, until Rosa unfurled herself, slid down to the pavement and noticed him standing there.

'Luke? Hi. You OK?'

'Because I'm in running gear, you mean?' He managed a smile. He had to be strong now. Play out some of the lessons that Alec had really helped him a lot with already. Alec was also right that the Smiths were a tight couple and they would be so much better as friends than foes.

'Yes, here.' He pushed some banknotes into her hand. 'The oner that I borrowed off ya. I did a couple of jobs yesterday. Bye then!' He nodded at them both then put his earbud back in and carried on jogging up the hill.

'Come on.' Rosa went to lift one of Josh's cases.

'Oi, get off that this minute, lady.' He put his hand to her tummy. 'How is Mr Bump doing now then? I can't tell you how worried I was the other night.' He walked through and put his cases in the back kitchen out of the way. Then, on looking up at the ceiling, he observed, 'You've moved the camera slightly.'

'Blimey, you're worse than PC Poirot. You'd got that camera so well hidden, I didn't even realise it was there until the other day.'

'Why did you suddenly notice?'

'Oh, er…they say you nest, don't you, when you're pregnant and I had my feather duster out.'

'My pregnancy book said it was much closer to the birth that you are supposed to start washing your net curtains and cleaning the skirting boards. This is a bit early.'

Rosa mock-swiped him. 'I'm going to burn that ruddy pregnancy book.' She then put her arms around him. 'I literally love that you are home. I have missed you so much.'

'You still found time to see Lucas though and lend him money,' Josh blurted out, surprising himself that he had spoken his thoughts aloud and so brutally.

Rosa took a deep breath then filled the kettle and flicked it on. 'Josh.' She paused to make sure her words came out as she wanted them to. "The poor bastard has just lost his mother. I was at the scene when she was gravely ill. I'm not going to lie; he has feelings for me, and he told me so outright. But the new Rosa, the non-drinking, the think-before-she-acts Rosa, told him straight that I was very much in love, with you. He didn't ask me for the money. He told me he hadn't been working, so I lent him a hundred quid to take away the immediate pressure of not having to work while he was arranging the funeral.'

Rosa turned away and took out her prettiest mugs from the cupboard and the special cake she'd been keeping for Josh's homecoming.

She went on: 'Now, let's concentrate on us, shall we? And just as importantly, tomorrow morning we need to discuss who is going to take over this shop and give us the freedom to move and concentrate on the café.' She stopped to make the tea as Josh stared right at her. Hot whined for attention as Rosa carried on, 'And, aside *that* monumental decision, we also need to focus on getting our general future in order so that we can be the best parents that Mr or Miss Bump could ask for.'

Josh carried on staring right at Rosa without talking, then started clapping. He had tears in his eyes. Rosa, now slightly bemused at her husband's actions, let Hot out into the back yard before asking, 'What is it, Josh?'

'I bloody love you, Rosa Smith.'

'And that deserves a round of applause?'

'I love your confidence. I love your truth. I love your kindness.'

'They've always been there; I just wasn't sure how to get them out there.' Tears formed in her eyes now. 'I need to get something else out there too. Something SO massive. But before I do, let's go upstairs and just make love, can we?

CHAPTER FIFTY TWO

'Polly Cobb – just look at you. You, haven't changed a bit.'

Mary winced on hearing her nickname. The nickname she used to use in her deluded alcohol-soaked days of emotional suicide. Composing herself, she put her fingers to her lips to check that her new lipstick was still in place. It felt weird to have something on them. Her lashes felt heavy with the mascara she had not worn in a decade either. She had even curled her long black hair with the tong things that Rosa had given her last Christmas. Feeling the need for her inhaler, as a comfort rather than a cure, she put her hand on it in her bag to check its whereabouts, then left it there.

'Kit Webb. I'm surprised I even remembered your name.' Mary bit her lip at the remembrance of when sleeping with men and not having much recollection of it became the norm in her twenties. She also very much remembered waking up sore and bruised after being with this man: that was the reason she hadn't wanted to tell him that he was the father of her child. Taking in his contoured features and then his perfectly formed full lips, she could not only see a classically handsome man before her but also could tell that he was the father of her child.

'Well,' he replied, 'I remember us going bowling, then going back to the pub where you worked and,' he smiled, 'you were a stunner – had all the chat too.'

'Yes, and then we did more than just bowling together, I guess.' Mary attempted a smile, then yawned, hastily hiding it behind her hand. She'd had less than three hours sleep last night, with the worry of this meeting playing on her mind.

'Yes, according to my son, we created a daughter together. Let me get you a drink.' Christopher Webb stood up. His white hair was covered by a smart hat, his long black coat still on, despite the roaring fire in the cosy pub in Polhampton. 'It's the least I can do with you getting the bus out here.'

'Well, you've come all the way from North Devon.'

'It takes less time than the old Cockleberry Bay bus, I should imagine. Anyway, what's your poison?'

'Just a ginger ale with lots of ice, please.'

Christopher returned to their table with a pint of bitter and Mary's sparkling drink. He sucked away on an empty pipe.

'Why didn't you tell me?' he asked.

Mary really didn't know what to say. She was grateful for Christopher when he started speaking again.

'How Rosa found me was because my name was on the birth certificate, so you were obviously certain the father was me.' He could see the pained look on Mary's face and put his hand on top of hers. 'I'm not here to be angry or cross or any of those things. I bury people every day. I know that life is short and that the here and now is where we should be living, not the past. I guess I'm wishing you had told me, as I could have helped you. Could have been a part of Rosa's life. She seems like the bonniest girl.'

'You've met her already?'

'Just in passing.' Christopher sighed. 'She didn't know who I was then. Have you spoken to her about me yet?'

'No, I've been avoiding her. You see, she left me a message, told me what she knew. I wanted to talk to you first and, shameful as this sounds, I don't remember much about that night I was with you,' Mary managed to say. 'In fact, I don't know *anything* about you really – and, well, she deserves the full truth now. So, when did you get this letter from her? I was going to say I can't believe that Rosa went through my private things, but now she's pregnant...' Mary remembered her asking about her dad '...well, I expect she wants to be able to tell her child who she is, who they are.'

'In short, I didn't get the letter.'

'I don't understand.'

'The letter was sent to my London address, the place I inherited from my parents. I was living in Devon then, but Nate – my son – he stayed there. He's always been a troubled one, which, sadly, has a lot to do with his mother leaving us both. He didn't want to move down to somewhere "where everybody is already half-dead" – his words, not mine.'

'He and his half-sister have more in common than they think.' Mary sounded woeful.

Christopher nodded. 'Yes, they do. Anyway, he opened the letter to me in which your Rosa wrote that she hoped she had found me, but also in it she mentioned about the shop that she had inherited. I think in his deluded mind, my boy thought maybe he would be in for some of the bounty, as they could be related. Then when he came down here to work for Sea and Save and get closer to her, he heard that Rosa was giving the shop away. He must have been delighted. Nate then took it upon himself to do some proper digging, to see how best he could benefit – whether just to bid for it or reveal himself to her. All the while I was completely oblivious to this.' Christopher sighed. 'There was I, feeling rather proud that he was working for a charity, finally acting like a responsible adult. But then I got a phone call of the kind I am very used to getting – and it was only because he said that he had been beaten up and had no money that I came down to find him. I've got him out of many a scrape before, as you can imagine.'

Mary nodded. 'What a tangled web he was weaving.' She then laughed out loud. 'Ha! Excuse the pun, Mr Webb.'

'That laugh. It's exquisite.'

Mary felt herself redden slightly. 'So, he confessed all this to you, then?'

'Yes, and I believe, to Rosa, yesterday. Hence her recent message to you, no doubt.' Christopher took a drink from his pint glass. 'The twist in the tale is rather a lovely one though. Because when Nate realised just how great a girl Rosa is, he couldn't dupe her. In fact, he feels a compulsion now to protect her. "Peas in a pod", was his description of them both.'

'I'm guessing Rosa is not angry with him, then?'

'No. Your girl has a big heart and somehow she understood. You see, he always knows he can come to me if he has money troubles. But he tries not to, and that's when he thinks gambling is the answer. He thought getting the shop was another easy way of sorting himself out.'

'She will understand more than anyone, because of her past. In fact, if anyone can help and guide him, it may well be her.'

'I can only bloody hope so.' Christopher drained his glass. 'Relationships, eh? Whatever form they come in, they certainly need work. Did you ever marry, Mary?'

'No.' Mary felt suddenly sad. 'Spinster of the Cockleberry Parish, me. Quite happy with my cat.'

'Really? You just haven't been swept off your feet by the right man yet.'

Mary felt herself redden again; was he flirting with her? It

256

had been so long; she wasn't even sure what that was any more.

'And you?' she asked daringly.

'My long-term partner and I split a couple of years ago, but I'm a hopeless romantic. I still believe there is a lid for every pot out there.' He paused. 'Mary, I wanted to talk to you about that night.'

Mary went to her glass for comfort, but it was empty. She reached for her inhaler and took a big drag. Christopher Webb mirrored her by sucking on his empty pipe. She was scared at what she might hear.

Christopher took his time before beginning to speak. 'After we spent the night together, I woke up the next day worried that you would think badly of me. The night before, I'd met you for the first time at the pub where you were working. The next day was your day off, so we went bowling and then drinking – and of course when you said I could stay over, being a twenty-something lad, I wasn't going to say no, was I? The thing is…the person you had slept with before me had been rough with you, you told me. I said then of course there was no way I wanted to make love to you in case it hurt you, so we'd sleep apart. You insisted. I was weak. I was especially gentle with you, but then somehow the condom came off and, well, I said maybe you should be worried. You didn't care, Mary. I even came in the pub the next night to see if you were OK, but you swore at me and I guess, in your drunken state, convinced yourself that I was the baddie.'

'The demon drink, eh? Life could have been so different.' Mary cringed at the thought of her previous drunken antics. But it wasn't really the demon drink that was to blame, it was her own demon within: the pain of losing her mother in childbirth and, subsequently, her father. The only way she could subdue this pain was by drowning it in drink.

'No, it couldn't and wouldn't have been different, dear Mary. It wasn't the right time. Knowing what I know now about life, you needed professional help. We are where we are. Me with two beautiful kids now and you with your Rosa.' He laughed, breaking the tension. 'If life was perfect, it would be pretty boring.'

'Yes, but what happened was about as far from perfect as it could have been. I lost my child. Worse still, she lost me.' Mary looked Christopher in the eye. 'And we both lost you.'

The kindly man put a hand on Mary's trembling one. 'As I said, we are here now and there is time to rectify everything. For all of us.'

'I need to speak to Rosa.' Mary sighed.

'And I've made the decision that I'm going to leave Rosa to come to me. It sounds like she has a lot on her young shoulders to deal with at the moment.'

'Yes, Grandad, she has. And knowing my daughter as I do now, I'd really appreciate that.'

'Of course – and oi, less of the "Grandad".' This time, they both laughed. 'And Mary?' Christopher looked directly at her. 'Seeing as we are going to be sharing that joy, maybe we should do this again, sometime?'

CHAPTER FIFTY THREE

'Pigs in chuffing Blankets? What does that mean anyway?'
Thankful that it was Sunday and they could spend a whole
day in peace together, Josh and Rosa were sitting at the table
in the lounge going through the few entries they had had for
the shop. As expected, Josh had been slightly shocked at first
on hearing the new family revelation, but, in true matter-of-
fact style, he said that whatever happened they would cope,
and if Rosa wanted him to be there when she met with Mary
– or her dad, for that matter – to talk about it, then of course
he would come along to fully support her. Josh also stressed
to her that although Nate had initially thought he had a claim
on the shop, he truly didn't. Legally, it had been left to Rosa –
and if she wanted to gift anything to him it would totally be
down to her.

During their talk on the clifftop, Nate had, however, made
it clear that he was so happy to have Rosa as a half-sister that
he was going to talk to his dad about living with him in North
Devon and paying his way properly. He also said that he had
never expected to have such a rapport with her, to feel so close
to Rosa in such a short time, and that she had inspired him to
be a better man already.

'You must have had Pigs in Blankets at Christmas dinner at home before, or somewhere surely?' Rosa asked now.

'Nope.'

'It's mini-sausages – a bit like Hot's puppies, really – wrapped in bacon.'

'Oh, *them*,' Josh tutted. 'Mum just used to call them just that: sausages wrapped in bacon.'

Rosa laughed. 'I learn something new about you every day, husband.'

Hot was sleeping soundly in his bed until the shop doorbell went, and then he struggled up, all agog to see who was troubling them on a non-workday. Josh nipped downstairs and returned with another envelope, which he gave to Rosa, saying, 'Talk about last-minute.'

Josh then opened his laptop, going to the spreadsheet entitled 'Shop'. He laid out all the envelopes in front of him. 'I'm going to type out all the main points and then we can go through them in order. Are you happy with that, dearest?'

'Do as you will, my darling. You know me, I just want the bare facts and then I can make my final decision.'

'OK.' Josh spoke aloud as he gazed at his spreadsheet. 'I will put in the biggest charity money order first.'

'But that's not how I'm choosing,' Rosa objected. 'That's just an extra bonus.'

'I know, my little chinchilla.' Josh blew her a kiss. 'Rosa Smith will no doubt be following her heart, as she does with most things.'

'Yes, she will.' Hot was now snuggled next to her as Rosa went to lie on the sofa, having a rest at her husband's insistence.

'So, we have Frosty the Snowman, who wants to donate the massive sum of one thousand pounds to Polhampton Paws, a rescue centre for dogs and cats. He or she wants to sell crystals and designer dog blankets. And, their reason for wanting it is…'

'I don't want to hear all the reasons now.'

'All right, Miss Stroppy.'

'Well, I've read them already.'

Josh continued to talk aloud as he worked on the spreadsheet. 'So, next is Rudolph the Red-Nosed Reindeer. Now he – or I guess it could be she – is donating seven hundred and fifty pounds to – wait for it – the Carrot Footprint, who are a charity campaigning for a safer planet. They want to set up a plant-based healthfood shop.'

'Hmm. Would the locals of Cockleberry really be ready for that, just yet?' Rosa wondered.

'Maybe Vegan Vera is putting her stamp on it.' Rosa grimaced at even the mention of that woman's name, but said nothing as her lovely husband went on, 'Next is – ooh yes, here they are – Pigs in Blankets, donating two hundred and fifty pounds to the Cockleberry Bay Residents Association. Nice.' Josh carried on typing. 'And a beauty salon. Can't really see how that will work, unless they intend to use the flat as treatment rooms.' He took a slurp of his now cold coffee. 'And, last but by no means least, we have Quality Street. My favourite chocolates. Did you get any, by the way? We must have a tin for Christmas.'

With a massive sense of relief, Rosa was now intently reading the envelope that had just been put through the door.

Josh carried on talking to himself. 'So, Mr or Mrs Quality Street, they are donating one hundred pounds to the local Lifeboats and they want to turn the shop into a DIY store.' At the mention of a DIY store, Rosa smiled. That had to be Danny. When he had called her the other day, he did say that he knew it was closed bids, but he wanted her to know, anyway.

Josh noticed how quiet Rosa had become. He looked over at the sofa where she was still reading the letter from the envelope he had given her. The tracks of her silent tears were evident.

'Oh, my darling, what is it?'

'I now know the two we are taking to the grand finale on Christmas Eve. And you, my gorgeous husband, will just have to trust me on this one.'

CHAPTER FIFTY FOUR

'I can't believe you got us through to the final. You're a canny one, you are.' The Managing Director of Costsmart Supermarkets lay back in his comfy office chair, feeling well pleased.

'She thinks she's clever, the one who runs it,' his caller said snidely, 'but she was easier to fool than my mother when I was a teenager. And I knew the charity I chose would pull at her silly little heart-strings. I wrote a pledge that would be Oscar-worthy too. We've got this!'

'I bloody hope so. My job nigh-on depends on it.'

'Have you got my cash?' the caller then demanded.

'Just let me know when the shops is ours and I will transfer it.'

'I would rather have it in cash.'

'OK, OK. Well, thanks again and good luck at the grand finale, although by the sound of it, it's in the bag.'

'Paper ones not plastic, of course, to keep all the do-gooding environmentalists happy.' The caller sniggered.

The managing director was amused. 'Somehow,' he commented, 'I don't think you'll be going to heaven.'

'Somehow, I don't care. Merry Christmas, Mr Badger.'

'Merry Christmas...Frosty the Snowman.'

CHAPTER FIFTY FIVE

Ritchie was zipping up Theo's little blue anorak when the baby let out a noisy fart, causing all three of the little family to laugh.

'He gets that from you.' Titch shook her head then looked in the mirror and picked at her teeth. 'Bloody raspberry pips in that Co-op jam.'

'You are coming to see Rosa do her pitch, aren't you?' Ritchie asked.

'What time is it starting again? Mum said to drop him at Auntie Betty's, as she's up there with her finishing off the wedding cake and will then come down to the event. When are you at work?'

'I told you last night, I'm going in a bit later. Dad's doing the prep for me. We have to support our mate.' When Titch sighed, Ritchie kissed her gently on the cheek. 'Are you all right, my little love? You seem a bit out of it.'

'I'm just tired, that's all – and we are getting married in three days in case you had forgotten.'

Ritchie put his long arms around her. 'I thought we were all set.'

'We kind of are,' she replied. But it wasn't the wedding that was causing her to feel such melancholy, it was the recollection that, even after Ritchie's gentle persuasion that she bid for the shop, she had made the decision not to do so. Had made the decision to miss out on the chance of following her dreams and finding a secure home, somewhere that she, Ritchie and Theo and their pets could call their own.

At that moment, Saveloy and Mr Chips came scampering in from the kitchen and started to yap at their feet.

'Come on, let's hurry up and see if your mum and Bet will take these two furry monsters as well,' Ritchie said, 'and then we can get ringside seats for Rosa. You know how your mum and Bet dote on the lot of them.' Secretly, he thought the two ladies wouldn't get much done once their tiny charges arrived. 'You'll probably get the chance to fit in a kip yourself later, I reckon.'

'Ooh yes, that sounds like the perfect plan.'

'You should wear that new sparkly Christmas jumper of yours, seeing as it's Christmas Eve and everything. Make yourself feel better.'

'All right, but Ritchie?'

'Yes, my Tinkerbell?'

'Be an angel and change Theo's nappy first, can you? I think he followed through with that fart of his.' She threw one at her husband-to-be, causing the little wieners to try and catch it and start barking like crazy again. 'And Ritchie?'

Her obedient fiancé, already starting to take off the anorak he'd just put on Theo, his soon-to-be adopted son, looked up at his pretty, blonde, cropped-haired lover. 'Yes, She Who Must Be Obeyed?'

'I bloody cannot wait to be able to call you my husband.'

CHAPTER FIFTY SIX

Christmas Eve and the Cockleberry Bay Village Hall had not seen so much activity since the adult version of the nativity play twenty-five years ago, when Joseph had outed his wife for having an affair with the Angel Gabriel; in his hurry to escape the humiliation, the latter got his wings caught in a wise man's stick and fell off the stage, breaking his ankle.

The atmosphere was alive with anticipation. The hum of the early crowd reverberated around the old wooden structure. The village hall was now home to play groups, the local am-dram group, dance lessons, Sunday school, yoga and martial arts classes. There was also an underlying excitement from some of the youngsters and, if they were honest, some of the oldies too, since it was cold enough for snow. And snow was a rare occurrence in the south-west, let alone on Christmas Eve.

Sara and a happy-looking Nate were already doing a roaring trade in hot drinks and mince pies, which they were serving from the hatch at the back of the room. It was Rosa's idea to do this and split the profits between all the afore-mentioned charities.

A subdued Danny was outside having a cigarette. After Rosa had explained that Nate was family, she had asked him to apologise, if he didn't mind. She said she knew that he was only trying to protect her and the shop. Rosa had also briefed Nate and warned him that if it was all going to kick off again, to make sure they were well away from the village hall and the prying eyes of the press. Luckily, just a few words were expressed, and the currency of fists had been exchanged for what looked like Nate pushing something – which could well have been cash – into his back pocket. Honour among suspected thieves and all that. Rosa was hoping that the two of them would make good friends, now the score had been settled.

Barry Savage was sitting up on the stage being briefed by his assistant, Charlotte, his large stomach protruding in his bright red Christmas jumper. It made a refreshing change, Rosa thought, from his whiffy, loud-checked suit.

The only information that Rosa had given in advance was that they had already messaged the two contenders concerned to be there at nine a.m., ready to go up on the stage and learn their fate. It seemed almost incredible that, in less than an hour, somebody else would be the proud owner of the Corner Shop in Cockleberry Bay.

Charlotte had also thought it quite strange that Rosa had specifically requested a projector and screen so that she could show a few photos of the shop from back when Ned and Dottie had it, right up to the present day. It was radio, after all. The listeners wouldn't benefit from it. However, being young and enthusiastic, the girl bought into it, agreeing that she would eventually link it up to the website as there would be a lot of people listening online too and they could be instructed to take a look in their own time; it would encourage those listening to the podcast to follow suit, too.

Alec had now joined Sara and Nate, so Josh went over to chat with his friends as Rosa made her way up onto the stage.

Wham's 'Last Christmas' was playing over the airwaves and some of the gathering crowd were singing along. The radio station had even lined up chairs in anticipation of a big crowd. Mary was sitting as far away as she could at the back, with Hot, who was being surprisingly good. Jacob and Raff were also near the back, looking on like proud parents. They knew how much this meant to Rosa and weren't going to miss a minute. Rosa waved to them as Charlotte and Barry talked her through how the next half hour was going to work.

Scott Wilde and Kelly from the *Gazette*, phones on, were both recording live, ready to get another scoop in a national newspaper if they could, and Scott had already started snapping to make sure they got as many good photos as they could. Rosa glanced out at the crowd and suddenly noticed Bergamot swanning in and taking the seat that had her name on it, right at the front. With her lips as full and red as jelly ones and her red faux-fur coat, plus matching red locks cascading down her back, she looked like the evil fairy in *Sleeping Beauty*.

As the song started coming to an end, a breathless Ritchie appeared through the door, shepherding Titch to sit near the front. He winked at Rosa and stuck his long legs under the seat in front of him. Just as one of the producers started to shush the crowd, the back door opened noisily. An embarrassed Lucas came in and sat down at the back next to Mary, then, on catching Rosa's eye, he smiled, then made a funny face and mouthed, 'What the fuck?' as he pointed to the back of DC Clarke's head. The policeman was sitting in front of him with a woman whom he assumed was his wife.

'So that was "Last Christmas" from Wham,' Barry Savage piped up. 'God bless the talent that was George Michael's – so very sad, folks. But we are here to be happy today, not sad. To celebrate somebody receiving the most amazing gift from this little lady here. Welcome, Rosa Smith, from the Corner Shop in Cockleberry Bay, who, not last Christmas, but two Christmases ago, arrived here in Cockleberry Bay after inheriting the shop from her estranged great-grandfather.'

'Hello,' Rosa replied, feeling a sudden rush of nerves at what she was about to announce.

Barry was more animated than Rosa had ever seen him. 'And part of her inheritance was that she couldn't sell the shop but had to give it away to somebody who deserved it. Now, this is what we are doing live on air on this cold Christmas Eve morning in Cockleberry Bay, and I am so happy to be the bringer of such great news.' There was a ripple of applause from the live audience. 'So, Rosa tells me that she had fewer entries than expected, and that this was probably down to the fact that she put a certain proviso on gaining the shop; this proviso states that the shop cannot be sold for at least ten years after today's date. We wouldn't want anyone getting it in an underhand manner, now would we, Rosa?'

'Thanks, Barry, and no, we certainly wouldn't. My great-grandfather not only worked hard to make a good life for himself and his wife, and the locals of the Bay, but also he wanted to make my life complete. I have promised in turn that I will do right by him, and hopefully continue to make him proud, moving forward, now and forever.'

Mary welled up. Her friends hugged her. Josh said, far too loudly, 'Go, Rosa.'

Barry took over. 'So, Rosa informs me that the charities which are going to benefit today, with a total of an amazing two thousand, one hundred and fifty pounds, are as follows: 'The Local Lifeboats.' A round of applause. 'The Cockleberry Bay Residents Association.' A small cheer. 'The newly set-up Carrot Footprint, who are another local charity campaigning for a safer planet.' A small ripple. 'Polhampton Paws, a dog and cat shelter, and not forgetting Sea & Save, who were the saviours of Cockleberry Bay's very own beach and wildlife earlier this year.'

A resounding cheer and thunder of applause went around the wooden building, which was at last starting to warm up with its old-fashioned overhead heaters.

'So all of you – and you know who you are – either here or listening in, please get your donations to your listed charities as soon as possible, to make all those carrots, animals, beaches and boat people happy.'

Rosa cringed; Barry might be in a buoyant mood, but he was still as ridiculous as ever in his choice of words.

Tugging his bright red jumper down over his massive belly, he announced, 'So on that note, let's play another song, shall we, and when we come back in a few minutes' time, we will hear why the two finalists think they should run the shop – and more importantly to the locals here and listening in – what they will be selling.'

Rosa got down from the stage and went straight over to Josh. He cuddled her gently and then cupped her now little visible bump with his big hand. 'Mr Bump will be so proud of you.'

'Or Miss,' Rosa corrected him.

'So, are you going to tell me who the finalists are now?'

Kissing him on the nose, she ignored her husband, then went to see Mary and make sure Hot was behaving himself.

'I'm so proud of you, duck. Queenie would be delighted, and if my mum, your poor Grandma Maria had been around, she would be too. In fact, all of us are proud of you, darling. Right, I'm just going to take the hound outside, so he doesn't start creating.' She stood up and put Hot on his lead. Lucas was just coming back from the toilet.

'Do I get a snog when you award it to me then?' he grinned.

'Ha, bloody, ha. Good to see you smiling though.' Rosa bit her lip. 'You're looking well – must be all that running.'

'Yeah, I've…er…I've met someone. It's early days, but I needed a distraction, you know.'

Rosa wasn't sure how she felt at this news. She swallowed down what she really wanted to say about it all being a bit quick, instead put her hand on his arm and said, 'Whoever it is, she's a lucky girl.'

Charlotte had now jumped down off the stage to get Rosa back up. Barry was live on air again, singing along to Bruce Springsteen's version of 'Santa Claus Is Coming To Town'. He suddenly bellowed, 'But it's not Santa Claus who's coming to this town, is it, Rosa? Or maybe it is, with the funny Christmas names you requested. Hahaha. Come on, tell us all what we've been waiting for. Spill it. Who are the two finalists, one of whom will be winning the amazing prize of not only a shop but a flat too?'

Rosa looked down to the front two rows, where an evidently pregnant Vicki Cliss was now waving back at her. She looked to Ritchie, who nodded nervously. Holding a bright orange envelope and a silver one with gold stars on it aloft, Rosa then asked: 'So, can Frosty the Snowman and Tinkerbell make their way up here, please?'

Danny's mouth dropped to the floor, both in shock that it wasn't him being called, and also due to the fact that the woman he had shagged in Rosa's back kitchen was there right in front of him, making her way up onto the stage as if she was about to collect an Oscar. Especially after he'd confessed to Rosa what he knew about her on the phone the other day.

'Go on.' Ritchie gently eased Titch up off her seat. 'That's your envelope, isn't it?'

'But…' Titch looked completely confused. Then: 'No! You

bugger!'

'Come on, Titch.' Helping her best friend up onto the stage, Rosa forced down the emotion that was already rising within her. She needed to keep a clear head in order to deal with another matter first. 'Ah, and Bergamot,' she said sweetly. 'Who'd have thought it, eh?'

Titch stood awkwardly next to the scarlet woman before Charlotte hurried the two to sit with a microphone in front of them at the table that had been set up on the stage.

'So, Rosa, why these two glamorous specimens? Do tell!' Barry hadn't quite grasped the new way of how you could or could not address women on a global stage.

'Well, Bergamot here,' Rosa began. 'What can I say? Polhampton Paws. With my love of dogs, what a great charity – and the fact that you want to sell crystals, which you know are very close to my heart too. And as for doggy designer blankets, how could I not choose you?'

Scott and Kelly from the *South Cliffs Gazette* pricked up their ears. They sensed from Rosa's tone that something else was coming and it was something they were going to love.

'Charlotte, can you start the video clips running, please,' Rosa asked pleasantly, and with relief that there were no children in the audience.

You could hear a pin drop in the room. The audience's jaws were hitting the floor. On seeing the film, Danny backed out of the door, although his dignity remained intact, since his identity was not shown, aside a white bottom moving in and out of the screen with the very evident and ecstatic face of Bergamot Hamilton-Jones doing what we all do, but usually in private.

Charlotte went to stop it, but Rosa wouldn't let her, for in the clever edit that Nate had helped her with, you then saw the vile woman sneak back into the kitchen and steal the Corner Shop's day's takings that Danny had dutifully left in the microwave for Rosa, as instructed by Jacob.

The producer, who was now bright red in the face with stress, went straight into a song. Barry, knowing that this was more than a ratings winner, that it would probably see him promoted to a regional station, was laughing fit to bust out of his Christmas jumper. DC Clarke had stood up and, loving the drama of having such a crowd to play to, he strode forward to arrest Bergamot for theft.

He called up to Rosa: 'I don't understand. You didn't report this.' Rosa picked up the handheld microphone that was on the table so that everyone in the room could hear.

'No, I didn't report this crime, DC Clarke, because I thought this public revelation of her guilt would be far more of a punishment. A public flogging, so to speak. Because not only had this deluded woman stolen a whole day's takings from me, if she was the winner here, she had planned to get the shop, then illicitly sell it directly to Costsmart Supermarkets.'

There was a collective gasp from the audience.

'How did you know that?' Bergamot gasped. She felt sick.

'I won't name names, but pillow talk – or should I say kitchen talk – can sometimes be a very dangerous thing. Now just get out of my sight, and you are to give every penny you pledged to Polhampton Paws – and I also want the shop takings back.'

The song-playing came to an end. 'So that was Rudolph the Red-Faced – ha-ha – I mean Red-Nosed Reindeer.' Barry was joyous. As were Scott and Kelly, who had enough words for the paper to cover the whole of the quiet Christmas period and way into the New Year. Bergamot stormed out with the policeman just as Danny sneaked back in, to a handshake from Nate and a thumbs-up from Rosa.

'And now to Titch Whittaker,' Barry said smoothly, 'who, if

I'm not mistaken, Rosa, is going to be the proud new owner of the Corner Shop in Cockleberry Bay.'

'Yes, yes, she is!' Rosa said jubilantly.

Ritchie rushed up onto the stage next to Titch. Josh, Jacob and Raff had come to sit right in the front row too. The gangly one spoke up first.

'My wife-to-be had no confidence about running the shop. She overheard something – incorrectly, I must believe – about her not being good enough.' Josh squirmed in his chair. 'Now this little lady here may be small in stature, but her heart is big. She's a survivor, see. Her dad and her brother died, and she still got up, brushed herself down and kept going. Our baby was very ill too, but never once did she complain or moan, just did what she had to do for her little man until he was well again. She's really great in a shop, too. Got the gift of the gab. Can charm the birds out of the trees, this one, and as for managing stock and stuff – she can do that as well. She can do anything in my eyes. Well, anything apart from fill out the form to try and get the shop, which was her dream.' He held Titch's hand. 'I haven't got much to give you, not yet, but what I can do is try to be the best husband to you and dad to our little Theo. So, when I knew that I could help to make this dream of yours come true, then I just had to do it.' He kissed Titch on the forehead. 'And you know I will support you fully in whatever you choose to do in life. I believe in you.'

There wasn't a dry eye in the house.

Titch leaned forward to the microphone. 'I managed to add the charity name myself, at least.' The audience laughed at this. 'And got as far as saying that I would keep the shop just the way it was. But that's enough about me. This is more about Rosa than anyone else here. My dear, best friend. Possibly the nicest woman I've ever met in my life. Sorry, Mum.' Titch then confided, 'She's not here, so that's OK.'

Another laugh went around the room. The producer was so happy to be getting this heartfelt speech after what had just happened that she let it run.

'Rosa has been on a long and painful journey too,' Titch resumed and looked down at Mary, who nodded. 'She was brought up in a succession of children's homes. Never thought she would make anything of herself – until Ned, her great-grandfather, left her the shop, that is. Running the Corner Shop in Cockleberry Bay was to be the making of her. It led her to being happy with her wonderful boyfriend – now husband – Josh, and it also led her to Alec – Dr Alec Burton, our local psychotherapist and friend to all of us in Cockleberry Bay.'

Alec and Sara were both trying to keep it together now.

'It was Alec who helped her when the demon drink ruled her emotions. Then there was Jacob and Raff and Vicki, even Darren the lifeboat man.' Titch waved to a bald man at the back of the room. 'They all had a part in helping her make her the best version of herself – not that there was one thing I didn't like about the old one, by the way. But what's important now is that the "new Rosa" is happy, and I know she won't mind me saying, now that she's sixteen weeks gone, that she's pregnant.'

There was a small round of applause as Titch continued, 'It will be an honour for me to take over the shop from you, Rose. You can always have your say, you know that too. But why am I even mentioning that? You won't be able to resist.' They both laughed, and Hot let out a loud bark from the back as Titch finished with, 'Mr Sausage obviously gives his approval too.'

Rosa, by now bubbling over with pregnancy hormones, reached for the big gold key that *South Cliffs Today* had made for her, and with tears in her eyes, she steadied herself before she spoke again.

'So, here's the key to the Corner Shop door for you and your little family. I cannot think of anyone in the world I would rather take over the shop. From the day I arrived in the Bay, Titch Whittaker, you were there for me. Rose, you called me, and Rose is what you will always call me. Our quirky friendship was built on trust, understanding and kindness.' Rosa's voice started to waver. 'I love you, mate, and I cannot wait to walk you down the aisle in a few days' time.'

Barry then thanked Rosa and all who had taken part before closing the show and returning it to the phone-in gardening programme back at the studio. As the dreamy sound of 'The Power Of Love' by Frankie Goes to Hollywood blasted through the speakers, there was a cry from one of Vicki Cliss's boys. The children had just arrived with her husband and were shouting, 'It's snowing! Father Christmas is coming and it's snowing!'

CHAPTER FIFTY SEVEN

As the wedding party walked animatedly down from the Cockleberry Bay church, the fifty-strong choir could be heard across the beach from South Cliffs to West Cliffs. So powerful was the delivery of 'As', it brought joy to everyone's soul. The group were swaying along as they sang on the beach right outside ROSA'S, not showing any sign of cold or discomfort as delicate flakes of snow fell on to the singers' matching navy fur coats. It really was a wonderful sight to behold.

'On my God!' Titch was agog with happiness as she clasped Rosa's hand. 'You walked me down the aisle, that was beautiful enough, but this… Oh Rose, this is everything I dreamed of and more.'

Ritchie then grabbed Rosa's arm and swung it high as they carried on walking down the steep hill towards the beach. 'Thank you, thank you so much for helping to make our special day so perfect.'

'Ritchie Rogers, don't you be getting all soppy on me too.'

The revellers then all made their way into the café, where Nate was busy overseeing getting the choir fed and watered, and making sure that the whole place was warm and cosy. Special wedding candles were on every table and a beautiful Christmas tree stood in the corner, with wedding gifts underneath that guests had dropped in earlier. Jacob and Raff, who'd had to work and were back at the Lobster Pot with the Duchess and the two pugs, had sent a huge, silver-wrapped gift with a photo of them all attached to it, with the message: *Love and Congratulations to Mr and Mrs Rogers from the Lobster Pot.*

Titch gaped in astonishment as she looked at the tables where red and green festive vases were full of bright yellow blooms. 'Daffodils? How did you manage that? This is just too much.'

Rosa smiled. 'No, what is too much is this bloody bridesmaid's dress. It's SO tight, I need to change out of it before I burst.'

Josh followed Rosa out the back. 'Look at you undressing for me already.' He stood behind his wife and kissed her neck. 'Happy?'

'So bloody happy. We can concentrate on us now, and me knowing that the shop is safe in Titch's hands – well, it's just the best scenario all round.'

'I should never have doubted her,' Josh said ruefully.

'It's all good. Look at me.' Rosa stuck her stomach out. 'I've never had a belly before.'

Josh leaned down and kissed it. 'You're beautiful inside and out, and this time next year we will have a little family of our own. I love you, Rosa Smith.'

'And I love you too, but we'd better get out there, we've got a wedding to run.'

With the choir on a coach on their way back to Exeter and the guests tucking into the wedding gift from Ritchie's parents of a hot fish-and-chip feast, Rosa wriggled along a bench beside Mary. 'You OK, Mother?'

'This is wonderful, darling. I am so proud of what you've achieved. In fact, I'm just proud to call you my daughter, full stop.'

Rosa tutted. 'We've got a good thing going now, Mum, you and me. Now eat up and enjoy yourself.'

Mary put her fork down. 'Rosa, about your dad.'

'Not now.' Rosa went to stand up.

Mary stayed her with her hand. 'I met him. He says if and when you are ready, he will be there for you.'

Feeling a wave of emotion go straight to her throat, Rosa stood up and kissed her mother on the forehead, saying chokily, 'That's good, Mum, that's great.' She went outside to take in a breath of fresh cold air. Not realising that anyone else was out there, she stuck her tongue out to catch snowflakes, just as she used to do as a child.

'Be careful where you're sticking that,' said an amused voice.

'Well, I won't be sticking it anywhere near you, Luke Hannafore, that's for sure. Look at the trouble that caused.' She smiled. 'I didn't realise you were joining us?'

'I didn't either, but I bumped into Titch the other day and she said to come down for drinks after the food if I wanted to. Seeing as I'm staying down here, I thought it would be good to start drumming up some business.'

'Aw, that's great news. So, will it be plumbing or will you be taking the helm at the Ship again?'

'Tom and I have chatted, and we've decided to turn the old pub into a boutique hotel. Mum left us a pretty packet, so we can do it up for a high-end market. I also got talking to that Danny fellow, with the scar, in the Lobster Pot the other day. He's one of us, Rosa. He's all right. Handy by the sound of it, in more ways than one.' They both laughed in understanding. 'He's going to help me do it up and I'm sure I will find a job for him when it's done. Him and his son can have a room there. Genius, actually.'

'That's brilliant news, and relieves my slight guilt about him not getting the shop.'

'Oh, shut up, Rosa. You know and I know it had to go to Titch. It was obvious.'

'Don't be a smartarse. Where's your new girlfriend, anyway? Is she coming down?'

'Nah, she's working tonight.'

'But it's Christmas.'

'She's a copper.'

Rosa, now shivering slightly, opened her eyes wide. 'You with a policewoman?'

'Yes, she's fit. You met her. She was in the room when you were being questioned that day.'

While Rosa took this in, Josh appeared at the door. He acknowledged Lucas, then putting his arm around Rosa, he ushered her inside. 'Come on you, it's freezing out here.'

Rosa winked at Lucas and dutifully followed her husband inside. She then went through to the kitchen, where Nate was busily hand-drying glasses and putting them on trays.

'All right, bruv?' she said in a comical voice. 'How's it going?'

'All good. You know I love working here. I'm in my element.' He stopped what he was doing, wiped his hands, then placed them on Rosa's shoulders. 'I have to thank you, sis.'

'For what?'

'For not showing me a red card straight away, even when I was acting like a complete arse.'

'You can't kid a–'

'Kidder.' Nate finished her sentence.

'This isn't really the time,' Rosa went on, 'but, well, I've had a chat with Sara and found out that she's ready to hang up her apron.' Nate stood back and looked at Rosa quizzically as she continued, 'She wants to pursue some of her art projects. So, er, we were wondering if maybe you'd like to work here full-time?

280

I'll be part-time overseeing things, but with a baby on the way I need someone I can trust to run the business.'

Nate ran his hands through his curly brown locks. 'Are you serious?'

Rosa nodded. Seeing her brother's face so full of love for her and lit up with excitement at the challenge of running ROSA'S, made her feel warm inside.

'That is possibly the best Christmas present I have ever had – and yes, of course, I would love to take it on.'

Hot, Saveloy, Mr Chips and Theo were now all causing chaos. The bridegroom rounded them all up, then stepped back as Titch briefed Ben, Theo's real dad, and Ben's stunning new girlfriend on baby and dogs, and as planned, the young couple left with their noisy charges and headed back to Alec's place, where they would all spend the night. Hot, of course, was to stay and carry on running around under everyone's feet until the last reveller was ready to leave.

'All sorted?' Ritchie kissed his new wife on the cheek.

'I'm a bit worried,' Titch admitted, 'but Ben is a doctor so I'm sure he won't panic about anything.'

'He's only up the road, it will all be fine. Now come here, you.' Ritchie pulled his new wife into him and squeezed her tightly. 'Mrs Rogers, I do presume.'

'Speech, speech!' a few shouted from the tables as they noted the happy couple in a warm embrace.

'OK. OK. You noisy lot.' Ritchie lifted a glass of champagne from the counter. 'Firstly to my wife. My love, my best friend, the brilliant mother to our amazing Theo, and the magnificent new owner of the Corner Shop in Cockleberry Bay. My wife!'

He lifted his glass as the room echoed, 'Your wife.'

'And now to Rosa.' Rosa gave a little wave from the back of the café. 'A beautiful soul, whose kindness, love and generosity has not only seen us celebrate in such a marvellous fashion today but who has gifted us a shop and a home and ensured a bright future ahead for all of my family. If diamonds were people, then she would without a doubt be a priceless one.'

He lifted his glass as the room roared its response.

'*To Rosa!*'

EPILOGUE

Six months later

Titch poked her head around the hospital curtain. 'Knock, knock, can I come in?'

Rosa smiled back at her; she had never looked more serene or beautiful than when holding her first child in her arms.

Josh stood proudly beside her. 'We'd like to introduce you to Benedict Christopher Smith,' he said, a huge grin spreading across his face on saying his baby son's name out loud.

Titch's eyes filled with tears. She kissed first Rosa, then Josh, and on looking closely at the dark-haired bundle of joy before her, lightly kissed him. 'He's perfect.'

Rosa, too, was welling up. 'Benedict was Ned's full name,' she explained, 'and I couldn't not add Christopher, could I?'

'Very posh. Oh, and one more thing.' Titch grinned. 'You do realise what all this means now, don't you? You are officially inaugurated into the "No telling anyone anything bad about it" Parents' Club.'

Rosa looked down at the dear little boy sleeping soundly in her arms, then to her handsome husband standing by her side and said quietly, 'And there's nowhere that I would rather be.'

Word-of-mouth is crucial for any author to succeed. If you enjoyed your time down in Cockleberry Bay, please could you leave a review on Amazon. Even if it's just a sentence or two, it would make all the difference and would be very much appreciated.

Love, Nicola xx

In memory of Eden
27 December 2001 – 13 November 2019

Please support www.youngminds.org.uk

ABOUT THE AUTHOR

The Gift of Cockleberry Bay is Nicola May's eleventh novel and is the third of the bestselling Cockleberry Bay trilogy. She has won awards at the Festival of Romance for *The School Gates* and *Christmas Spirit*.

Nicola likes to write about love, life and friendship in a realistic way; she is not afraid to tackle the big themes, such as infidelity, addiction and infertility, describing her novels as 'chick lit with a kick'.

Living near the famous Ascot racecourse with her black-and-white rescue cat, Stan, she enjoys watching films that involve a lot of swooning, crabbing in South Devon, eating cream teas – and, naturally, enjoying a flutter on the horses.

Find out more at www.nicolamay.com
Twitter: @nicolamay1
Instagram: author_nicola
Nicola has her own Facebook page

BY THE SAME AUTHOR

The Cockleberry Bay Series:
*
The Corner Shop in Cockleberry Bay
Meet Me in Cockleberry Bay
The Gift of Cockleberry Bay
*

Working It Out
Star Fish
The School Gates
Christmas Spirit
Better Together
Let Love Win
The SW19 Club
Love Me Tinder